ALL THE
OLD LIONS

A Thea Barlow Wyoming Mystery

Book One

Carol Caverly

Cover and Book design by eBook Prep
www.ebookprep.com

May, 2015
ISBN: 978-1-61417-731-9

ePublishing Works!
www.epublishingworks.com

DEDICATION

For Midge, with fond memories of those wonderful early years of Wyoming Writers

REVIEWS & ACCOLADES

"…a modern story of murder and mayhem in the colorful west."
~*Romantic Times*

"A suspenseful tale leading up to a real "Perils of Pauline" climax."
~*The Denver Post*

"…an entertaining excursion into the modern west."
~*Gothic Journal*

"Caverly's books are a step up from cozy. Good stories, interesting characters and settings, a touch of romance, and a little humor. Lots of fun!"
~*Mysterious Woman*

CHAPTER 1

I felt duty-bound to rebel.

Being a born and bred city person, Chicago was my security blanket and I resented being sent out to the western wilderness on a fool's errand—Roger should have gone himself.

Of course, my rebellion meant nothing to Roger Sweeney, President, self-serving head honcho, overweening Grand Muckity-Muck of the Sweeney Publishing Group. As the tides of fortune would have it, Roger was also my boss and a distant, but reluctantly claimed, cousin.

I'd barely had a chance to say a word before he started bellowing.

"Look here, Thea Barlow, I didn't give you a job so you could sit around on your butt deciding what you will and won't do. You work for *me*, remember?"

Nepotism is not all it's cracked up to be.

Roger had been obnoxious as a child and hadn't improved much with age. Taller, of course, and the baby fat had solidified decently enough, though he was still soft around the middle—something I liked to remind him of, now and then. Whatever had made me think we could work together?

I like to believe my opinion of Roger has nothing to do with his being three years younger than my twenty-eight, and a hot-shot MBA in complete control of his own little world. A year ago I could have honestly said there wasn't a jealous bone in my body. Now, I'm as unsure about that as I am of everything else in my life.

"Uncle Charlie doesn't want to see me," I said stubbornly. "He wants to see you."

"Ha! He set you up as the protector of his precious magazine, didn't he? And you can bet he's just itching to get his two cents worth in about this new project. He'll give you the big bear hug and ho, ho, ho, then load you down with advice and directives. You can count on it." Charlie's constant meddling really rankled with Roger.

Uncle Charlie hadn't given up the reins easily when he handed over the foundering Sweeney Publishing Group to Roger, his nephew. Charlie hied himself off quickly enough to retirement in his beloved Black Hills of South Dakota, but he kept the phone wires burning, and demanded his full share of cosseting.

Western True Adventures, a rather tacky, old-style pulp magazine, was Uncle Charlie's pride and joy. Begun as a hobby, it became the base of the Sweeney Publishing Group and remained a small but steady money-maker for forty years, which is more than can be said for his other projects. Now he was afraid Roger would dump the magazine or try to turn it into a fancy slick.

"Besides," Roger went on, "Uncle Charlie doesn't care who he sees as long as he has a live audience once a year. I've made the visit twice. It's your turn."

Roger tried to put a magnanimous look on his handsome face. Handsome, that is, if you like the sleek and oily type. "For someone with no experience, you've done a better job with that damn magazine than I expected."

Roger didn't offer praise without a purpose. I waited for the double-whammy I knew would follow.

"You could use Charlie's input on your whorehouse project. I shouldn't have given you full responsibility in the first place. I might have to turn it over to someone else."

"Of all the rotten…" He knew what that project meant to me, but his not-so-subtle threat worked, as he knew it would.

"You can fly into Rapid City," he said, "spend a few hours with the old man and fly back. And don't snap those big brown eyes at me, either. Hell, Thea, I'll even throw in a few extra days, if you like. A little vacation will do you good."

"You're all heart, Roger, but no thanks," I wasn't going to be appeased by a bit of bribery.

However, later in the afternoon, a surprising call from Minnie Darrow changed my mind. Minnie Darrow was a crucial part of what Roger disparagingly termed my "whorehouse project." Minnie, a Little Old Lady from Ioway(as she put it), had first proposed an article for Western True Adventures about an old time Wyoming bordello called Halfway Halt. Minnie had found a journal kept by the house's notorious madam, Jersey Roo. I may be a neophyte in the publishing business, but I'm smart enough to know that choice bits of primary source material don't surface all that often. I thought her idea was worth more than a magazine article and approached Roger with a proposal of my own for a series of soft-cover books that would sell on the racks next to *Western True Adventures*. Minnie's history of Halfway Halt would be the first book in the series. Roger liked the idea and told me to follow up on it.

That afternoon when Minnie called I could barely hear her. The line was full of static. "You're calling from where?" I yelled. "Wyoming? Hijax, Wyoming? You've moved? You're living where? In Halfway Halt?" I sounded like a parrot, squawk and all.

An hour later I staggered into Roger's office and plopped into a chair.

"I'll take those extra days, Roger," I said. "I'm going to spend a day with Uncle Charlie, then rent a car and drive to Wyoming to see Minnie Darrow."

"Wyoming? I thought she lived in Iowa. What are you chasing off to Wyoming for?" The parrot syndrome was breaking out all over.

"Minnie has moved from Iowa to Wyoming and says she's living in Halfway Halt."

"The whorehouse? It's still in business?"

"Of course not," I answered automatically, but I hadn't thought to ask, just assumed she'd bought what had once been... Hadn't she said something about renovation?

"Anyway," I said, "I told her I'd be out in the area. She seemed eager to see me and invited me to stay with her a couple of days."

Roger raised an eyebrow. I ignored it.

"Look, Roger, something weird is going on out there and I want to know what it is. When I reminded Minnie that her manuscript is due by the end of the month, she got evasive. She sounded scared, and I could swear she was crying. Said something about making a big mistake. If she doesn't meet her deadline I'll be in a hell of a mess."

Roger shrugged. "You can always call her."

"There isn't a phone in Halfway Halt. She said she

was calling from town."

Roger glared at me. "You better not foul this up, Thea. I'm counting on that book."

One of the unexpected pleasures of my job was a new-found fascination with the Wild and Woolly West, so Uncle Charlie's enthusiasm found a ready audience in me. He, in turn, was fascinated by the little I could tell him about Halfway Halt, and eager to see Minnie Darrow's completed manuscript. He assured me the book would find a solid group of readers in the small, but faithful, Western market.

So after an enjoyable day of listening to tales of daring-do and touring the Black Hills, I set off for Wyoming in a rented Ford Escort. Images of midnight campfires, strawberry roans and cowboys in tight jeans filled my head. But not for long.

By afternoon I felt as if I'd been driving forever. I wasn't prepared for the vast stretches of emptiness that seemed to be all that Wyoming contained.

Hours earlier, the air-conditioning in the little Ford had given up the battle and left me to swelter in the blazing July heat. Perspiration trickled down my neck and between my breasts. I drew my white gauzy skirt as high up my thighs as possible and undid another button of the matching blouse. I'd already discarded the woven sash, and tossed it in the back seat.

Frequent signs announcing NO SERVICES FOR 68 MILES, or something equally appalling, left me hunched over the wheel alert for further indications of rebellion from the Escort.

Chalk hills, and buttes capped with blood-red rock erupted like pustules from earth baked to an unhealthy gray. Periodically, thunderheads passed overhead, bringing momentary relief from the glare, but with the creeping shadows came an overwhelming sense of aloneness. For the first time I understood the true meaning of "in the middle of nowhere."

The small town of Hijax, dismal though it was, seemed like an oasis when I finally got there. I needed a long cold drink and a restroom. It was also time to check the map and make sure I knew how to get to Minnie's from Hijax. Halfway Halt, according to Minnie, was way out in the country somewhere.

I pulled into the nearest parking place and stepped out into gritty, boiling heat that was no worse than the inside of the un-airconditioned car. Holding my limp skirt away from my legs to catch the breeze, I surveyed my choices. There weren't many. I could see all of the few blocks that comprised the business district from where I was standing. Lots of bars, a clothing store, a hotel, Bev's Beauty Hut. The only building that looked as if it had been built within the last forty years was a pretty nice bank on the far corner. At least it had a tree—or maybe shrub was a better word—in front, and a planter that didn't have any flowers in it now, but might some day. Across the street was a brick store in slightly better shape than its mates on either side. It sported a Walgreens sign and two slick red circles announcing Coca Cola was sold there.

I started to cross the street, then decided that I hadn't come all the way from Chicago for another Walgreens. Instead, I headed for the Clarion Hotel, which looked like it could have been one of the town's original buildings.

A cafe adjoined the old red stone building, but curiosity led me through the hotel's main entrance. Three old men in overalls sat in front of the large window, puffing cigarettes and watching the street. Their weathered faces were as dark and cracked as the chairs they sat on. An oscillating fan on the registration desk fought a losing battle with the biting drifts of smoke that wafted through the lobby.

A pleasant-looking woman with one of those sculptured looking hairdos (Bev's Beauty Hut?) sat behind the desk reading a newspaper. Business was not hopping. The woman stood when I came in and eyed me with bright curiosity. She looked surprisingly crisp and fresh in a navy and white dress.

"May I help you?" she asked.

I smiled wanly. "I'm looking for a restroom and a big glass of iced tea—in that order."

She smiled sympathetically and directed me down a dingy hallway, and when I returned, pointed me to the door of the restaurant, saying, "It's hot out there all right. Have you come a long way?"

"A million miles at least." Another time I might have stopped for a chat, but not now. I needed that drink.

The restaurant contained nothing that could have been called decor, and smelled nicely of charred beef. It was empty except for five men of various ages gathered in the large corner booth. Across from them, a man in a brown and tan uniform sat on the end stool with his back to the lunch counter, clearly a part of the group. The good-natured joshing flowing between them slowed as I walked across the bare boards. I sat a couple of stools away from the man at the lunch counter. A sheriff, I saw, reading his badge. We exchanged smiles and nods. He was tall, not fat, but bulky-looking, with sandy hair that was beginning the march back to the sea. He had inquisitive eyes, and one of those round, guileless faces that never seem to age.

"Hello. Hot enough out there for you?" he said. "You must be new in town; at least, I haven't seen you before."

"Aw, come on, Hank," one of the men at the table

called out. "You can do better than that!"

"That line's older than Hickam's barn," chimed in another, followed by hoots of laughter from all of them, including the waitress who strolled over and took my order for iced tea.

The sheriff was unperturbed. He turned his back to the jibes and continued.

"On the other hand," he said, "you could be lost or something. We don't get many tourists passing through here. And if you *are* lost, well I'm just the man to help you. Sheriff Henry Beesom, here. Otherwise known as Hank." He stuck out his hand.

I shook it, and received some friendly catcalls from the peanut gallery. "I'm not lost yet," I said with a laugh, rather enjoying the teasing, "but I don't want to get that way, either. Do you really know everyone in town, Sheriff?"

"You better believe it—county, too. Try me."

"Maybe you can help."

I took a long drink of tea, then fished the road map out of my bag and spread it out on the counter between us. "I think I know where I'm going, but it never hurts to be sure. Do you know where Minnie Darrow lives?"

"Darrow!" the waitress said with an incredulous squeal. "Minnie Darrow?"

Startled, I glanced up from the map. "Yes. Is there something wrong with that?"

She shrugged and replenished my tea, sloshing some in the process. The men's conversation had stopped; their attention was palpable. I glanced over my shoulder in the other direction and saw the woman with the stiff dark hair standing in the doorway, watching us.

"Is there a problem with Ms. Darrow?" I asked again, this time of the sheriff.

"No. Not at all. And of course I know where she lives. As I said, I know where everyone lives." His tone was light, but neither it nor the big grin he gave me hid the fact that the high-spirited fun had disappeared from the room, and a hard edge had crept into the back of the sheriff's eyes.

"Let me see what you have," he said. He slid the map closer, found Hijax with his finger and traced the road out of town. "Here we go. You drive about fourteen miles north of town and take this county road—yep, you've got the right one marked—and it's another fourteen, fifteen miles to her place. You'll find the turn-off with no problem." He shoved the map back toward me and asked, "Minnie a relative of yours?"

His face was bland and still puppy dog friendly, but I wasn't fooled. I could play this game, too.

I said, "No, Minnie's not a relative." And nothing more.

"You're going to be around these parts awhile, then?"

The room practically vibrated with curiosity, all ears out on stalks. I'd heard about the nosiness of small towns, but this was beyond belief.

I drained my tea, rose, and smiled excessively at everyone. "Thanks. I'll be on my way."

The sheriff held out his hand again, which I took.

"Pleased to meet you," he said with another ingratiating smile. "What did you say your name was?"

"I didn't, Sheriff. And thanks so much for the directions. Goodbye now."

I just wish I hadn't looked back, but when I got outside the urge was too great. They were all there, standing at the window, watching me. The woman from the hotel stood with shoulders hunched, arms wrapped tightly around her middle and a scowl on her face. The sheriff leaned against the glass on his elbow, chewing his thumb. The waitress seemed to be arguing with two of the men, her neck stretched toward them, spitting out words, her finger jabbing in my direction. Something chilling about the silent tableau sent a shiver through my body. *That's the devil dancing on your grave*, my mother would have said. Not exactly a welcome thought at this point.

Minnie, what is going on?

At least the sheriff was right about the turnoff; I found it easily enough. The map indicated a gravel road. Ruts and boulders would have been more accurate. Odd pinkish-colored stones, some larger than a fist, covered the roadbed. The Escort bucked and bolted over the rough surface, shooting out of control when least expected.

It took all my strength to keep the car from being tossed onto the loose piles of gravel gathered on either side of the single set of tire tracks that ran up the middle of the road. Either the road was seldom traveled, or no one else was bothered by blind curves, but when the single track began a steep climb up and around a hill I knew I had to move to the right edge.

Warily eyeing the drop-off, I eased the tires through the loose stuff, fighting the wheel, trying to force my lightweight car in the proper direction. Halfway across, thinking I'd finally gotten the hang of it, I raised my eyes and saw a blue pickup truck hurtling straight at me.

I jerked to the right; the truck swung to the left. If I hadn't committed the cardinal sin of stomping on the brake I would have been all right, but brake I did, and sent the Escort in a sickening backward slide across the narrow shoulder. One rear wheel caught in a shallow ditch. The car shuddered, and stopped.

I gasped for breath, heart pounding like a trapped bird. I couldn't have moved if I'd wanted to. I dropped my head to the steering wheel and waited for all the adrenaline, or whatever it was, to switch off.

The Escort's door flew open. "My God!" a voice thundered in my ear.

I'd only thought I couldn't move. With a startled yelp, I flung myself across the crazily canted seat.

The man grunted. "You're not hurt." It sounded like an accusation. "The way you were draped over the wheel, I thought you were dead."

Head, shoulders and black cowboy hat filled the doorway. His face was dark with tan and beard-shadow, dominated by a square jaw and heavy, sharply arched Tom Selleck eyebrows. Unfortunately, the resemblance ended there.

"I'm not hurt, no thanks to you." My voice trembled with anger. Fear had turned my body into an unmanageable lump of sludge. I tried to slide back under the wheel and lost a sandal in the process; the limp skirt twisted around my hips and crawled up my back.

"Stop looming over me." I yanked furiously at the flimsy material. The motion popped open the rest of the blouse buttons and sent my fingers flying. He had the grace to retreat, but not before I saw a grin pull at his mouth.

"You could have killed us both," I snapped.

"You're right. I'm sorry," he said, smoothly polite.

"Somebody should show you people how to build a road. Even without *insane drivers* this one is stupidly dangerous." I righted myself in the seat. The buttons that mattered were fastened and my legs covered decently enough.

He hunkered down by the open door so we were eye-to-eye, and pushed the incredibly dusty hat off his forehead, exposing a white band where the sun hadn't reached. Heavy-lidded eyes gave him a lazy appearance, deceptive, probably, from the tough look of him.

"All right," he said, "I apologize for the road and for my driving. I just want to make sure you're not hurt."

"I'm perfectly all right." Exhaustion took over. Whatever fueled my anger had burnt out.

"Let's see if you can walk."

"No, I'm fine. Just leave me alone." I leaned back and closed my eyes.

"Look, I haven't got all day," he said finally. "I've had enough of harebrained women today to last a lifetime." He reached in and grabbed my arm.

My eyes flew open and I shook free of his hold. I didn't need to be reminded that I was a million miles from nowhere, and he a total stranger. My flash of fear must have been evident; he dropped his hand as if he'd touched an explosive device and stood back.

"You've hurt your knee," he said, pointing to my scraped shin, which must have banged against the steering column. "I'm not leaving until I've seen you walk." Exasperation crisped each word.

The abrasion was more vivid than debilitating. However, being a Grand Master of Stubborn myself, I recognized champion stuff when I saw it. I struggled out on my own, wincing when my bare foot touched the gravel. With an eloquent grimace of disgust he reached into the front seat and retrieved my sandal, gingerly supporting my elbow as I slid it on.

He was so obviously incensed by my show of fear and general bad attitude that I felt a smile building and shreds of good humor returning. I walked the few feet he seemed so determined to see and windmilled my arms, and flexed my knees for a bonus. Actually, I was rather relieved to find that, other than the usual aches and miseries from riding too long in a small car, my body was all in one piece and worked as well as could be expected.

I turned, ready to make amends for my foul humor. "There. You see, everything works."

But he was staring at my car. Heart-in-mouth I did the same; it clung perilously close to the edge.

"Oh, please," I begged shamelessly. "Would you drive it back on the road for me?"

"Sure. Where are you going?"

"To Minnie Darrow's."

He swung around. Raw hostility filled his face. I caught my breath.

"I should have known," he muttered, then folded his long body into the Escort. He slammed the gear in place and gunned the motor. With a spray of gravel and debris the car lurched back on the road. He was still scowling when he stepped out.

"Look," I said before he could walk away. "What is all this about Minnie Darrow?"

He took a cigarette and a kitchen match from his shirt pocket. The cool, gray-brown eyes never left my face as he fired the match with a quick snick on his fly zipper. He lit the cigarette and exhaled a cloud of smoke.

"If you're smart, you'll go back where you came from." He tossed the dead match to the gravel and ground it in with his heel. "I don't know who you are, or what you're here for, but we've got enough trouble without anyone else adding to it." His calm manner was belied by rigid tendons that stood out on his neck and wrists. Abruptly, he turned, stalked back to his truck, and climbed in.

"Wait!" I called, shocked out of my stupor. But he drove off, leaving me to choke in his dust.

CHAPTER 2

My mind reeled with questions. What was I getting into? Who was this guy anyway, and what did he mean by trouble? And how could my presence add to it? I tried to remember what Minnie had said on the telephone, with little success. She had been upset and I thought she sounded scared, but that had been my interpretation. I should have asked more questions and done less mother-henning. And what about the people in the restaurant? Had their reaction to Minnie Darrow's name been more than the rude curiosity I'd taken it for?

As if on signal, the thunderheads returned to darken the sky; tendrils of shadow reached through the trees and across the road. Silence bore oppressively down around me, broken only by the clack and whir of insects.

With an uneasy glance over my shoulder, I hurried to the car. Ten more miles, maybe, then I'd get some answers from Minnie. And if I didn't like the look of things, I reassured myself, I could always leave.

The car careened down the road; heavy pink dust boiled up in clouds beneath the tires. A misty haze prickled my nose and clung to skin and clothes with gritty tenacity. It was stifling.

Roger was right, I thought morosely, this side trip was a stupid idea. I could be getting into some kind of unsavory mess, and what did I expect to gain?

The manuscript for one thing. If it was finished, I could take it back to Chicago with me and stop worrying about deadlines. If not, ugh, I didn't even want to think about that possibility. All the old doubts came flooding back. What did I know about publishing anyway?

Leaving my chosen profession of teaching had been traumatic enough without throwing myself into a new field where I had no expertise. No wonder my confidence was in shreds.

It had only taken four years of force-feeding junior high kids to realize that my dreams of imparting knowledge to hungry little minds were just that—dreams. Facing the fact that I was totally uninterested in the vast sea of reluctant learners left me shattered, as if the loving, giving side of me had been hopelessly damaged in the process. At least I had enough sense to know my usefulness as a teacher was limited, and the time had come to change course.

The job market landed another blow. The only people impressed by my literature degrees and teaching credentials were my parents, who were eager to welcome me back to the bosom of suburbia. When Dad finally accepted the fact that I wasn't going to move back in and help him run his constant string of local campaigns—Water Board this time—he urged me to approach the Sweeney Publishing Group and Roger. After a particularly harrowing string of rejections, desperation won out, and here I was. For better or worse.

My blouse stuck to my back in an uncomfortable wet blotch. I tried to run my fingers through my tangled hair. Always unruly, it was practically standing on end, windblown, matted with sweat and dust. Balls of grit rolled under my fingers when I brushed them across my cheek. I wanted a shower. I wanted to sit on something that didn't careen around like a drunken horse. I wanted to put my feet up...a cold beer would be nice.

Damn it, what I really needed was a success, I thought, trying to pull myself from the dumps. And with Minnie's manuscript for the lead title the book series would be a success. I was sure of it. Minnie was a good, dependable writer who'd been turning out nicely-researched articles for *Western True Adventures* for several years, well before I came to work at Sweeney. She wouldn't fail me.

Of course, I knew nothing about Minnie's personal life except that she had grown up in Iowa and was raised by an older sister who had died several months ago. I had no idea if Minnie was married, or how she earned a living. She certainly couldn't support herself with what Sweeney paid for a few articles. For all I knew she could be the Mayflower Madam of Iowa. And did it really matter? I felt the old enthusiasm stirring. After all, there is something wonderfully fascinating about Ladies of the Night and their various dens of iniquity.

And as for the Cro-Magnon who'd run me off the road...well, so much for the code of the West. Who needs John Wayne, anyway?

I spotted Minnie's mailbox with the relief a racer must feel when he sees the checkered flag. The last lap. Turning onto a dirt road that seemed as smooth as city cement after all those rocks, I followed the narrow track up an incredibly steep incline threaded through thickets of pine trees and scrub. The Escort groaned as I shifted into second gear.

"Come on, baby, we're almost there."

A sharp turn brought me to the top of the hill where the road disappeared abruptly at the edge of a clearing. An immense hewn-rock house rose from the naked ground, a desolate relic. Two tall posts and a few scattered pickets were all that remained of a wooden fence. There was no yard, or grass, or obvious place to park, so I stopped by one of the sentinel posts, put on the brake and stepped out.

A wooden verandah ran across the front of the house and wrapped around the corner. Several supporting posts were missing, causing the roof to sway in a frowzy line across the stark facade. Crude letters carved or burned into the lintel above the steps were barely discernible: Hal way H lt.

There was a daunting aura about the crumbling sandstone, an eerie look of flatness, as if there were nothing behind the limpid curtains hanging in the windows. A trick of the light, perhaps. Nevertheless, I was strangely reluctant to approach the house, reminded of something Minnie had told me, some old-timer's description of the house: "Halfway to heaven or halfway to hell, depending on which way you was going." It sounded like an epitaph.

Stalling for time, I took a small hairbrush from my shoulder bag and cleared the tangles from my hair. Every sound—the bag's zipper, bristles pulling through hair—seemed magnified in the intense silence. I looked around warily. Like the road, the trees stopped at the edge of the clearing. Beyond the house stood a ramshackle barn and out-buildings in various stages of collapse, then the hill rolled endlessly away into a distant purple horizon.

The scene had the look and feel of an Andrew Wyeth painting, that same sense of decay and sorrow hiding under rustic tranquility. Nothing moved. I wanted to yell or throw something.

Instead, I retrieved my sash from the car and slammed the door with a satisfying bang, then yelped with surprise when something wiggled against my legs and licked my hand.

A black and white shepherd-type dog had come out of nowhere to squirm against my feet, begging for a kind hand, but not expecting one, poor thing. I dropped to my knees, relieved to find some other living thing in this godforsaken place, and lavished him with coos and hugs. The dog moaned with ecstasy, lolloping me with a long, wet tongue. Obviously, I had a friend for life. I had also added the pungent smell of dog to other sins of disarray.

Brushing at my skirt again, I tied the sash and headed for the house. The porch listed at one end, but seemed sturdy enough. I knocked on the door and squinted down the length of the porch, trying to picture what it must have looked like in its heyday. Wicker furniture maybe, a swing, virile cowboys lounging on the railing ogling wrapper-clad hoydens.

The door opened without warning and caught me daydreaming.

"Oh," I said stupidly, and stumbled over the dog, which groveled at my feet. "Ms. Darrow?"

"Yes?" She held the door partially open, a plain statement of "name your business, or be on your way."

"Thea Barlow." I held out my hand.

She barely came up to my chin, a little dumpling of a woman, one of those who age in a lump, with bosom, waist and hips becoming one. In spite of her shape, or perhaps in defiance of it, she wore denim pants and a white shirt with a red farmer bandanna at the collar. Her hair was a lively mass of graying curls that bobbed with every movement.

She ignored my hand, so I added, "I'm from Sweeney Publishing Group."

"Oh! Thea, of course." She sprang into animation, her smile revealing a deep dimple in her finely-lined, doughy cheek.

"I'd forgotten this was the day you were coming." The sweetness of her tone did not quite reach the alert brown eyes that were giving me a thorough once-over. "You're younger and prettier than I expected."

With a start, she noticed the dog writhing belly down on the porch. "Oh! Don't let him in!" she said in a frightened little voice, and moved as if to shut the door in his face.

"Your dog?"

"Well, I guess so, if nobody comes to claim him." She glanced at him uncertainly. "He just showed up the other day. I have a bad ear and thought it might be a good idea to have a dog around to raise a ruckus if need be. Protection, you know." She drew me in and closed the door.

What she thought that obsequious beast would ever save her from, I'll never know.

"But I don't want him in the house," she said, nervously. "I've never had a pet before."

I could tell.

We stepped further into the oak-paneled hallway. Never having been in a whorehouse before, either new or old, the temptation to gawk was overpowering.

"So this is Halfway Halt," I said. "I was really surprised when you told me you'd moved out here."

A narrow stairway with a carved and burnished banister rose to the second floor. To my right was a large room with an enormous fireplace filling the far wall. But it was the room on the opposite side of the hall that drew me in, a magical Victorian parlor exquisitely furnished down to the finest detail. No whorehouse red here, but soft shades of rose and celery green that enhanced the elaborate whorls of a cabbage flower carpet. Tall narrow windows led the eye up to a high pressed-tin ceiling untouched by decorator's art. A grayness seemed to hover there, decades of mustiness that refused to be conquered.

"Do you like it?" Minnie rushed by me, fussing with the placement of a needlepoint cushion, moving a cut glass vase of peacock feathers an inch to the right, checking my face for a reaction.

"It's marvelous," I said. And indeed it was.

"Well, the woodwork needs more attention, but I've done the best I can with precious little help." She twitched the heavy lace curtain to better cover the window frame. "And I can't find a soul brave enough to tackle that ceiling."

She continued to fuss and I turned to the great room across the hall. Masculinity prevailed here. A few dark rugs were scattered over the wood floor, and heavy leather-covered chairs clustered around a fieldstone hearth streaked with soot. Shafts of waning sunlight filtered around the edges of brocade draperies providing a dim, hazy illumination. A magnificent mahogany bar filled the far end of the room, and at it, to my surprise, stood the cowboy of my dreams. He could have been a remnant from an old Western movie, one high heeled boot braced against the gleaming brass rail.

He wore a scarred leather vest that hung open over fawn-colored pants and a light shirt. But it was the hat that made my heart sing—a pale cream Stetson with a wide curving brim and a foot-high, uncreased crown. An open cigar box sat on the bar in front of him, and he studied something—a piece of paper or photograph—balanced on the box's rim.

He stood so still, and the picture was so perfect, that I thought he was a mannequin. I must have gasped when he moved, because he looked up, stared for a moment, then gathered up the cigar box and walked toward me with brisk, cocky steps.

The room was long and the lighting dim. The sound of leather heels against bare boards caromed off the walls. The appearance of youth dropped away as he approached. When he stood in front of me I could see he was just the husk of that mythic man I'd envisioned.

He was old and small, but finely made, dressed to the hilt and well aware of it. A black silk scarf circled his throat with the elan of an ascot, but looked nothing like one.

Sweeping off that incredible hat, he revealed a sparse thatch of bone-white hair and pale blue eyes that sparkled at my obvious appreciation.

"Oh, there you are, Helby," Minnie said, coming up behind us. "I'd like you to meet Thea Barlow. Thea is my editor, come from Chicago. This is Helby Enright, Thea. Lives up the road."

He gave a terse nod and offered a hand liberally sprinkled with age blotches, the skin rising in delicate parchment wrinkles. Well into his seventies, I thought. A slight tremor shook his fingers, but the grasp was firm.

"So, you're going to publish Minnie's book, then." It was a statement, not a question. The sparkle had died from his eyes, and his smile was as grim and cold as frosted iron. Not bothering to wait for an answer, he turned to Minnie.

"Here's my last lot of pictures, the special ones, I guess. Always kept them separate for some reason.

You can take your time; I'm in no hurry to get them back." With another arrogant nod, he replaced the magnificent hat and walked out the front door.

"A nice man," Minnie said. "Well now, come along to the kitchen, I've got to get dinner on."

The kitchen showed none of the efforts at renovation evident elsewhere. A fresh coat of apple green paint did its best to brighten an otherwise drab room filled with ancient appliances. The linoleum floor covering in front of the sink was worn to the board and showed enough layers of patterns to delight an archeologist.

"Get yourself a plate and cup and saucer," Minnie said indicating an overhead cupboard. "Sorry this kitchen's such a mess, but as you well know, I can't spend all my time painting and puttering." She took a platter of meat from the refrigerator and began sawing at it with a large knife. The roast had been cooked to the last degree of doneness and broke away in strings wherever the blade touched.

"You've done a beautiful job of decorating in the front rooms. I'm anxious to see everything." Actually, I was more concerned with her comments about time spent. Had her writing suffered?

I reached for the dishes, and fished silverware from a drawer. "How is your manuscript coming along? I'm hoping to take it home with me when I leave. But I am curious, how did you happen to buy Halfway Halt?"

I sensed her stillness even before turning to find her hunched over the platter, the knife poised motionless in the air. I could almost feel the deep breath she took as she straightened her shoulders. Chin up, she faced me.

"I didn't buy Halfway Halt, I inherited it. I was born in this house. My sister Lil was the owner...the...the last madam here. She raised me from the time I was two." Her cheeks were red and quivered with defiance.

She was obviously disturbed, but before I could assure her I wasn't going to faint from shock at her revelation, she rushed on with a flood of bright words.

"There's some beans on the stove, just set them on the table in the pan."

I went through the motions, wondering how delicately I'd have to phrase the questions I was dying to ask. Talk about primary source material! But what connection did Minnie's sister have to the infamous Jersey Roo? They couldn't have been contemporaries; Minnie's sister had only recently died. How old could she have been? How old was Minnie for that matter? In her sixties, maybe. Mental math was not my forte, and besides, I decided, the connection between the two was irrelevant I wanted the story of Jersey Roo's Halfway Halt before the turn of the century. Minnie could be as discreet as she wished about her sister's background for all I cared.

Minnie emptied a can of peaches into a bowl with an untidy splash. "Sorry I have to rush you like this, but I have a caller coming—interviewing him for my book, you know—and I want to be finished with all this when he gets here."

"An interview? Would you like me to sit in on it?"

"No. Whatever for? I'm fishing for information and don't want him scared off. I'll tell you about it later." She motioned for me to sit at the table and proceeded to fill her plate, passing dishes as she finished.

"Don't worry, Miss Darrow, I won't interfere," I said, rather taken aback by her bluntness. "Just let me know if I can be of any help."

"You can start by calling me Minnie." She eyed me speculatively.

I helped myself to an unappetizing portion of cold beans and peaches, and bypassed the dreadful looking meat. Cooking was obviously not one of Minnie's interests.

"You know," she went on, "I haven't exactly been welcomed in this town. The people around here are tight-mouthed snobs. I could use an ally. How long can you stay? A week or so?"

"Hardly." I chased a slippery piece of peach around my plate. "A couple of days at the most. What do you need an ally for?"

She glanced at her watch and pushed away from the table. "Sorry, dear, but I've got to get ready."

Halfway to the door she stopped and turned on a sweet little smile that made her look like a cupcake.

"Oh, and if you'd like to help, would you mind cleaning these things up a bit?" She gestured vaguely at the table. "I have to get ready." She hustled off into the hall, steely curls bouncing like a halo around her head.

Touché, Minnie, my dear, I thought with a laugh. It was going to be dog eat dog out here in the wild country, I could tell. But I didn't mind. It was a simple job and took only a moment, even with time off for a trip to the bathroom I discovered off the hall. I'd finished stacking the plates on the drain board to dry when I heard the sound of a car approaching.

Curiosity, or maybe a growing awareness of isolation that had been building all day, sent me through the other door leading out of the kitchen. A room that appeared to be Minnie's office separated the kitchen from the Victorian parlor. I crossed both and headed for the front window, where I peeked through the lace curtain with the anticipation of a child waiting for Santa Claus.

An old man lumbered up to the porch while the silly

dog humbled himself all over the ground at his feet. The dog must have gotten too close, for the man turned on him. Aiming a vicious kick at the poor animal's ribs, he used words I didn't have to hear to understand.

"Why, you old reprobate." I flounced into the hall ready for battle, but Minnie beat me to the door with the eagerness of a teenager.

"Well, Potts," she simpered. "Good to see you. Come right in."

He was a great hulking person with a florid face and jutting jaw. His pugnacious look was not in the least softened by too-short overalls that showed a considerable stretch of white work socks. His hands were huge with fat, finely lined, banana fingers clutching a limp cowboy hat.

"It's too bad you didn't get here earlier, you could have joined us for dinner," Minnie said, not indicating by even a blink of an eyelash how madly she had hurried to avoid just such a thing. "And I want you to meet my...uh...helper."

I felt my status slipping, but assumed it was for good purpose.

"Thea Barlow, meet Parson Potts. Thea's just in from Chicago," she added.

I mumbled something in acknowledgment and turned from the man's small piercing eyes.

"Come in the front room, Potts," Minnie said, taking his arm. "I have all kinds of questions for you...Thea?"

Whatever it was going to be, invitation or dismissal, I cut her off with a suggestion of my own. "Don't worry about me, Minnie. I'll take a look around," and slipped out the front door. I didn't want anything to do with that awful man.

Rover, or whatever his name was, crouched under

my car. His tail thumped on the hard ground when I called, and though he moved forward a bit on his stomach he couldn't generate nerve for anything further. I met him more than halfway, muttering vile things about the character of a man who would kick a defenseless animal, and revived him with silly words only a dog would appreciate. He joined me for a tour of the grounds.

Here his courage came to the fore; he was much braver than I. The barn was empty, but an acrid odor witnessed it wasn't always so. I stood at the door content to watch light sift through loose boards. The dog snuffled in the stalls.

"Hello!"

I whirled, and cried out as my foot caught on a loose board. A hand shot out and grabbed my arm, preventing a nasty spill.

"Sorry," he said with a rueful laugh. "I didn't mean to frighten you. I thought you heard me drive in." His lean patrician face might have looked arrogant in a different situation, but was softened now by well-used laugh lines that defined his eyes and sharply molded mouth.

In his thirties, I guessed, as we eyed each other with the lightning assessment that seems to be a ritual greeting between male and female. He was of average height with an interesting air of careless confidence, and that kind of slender, whippy build that somehow indicates a great deal of strength.

"No, I didn't hear you," I said, wishing I'd taken time to change my clothes and done something more than brushing to tame my hair; it was still in a state of astonishment from the trip.

I could see the tail end of a sleek Lincoln parked beside my Escort and Pott's pickup. The place was beginning to look like a parking lot.

"Just wondered if my Dad was here. Thought he might have parked around back. I'm Jim Enright."

"Hi. I'm Thea Barlow, wandering Chicagoan, taking in the sights." I gestured at the decrepit barn and surroundings. The dog had come to the door, eager to greet the newcomer, undaunted by previous bad experiences. Not real bright.

Jim laughed. "Your dog?"

"No, a stray, but I guess Minnie's going to keep him, if nobody claims him. Unfortunately, I think he's adopted me."

He shrugged. "People are always dumping dogs off in the country thinking someone will take care of them; more often they starve. Come here, boy."

The dog performed his duty as ice breaker very well with a ludicrous display of waggling and tongue lolling, then ran off to continue his investigations. We strolled after him.

Thinking I caught a resemblance, I turned the conversation back to where it began. "If your father happens to be a delightful vision from out of the past, then I can tell you he was here earlier."

"Delightful!" He threw back his head with a burst of laughter. "I can't imagine anyone using 'delightful' in connection with Helby Enright."

I was right then to recognize the slight arrogant tilt of the head and the blue eyes, though there was nothing sharp or frosty about Jim's. He seemed genuinely amused by my description.

"Well," I conceded, "delightful might not be the right word, but he looked very other-worldly. I was quite enchanted."

"The hat, I bet. He must have been wearing that gawdawful antique. Dad's a bit of a showman and it's no secret he prefers life the way it was lived fifty years ago. I suppose he and Minnie were hashing over old times again?"

"I guess so. Apparently he brought some pictures and things for her to look at."

"Not another scrapbook!" He chuckled and shook his head. "They go through those things like they were the Dead Sea scrolls."

"Not a scrapbook; treasures in a cigar box."

"Well, that's a twist, but whether it's a scrapbook, or a cigar box, don't let either one of them get you cornered or they'll show all that stuff to you. It takes hours. You have to hear how Digger Bill stole the neighbor's slicks to build his herd and how old Maudie Brown rose from her birthing bed to shoot a buffalo. It'll fry your ears and make your eyes roll with boredom."

"Oh, I don't know, sounds like it might be interesting."

"A lot of it is, if you can get past the begats and Aunt Tillie's sister's cousin's boys. I've heard it all too often, I guess."

I liked his droll delivery and also the strong sense of tolerant affection beneath his words. It reminded me of my grandmother and her velvet-covered memory book stuffed with frilly valentines. Granny knew the story behind each card and loved to tell me about them.

We followed the dog, strolling in a wide path past a collapsed shed and a small storage building of some kind, and ended up in back of the house.

The rear of Halfway Halt was as bleak as the front. Great slabs of peeling bark hung from a gnarled and twisted cotton-wood that shaded the back entry to the kitchen.

"Now there's something that's *really* out of the past," Jim said, pointing to a large grassy hump beyond the tree. He took my arm and led me to it. "I'll bet you've never seen a dugout before. There aren't many left."

I stood on the edge of a bank and looked down into a sharply eroded ditch. Someone long ago had taken advantage of the feature and dug a room into the hillside. Four crude wooden steps stuck in the side of the ditch led down to the entrance. The door itself was made from rough planks and opened directly into the hill, if it opened at all.

"It's over a hundred years old." Jim jumped into the gully with the dog close behind. A lizard, basking in the sun, darted under the door. Yuck.

"Want to look in?"

"No thanks," I shuddered and turned away. "There's probably a colony of those things hiding in there."

Jim threw me one of those satisfied male smiles and climbed the bank. I gazed across the gentle slope of land beyond the dugout where it rolled into an immense, softly-colored panorama that disappeared into the purple haze of distance. Stark and forbidding, but with its own compelling beauty. Off on the horizon a curl of smoke drifted against the pale sky.

"What's that?" I asked lazily, "a fire?"

"Where?" Instantly alert, he followed the direction of my finger, then just as quickly relaxed. "Oh, that. That's an underground coal fire, been burning for weeks."

"A what?"

"Coal underlies most of this country. In the old days a lot of the ranchers mined their own. In some places the coal is so close to the surface that lightning or a brush fire will start it burning. Sometimes a good rain will douse the fire, otherwise the deposit burns out and leaves a hole in the ground."

How strange...and wonderful. I felt as if I'd been dropped on another planet instead of another state.

The sun was fading and a crisp breeze took the bite from the heat. The knots bunched in my neck and my arms began to loosen and ease.

"Look," Jim said, with a sweeping gesture. "That's our land as far as you can see. Awesome, isn't it?"

"What about Minnie's?"

"She only has a couple of sections. See that line of fence down there?" He put one arm across my shoulder and tried to aim my sight down his other arm. "The one with the well in the corner."

I squinted gamely and nodded, though it all looked like hen scratchings to me.

"That's the end of Minnie's land. All the rest is ours. It always amazes me when I can look out on it like this. Makes you understand what the fever must have been like for the old guys—dad and Grandpa— when they were putting these spreads together. Those days are gone though, and the big places are breaking up. Divided up among families or sold to the coal companies."

"Who are letting their assets burn merrily away," I said, fascinated with this new tidbit of information.

"If you're really interested in that stuff, I could show you a large burn-out pit on our place. Dad keeps it as a curiosity; he likes to have the school kids out now and then for show and tell."

He was an easy person to be with. Too bad there wouldn't be time to explore the friendship further.

"Well, Thea Barlow, now that I've given you the two-bit tour, do you mind if I ask what you're doing here? Are you a friend of Minnie's?"

"I hope we're going to be friends, but I'm here for work."

"Work?"

He loaded the word with an incredulous amusement that immediately put my back up. I answered stiffly.

"I'm an editorial assistant with Sweeney Publishing Group. Minnie's doing a book for us."

"So it's true then; she's got a contract and everything? I'd heard she was writing a book, but you can hear anything around here. What kind of book is it?"

"History; Western history. She's quite good, you know."

"Local history?"

I nodded. There was no secret about what Minnie was doing, but suddenly I felt reluctant to go into details. Something had raised my antennae, some kind of electricity that seemed to indicate he was more interested in my answers than he appeared to be.

"So, old Minnie's going to rattle some skeletons, is she?"

"I hadn't thought about it that way, but yes, maybe she is. Does that bother you?" I asked, trying to appear as cool and casual as he.

"Not in the least," he said. "Believe me, in a community like this there are no secrets. Everyone knows everybody else's business, and has for the last hundred years. There might be things people don't want talked about, but it will do the buzzards good to have somebody shake their tails a bit."

He seemed to relish the idea and I could detect nothing other than amusement in his words.

"What exactly does an Editorial Assistant do?" His eyes had a warm and flattering way of traveling over my face, lingering on my lips, but always returning to capture my glance and hold it. Perhaps the tension I sensed was merely the good old pull between the sexes.

"This is Minnie's first book and she's a little unsure of herself," I said with a bit of improvisation. "I'm just checking on progress, ready to provide some direction if she wants it."

He glanced at his watch, took my hand, and said reluctantly, "Well, I better get going. Sorry I missed Dad, and I hope you're going to be around a while. I'm on my way to Cheyenne, have some glad-handing to take care of."

"Politics?"

"State legislature. You'll still be here when I get back?" His clasp was warm and firm.

"Probably not. I'm only staying a few days."

"I'm sorry." He loosened his grip, but didn't drop my hand. Again his eyes searched my face. He started to say something, hesitated, then settled for, "Well, goodbye then. Say hello to Minnie for me."

He strode off to his car, turning once for a final wave. A very attractive man.

I stretched and yawned, feeling the weight of the day descend in full force. The dog bounced around and followed me to the front door, but I was too tired to pay much attention to him. The time had come to get settled in. Like it or not, I would interrupt Minnie's interview long enough to find out where my room was. I eased backward through the door and shut it in the dog's face. I hoped he wouldn't feel too rejected. Turning, I rammed right into Parson Potts.

CHAPTER 3

"Oh, excu—" I gasped, not able to finish. He grabbed me in a vice-like grip, holding me off the floor while his eyes swept across my unbuttoned neckline and the flimsy material of my dress. His thoughts were evident: woman, the devil incarnate; and sin, sin, sin. A blush crawled up my face like some nasty animal.

"You're from the city, aren't you?" he growled, as if that doomed me to the seven pits of hell. "Have you been saved?"

I could feel the impulse in his hands, wanting to shake the city sin from me with great flicks of his heavy arms. Furious, I jerked out of his grasp. He opened the door, but stopped for a parting shot.

"We're God-fearing people around here," he said, shaking a fat finger at me. "We don't allow destructive forces to contaminate our young ones. You better mend your ways, Miss."

He shut the door just as Minnie came out of the parlor. "What's the matter with you? And where's

Potts? I wanted to show him—"

"The man is crazy," I said.

"Crazy? What did he do, start preaching at you? He's not crazy, foolish maybe and usually harder to get rid of than a burr. Now, when I want him, he disappears." She gave a little snort of disgust. "Eat you out of house and home, too, if you let him. Always comes calling at dinner time so you got to feed him." She smiled.

The smile traveled all over her face, bringing the dimple into play that brightened her plain features into a startling attractiveness. It helped restore my poise.

Her fingertips brushed my arm like butterfly wings. "Don't let Potts bother you," she said. "He's a harmless old man."

"I'm not so sure."

"He's lived here forever. In his young days he was quite a heller, according to my sister Lil. No worse than a lot of others, but still pretty much what you'd call a rough number. Somewhere along the line he got religion and the name Parson. Guess it stuck. Nobody calls him anything else."

"I don't care for the man. Anybody who'd kick a dog—" I stopped, realizing Minnie hadn't witnessed the incident.

But her thoughts weren't on the animal, they were far away in another world. "He knew me when I was little. He used to ride me around on his back like a horse. In these very rooms…" Her voice drifted away, feather soft.

The hall glimmered with the luster of fading sunlight and newly polished wood. I followed Minnie into the great room and watched as she trailed her fingers across the backs of the dark leather chairs.

Her voice was a whisper. "They used to stand me on the bar and clap their hands while I danced." She swayed to an unheard rhythm.

Hairs prickled on the back of my neck. My eyes drifted shut. I listened for rowdy voices, the thump of an out-of-tune piano, shrill cries of women vying for attention, and a tiny girl reveling in the commotion. The stench of stale cigars burned my nostrils and throat. My eyes flew open. But only Minnie was there, floating down the room with a light-footed two-step. Then she stopped, and pressed her fingertips to her temples in a shy, kneading gesture.

"I probably don't really remember," she said. "I was only two years old; but it seems like I do. My sister Lil filled my years with so many stories. Those stories are all the family I have."

My hand went out to her, compelled by an urgent need to make a connection, to defy the loneliness that seeped from the very bones of the old house. But the spell was broken.

She brushed past me. "Why are we standing here like fools? There's work to be done."

I was too tired to sort through her mercurial switches between politeness and blunt Iowa hardrock. I stood my ground.

"Actually, Minnie, I'd like to get my luggage out of the car. If you could show me where I'm to sleep?"

"Oh no!" She whirled, truly dismayed. "Oh, my goodness, I'm so sorry. It's been hours!" She rushed past me out the front door and insisted on carrying both the suitcase and tote bag.

"Whatever was I thinking about?" she muttered. "I'm so sorry."

I didn't have the heart to remind her she'd been thinking about Parson Potts eating her into the poor house. Besides, I was in complete sympathy with her impulse to starve the old reprobate.

She soon had me placed in a small but lovely room

at the top of the stairs.

"Minnie, this is beautiful." I was impressed. "Did you do all the decorating yourself?"

She nodded. "I don't know if I'll ever get it done. The place was a mess. Been sitting as good as empty for nearly sixty years. Took a couple of weeks just to get rid of the mouse and rat turds. But the Enrights took good care of it."

"Enrights?"

"Helby Enright, the old gentleman you met earlier. He leased the land from Lil ever since she left all those years ago. She put it in the lease that Halfway Halt had to be taken care of, too. They had a hired hand living here sometimes, but mostly it was boarded up."

She brushed her palm across the marble top of the cherry wood dresser, and smoothed the yellow flowered comforter. "I like things nice, and this furniture is from the old days."

"You mean from here? Original furnishings from Halfway Halt when it was…uh…in business?" I still wasn't sure how sensitive Minnie was about her sister's occupation.

"I don't really know." A breath escaped her mouth, something between a sigh and a chuckle. "My sister was many years older than I; the oldest in the family. Ma was nearly fifty when I was born. Guess I killed her; she died soon after. Lil was the only mother I ever knew." Two fingers smoothed the skin on her temple in a gesture I was beginning to recognize.

"This place—the land—was my folks' homestead," she said. "Dad built the house one of the few times he had money. Lil quit the…uh…" her chin rose defiantly, but then she ducked her head and followed my euphemistic lead, "her business and took me to Iowa, you know. Actually, she was run out of Hijax. I was very young, two or three. In Iowa she ran boarding houses and did bookkeeping for folks."

Ah, yes, I thought, the old familiar story: reformed prostitute with a heart of gold.

"That was Lil's bed. I like to think she brought it from Halfway Halt and now I've returned it. Anyway, they're the things she prized the most. I'm glad you like them."

It was difficult to believe that round, sweet-faced Minnie could have anything to do with madams, or red light districts, or houses of ill repute. Still, one had to wonder. What was Minnie other than a writer? What about those Iowa "boarding houses?" And the men hanging around here? I'd met three before I'd even said hello. The thought brought a smile. There were hardly three less likely men to be whorehouse habitués. Two were lucky to be getting around without walkers and the other, I felt certain, would have no problem coming up on his own with whatever delights tickled his libido. I was more curious about how the notorious madam, Jersey Roo, fit into the family maze.

But lethargy was taking over. Questions could wait. With more apologies, Minnie left me to my unpacking. Refreshed, but not revived, by a shower and shampoo, I grabbed a brief nightshirt and crawled into the marvelous brass bed. I barely had time to contemplate the wonders of sleeping in a bed-of-joy before I was deep in sleep.

After such an early bedtime I wasn't surprised to wake in the middle of the night. I lay there contentedly and sorted out the day's happenings while listening to the rumblings of the old house. Did it have a ghost? What kind of spirits would haunt Halfway Halt? Visions of scantily clad nimbuses giggling and scampering from room to room entertained me until my growling stomach begged for attention. Thoughts about the leftover bowl of peaches in the refrigerator took over; even the stringy meat had gained some appeal.

Would Minnie approve? Or would my raiding the fridge come under the same category as Potts eating her out of house and home? Potts, the old hypocrite, cadging meals, kicking dogs and spewing religious clichés all in the same breath. At least he seemed eager to talk to her. Hadn't Minnie said nobody wanted her in Hijax? What exactly did she mean by that? Tight-mouthed snobs, she called them.

Helby Enright and his son Jim seemed friendly enough. Then there was the clod who'd tried to run me off the road. Friendly was not a good description of him.

My stomach continued to grumble. Would Minnie approve was no longer the question. Would she hear? I slipped out of bed. The upstairs hall opened to the stairwell, surrounding it in a U shape. My room was at the right end of the U's base with a bathroom next to it, and another room at the far end. Minnie's, perhaps? Closed doors indicated four bedrooms on each leg of the U. I tried to be generally quiet, rather enjoying myself now, and trod on the ends of the stairs which—a childhood discovery—are less squeaky than the middle.

Halfway down, I heard a noise from below. I paused, wanting to identify the sound. Then, of course—the dog. I'd almost forgotten him, poor thing. He was probably lying by one door or another, as hungry as I, and feeling quite forlorn. I doubted if Minnie ever remembered to feed him. I skipped down the rest of the stairs. It wasn't terribly light, but I had no difficulty picking the way. I turned into the kitchen and froze in the doorway.

Someone was there, not two feet from me. My heart slammed against my chest. I flicked on the light.

"What the hell."

Fortunately, the man was just as blinded as I in those first few seconds, but I recovered first.

"What are you doing here?" I demanded.

He staggered back, a hand covering his eyes, but the tall, broad-shouldered shape was familiar. He looked worse than when I'd first seen him on the road after our near collision. His plaid shirt-tail hung out of the low-slung jeans and the dark beard-shadow had turned to stubble. He leaned against the doorjamb and dropped his hand. The hat was gone, but the eyebrows were unmistakable.

"What are you doing here?" I demanded again. My knees started to shake as his eyes wandered lazily over my thinly-clad body.

"Uh...water," he said hesitantly, his voice rough and slightly slurred. "I want—"

But I wasn't about to give him a chance to say anything. "You're drunk." My voice rose to a screech. "Get out of here, get out."

"Look, lady." He lurched away from the door and reached for me.

I whirled away. My hand grabbed something from the counter and threw it. It hit him harmlessly on the chest and clattered to the floor. A pancake turner.

I wanted to run, but couldn't. I just kept yelling, "Get out of here. Get out or I'll scream."

He steadied himself on the back door, glared at me, then turned and lurched out. I stood motionless, until the porch screen closed with a soft chunk, most likely the same sound I'd heard on the stairs. Then I bolted the kitchen door, ran through the hall to the front door, checked its lock, and raced up the stairs.

I knocked on the door I thought was Minnie's,

gulping to slow the ragged breaths that tore at my throat. I put my ear to the panel and heard steady snoring. I knocked again, but the snoring continued unabated.

I wished I'd flicked the upstairs light on. My eyes strained to see past the darkness gathered around the stairwell and the rows of closed doors. The harder I tried to see the more the doors looked as if they were opening and the shadows swirling with movement. Outside, the wind quickened, and moaned through loose boards and shingles. A cool draft curled around my ankles.

To hell with Minnie. I ran to my room, jumped into bed, and pulled the covers up to my chin.

I always wondered what I would do in a crisis, now I knew—blab my fool head off and run. If you can't hit them, talk them to death, that's me. But it wasn't funny. My teeth were clenched and my legs quivered.

I should have wakened Minnie. And where was he? Why had he followed me here? I hadn't heard a car, or had he walked in? That seemed more sinister. Was he still prowling around? I should do something. I ought to wake Minnie.

Ought or not, I knew nothing would get me out of that bed again, not even to shove something in front of the door, which is what I really wanted to do. Instead, I crept further down in the bed and pulled the blanket over my head.

Impossible as it seemed, I must have slept. When I burst from my cocoon, sun filled the room with heat, and with a rush, my fears returned. I threw on jeans and a skinny knit top, anxious to put my worry onto Minnie's shoulders, where it belonged. I raced downstairs and, in a nightmarish repeat, stopped short in the kitchen doorway.

CHAPTER 4

Last night's intruder sat calmly at the table nursing a cup of coffee between his hands. I opened my mouth to protest, then saw Minnie at the stove staring glumly into a frying pan.

She glanced up and grunted a greeting. "Help yourself to the coffee and have a seat. Get the butter and jelly, and set up the toaster." The added, "Please," was an afterthought.

I was glad for something to do. I felt incredibly stupid. But how was I to know the man belonged here? Chicagoans scream first and ask questions later.

Minnie said, "Thea, this is Max Holman; he works for me. Hired hand."

He glanced at Minnie with something that I supposed was a smile twitching the corners of his mouth.

"We've met," I said, grudgingly ready to make amends.

"Coffee?" he interrupted, holding out the pot.

"Yes, please." I eyed him warily. He didn't appear

hung-over, just sat there, shaved and combed, looking as innocent as Adam. An innocence, I might add, I've always held suspect. He wore another plaid shirt, with the sleeves rolled up his arms. There was nothing very handsome about him. Thirty, maybe; a tad weatherworn. The stubborn square jaw gave him the look of a "heavy", the bad guy, the one who always wears black gloves and a black hat. At least the edgy tension was gone, that sense of pent-up energy waiting to explode that I'd noticed on the road.

I sipped my coffee and began again. "We had quite an adventure last ni—"

"Toast?" He offered the fresh, warm slices he had just buttered.

A classy act. Very smooth and natural. If it hadn't been for the harsh words he'd thrown at me yesterday, telling me to go back where I came from, I wouldn't have been suspicious, wouldn't have thought his interruptions were intentional, that, for some reason, he didn't want Minnie to know he'd been in the house late last night.

"Eggs this morning," Minnie announced triumphantly. She brought the frying pan to the table and flopped three eggs on Max's plate and two on mine.

I've never been able to face an egg early in the morning, but these were things to be pitied. They actually looked crisp. As usual, Max Holman was watching and ready.

"More toast?" With an expressive roll of his eyes he offered another slice.

I took it, struggling to hold back a childish burst of giggles. With another eloquent grimace, he began to eat the horrors on his plate, and I approached a state of near hysteria. Excusing myself for a drink of water, I lingered at the sink until I could return and munch my toast with some composure, not entirely happy with how quickly he'd turned me into a giggling co-conspirator. Well, he hadn't won me over yet.

"Eat your eggs, now," Minnie lectured me. "Nothing but skin and bones. Need something to stick to your ribs."

The eggs were beyond me, but Max Holman came to the rescue. He switched our plates when Minnie got up to refill the coffee pot, and quickly devoured the mess.

"What are you doing today?" Minnie asked abruptly. I jumped. She had a way of making me feel as if I were back in the schoolroom—on the wrong side of the desk. But she was talking to Max.

He lit a cigarette, and tilted his chair against the wall before answering.

"Fix the well in the winter pasture; the stick's broken. Think I better check the south one, too."

"How about the fence that was down?"

"Fixed it yesterday. Looks good. Just the north end left to check and that can wait until the wells are fixed." He ran his hand over his chin thoughtfully. "You know, Minnie, cows don't trample fences that often and the wells…"

"You just don't like to fix fence, is all's wrong with you. You're soft."

He brought the legs of the chair down with a bang and I waited (more eagerly, I suppose, than was proper) for the explosion I expected to follow. But he ignored her jabs and changed the subject. Because I was there?

"The old psalm-singer come calling last night?" He stood and stretched, then rested his hand on Minnie's shoulder, saying softly, "Don't let that old guy bug you now, hear?"

"He doesn't." She sighed. "But he wasn't very

cooperative. I've been trying to find out more about that hanging, but he clammed right up."

"Hanging?" Max asked. "What hanging?"

"Here in Hijax, nineteen-thirty." Minnie's eyes narrowed, intent on his face. "They lynched some sheepherder on trumped up charges. You know anything about it?"

"For chrissake, you're not going to hash over that old scandal, are you? I'd think people would be sick of it by now. What's that got to do with your book, anyway?"

"They ran my sister, Lil, out of town over it."

Max's boiling glance swung from Minnie to me, but I avoided his eyes, and stared instead at a tiny pulse that thrummed on his neck. The volcano was stirring. He grabbed his hat and walked out.

Minnie stared after him. Then, as if surprised to see me sitting there, she said, "Well, why don't you go with Max this morning? You'll want to see some of the countryside, and he can show you around the place."

I opened my mouth to protest, but she rushed on.

"I need to finish up some typing before I let you see my manuscript. I think you'll be pleased with it. When you get back we'll go through the pictures Helby brought over. See if any will work for the book."

Before I could come up with a counter suggestion Minnie ran to the door and hollered out at Max.

"Wait for Thea. She wants to see the place." She patted me on the shoulder and said, "Run along now and have a good time." It seemed foolish to protest.

The blue pickup truck was parked beside the barn and Max was loading equipment in the back. He looked up when I approached, but didn't speak.

"I'm supposed to go with you." I said, sounding

rather ill-tempered, I suppose. I climbed awkwardly onto the seat, fully aware that I was probably the only person in the whole world who had never ridden in a truck before. Under other circumstances a drive around the property would have been enjoyable, but Max Holman made me uneasy. I hadn't forgotten the pointed interruptions, nor that he'd succeeded in his purpose. I hadn't told Minnie about our middle-of-the-night encounter.

Without a word, he got in beside me and drove off down the slope in back of Halfway Halt. Finally, he broke the silence.

"Sorry I gave you a scare last night. I met an old high school buddy I hadn't seen in years, and we kind of hung one on. Can't take it like I used to. If I'd known you'd be wandering around well, I'd probably have come for water anyway. I am allowed; water is not one of the luxuries of the bunkhouse."

"Then you don't sleep in the house?"

"No. I use the bunkhouse out back when I don't stay in town."

At least I wasn't responsible for his having to sleep under a tree or something. I tried to think which building might be the bunkhouse and finally decided on the one I'd thought was a storehouse.

He took his eyes from the road and glanced at me from under those heavy lids. "I hope you understand that I expect a return apology," he said dryly. "You scared the living hell out of me."

"Why didn't you want me to tell Minnie about it?"

"About what?" His puzzled frown looked genuine.

"Our little midnight run-in. I got the distinct impression this morning that you were purposefully interrupting me every time I broached the subject."

He shook his head. "Sorry, I didn't mean to. Didn't you tell her last night? You made enough noise to wake the dead."

"She's a heavy sleeper. A bad ear," I added wryly.

Was that it? Had he simply come in to wash, and run into me, who promptly over-reacted and had hysterics? My dignity didn't want to accept the logical answer, but I gave in with a laugh.

"All right. Apologies accepted and given, besides, I owe you for the eggs."

His smile when it came was devastating, softening his harsh, somber features with a brilliant flash.

"Anytime. I like to eat."

"You must have a cast iron stomach."

"Minnie would make a good army cook." Then, apropos of nothing, "You're from the city, aren't you?"

"What does that have to do with anything?" I said, back on the defensive. "You're the second person who's accused me of being from the city as if I'd sprung foamy-mouthed from Sodom and Gomorra. What's so great about country life?"

He grinned, then turned his concentration to crossing a rocky gully. I clung to the dashboard and armrest, amazed that the large truck could be maneuvered—even with a great deal of gear grinding—in and out of such a deep, narrow crevice.

While I hung on for dear life, he was apparently mulling over my cursory question.

"Country life," he said, urging the truck up the bank as if it were a horse, "is closer to the bone. Isolation brings out the best and the worst in people. Reality on a pinhead."

"Oh, come on now, a day in a city will show you more 'reality' then you'd find here in a month."

"I'm not talking about murders and muggings. It's the inconsequential's that count, the trivialities that reveal people for what they really are." His words seemed drawn from a deep well of cynicism.

"And you don't like what you find?" I asked.

He shrugged. "As a rule, no. But the exceptions are worthwhile."

Heady ranks, I thought, with a cynicism of my own. I doubted I'd qualify as one of the exceptions. And anyway, it was a strange conversation.

"Who else accused you of being a city girl?" he asked.

"Potts. I barely escaped being his next human sacrifice. Let me tell you, I'd as soon run across a stranger in Chicago's Grant Park at midnight, as run into your Parson Potts again. So much for your grand country life."

Again I was rewarded with the flashing smile and its accompanying shock wave. It gave him a wicked, piratical charm that made one overlook (or appreciate?) the heavy beard-shadow, strong, slightly crooked nose and overpowering eyebrows.

"Let's try again. You're with Minnie's publishing company aren't you? What do you do there?"

"Oh, a little of everything." The airy answer sounded bitchy even to me. I tried to unbend a bit. "Actually, I'm an editorial assistant, but I do more typing and gofering than I like. I'm hoping Minnie's book will change all that. I intend to show Roger Sweeney that I can handle a manuscript with the best of them."

With my usual finesse, I'd sunk from condescension to sophomoric bravado. Who did I think I was— Alfred A. Knopf? Proofreading was one thing, I'd corrected papers for years. But what about putting a book together? Was a lifetime of reading really enough? Could I bully my way through this as I'd bullied the neighborhood kids when I was young, making them sit in make-shift desks while I played teacher and got to write on the blackboard? And what if I discovered I disliked publishing as much as teaching?

I hated wallowing in the endless morass of doubts and uncertainties, hated feeling like a silly little wimp stuck in a quagmire. I needed that success, but what if I didn't get it?

An unexpected sensitivity, or perhaps monumental disinterest, allowed Max to let me ruminate in silence. He drove casually with one elbow resting on the open window frame. Squinchy wrinkles fanned the corners of his eyes, an indication that the constant business of scanning the countryside was a life-long habit.

A light, aromatic breeze drifted across my face. The air was hot, but not the damp, sluggish heat of Chicago that left a person limp and exhausted. This heat was harsh and dry, something you could lean into and survive. Even the dust that swirled behind us seemed clean and fresh in the brilliant light.

"What's that delicious smell?" I asked.

"Sage." He stopped the truck, leaned out the open door and stripped silvery leaves from a rough branch. He dropped them in my hand. We drove on. The bruised leaves filled the cab with perfume.

"Minnie shouldn't be writing that book," he said, taking me by surprise.

"What?"

"Minnie shouldn't be here and writing that book."

"Why?"

"There's talk enough about her as it is. If she goes ahead with that damned book everybody'll be down her neck."

"Everybody? Who's everybody?" I couldn't believe he was serious.

"The town, the community, the whole damn area." He was in deadly earnest.

"But why? I don't understand. What she's writing is ancient history. Who would care?"

"Some of the people concerned are still around."

"Oh, come on, how many hundred-year-olds do you have around here?"

"Eighty-year-olds; Lil Darrow was run out of town in the early thirties. And there are more of them left then you might think. To say nothing of their children. There are plenty who remember those days."

And what about you, I wondered, recalling his vehement reaction to Minnie's remarks about a hanging in Hijax.

"Minnie's book ends in the eighteen nineties and doesn't concern Lil Darrow at all. It's about Jersey Roo and her reign. Really, Max," his name kind of rolled off my tongue accidentally, "it's the old, Wild and Woolly West Sweeney's interested in, not what happened in the thirties."

An accurate statement, but of course, by now, I wasn't entirely sure myself what Minnie was writing. Had she turned her book into a paean to her sister instead of the rowdy frontier history I was expecting? I needed to see that manuscript, I thought, suddenly uneasy.

"This is a close-knit community," Max continued. "They don't like outsiders nosing around their family business. In town last night all anyone could talk about was your arrival. They want to know who you are and what you're doing here. Is Minnie really writing a book and does she really have Jersey Roo's diaries? They want to know what's in them and what Minnie's going to put in her book. It wasn't pleasant chit-chat."

"Of course she has the diaries, that's what prompted her to write the book in the first place. Is that so awful?"

He shrugged, and I wished he wasn't driving, that he didn't have a legitimate excuse to turn his face away. I wanted to see his expression.

He was still gazing out the side window when he spoke again. "I didn't know much about Jersey myself until last night, but believe me, I got an earful. A real hard-case woman. Came to town with the tents and established a thriving business right from the start. Her establishments got shut down and quietly reopened on a regular basis. One of those times, bankrolled by the leading lights in town, she bought Halfway Halt from old man Darrow. He was an ornery old coot. The story has it that he sold out to Jersey for the same reason she bought the place; to irritate Black Enright, Helby Enright's father. The Enrights live five miles up the road. This place cuts their land in two."

"But how did Lil get it back?"

"I guess she worked hard and saved her money." His laugh was grim. "All I really know is that Lil bought Jersey out and ran the place until she was shut down for good and moved away. But she hung onto her land. After Black Enright died, Lil leased the place to his son, Helby Enright; that's in the courthouse records. Helby held the lease until six months ago, when Minnie didn't renew and decided to live out here herself."

"And what is everyone afraid that Minnie will reveal?"

He shrugged. "I don't know. That their grandpas bankrolled a whorehouse? That a hallowed family name might be sullied by connection with Jersey or Lil, or ridiculed by tales out of Halfway? I don't know what they're afraid of; I just know that feelings are running high. Things are starting to get ugly."

But he had lost my attention. I was in the throes of

an IDEA: Controversy. Whether the townspeople's fears were based on fact or fiction was of little concern if the squabble could be turned to good purpose, right? Like some nation-wide publicity. An article in *People* magazine, maybe. *Small Town Explodes Over Whorehouse*, or something. Wasn't that the kind of thing that sold books? I needed to talk to Roger. If the idea was as good as I thought, maybe he could get something going from his end.

"There's nothing for anyone to worry about." I said absently, remembering that Minnie didn't have a telephone.

Then came the eruption.

"Great!" He pounded his fist against the steering wheel and managed to hit every rut and rock with jarring emphasis. "Tell the ignorant peasants there's nothing to worry about, the world's going to love their dirty linen—think it's funny as hell." He rocketed in and out of another dry creek bed.

His anger gave way to exasperation. "I don't give a damn whether you think it's ridiculous, or not. I've been trying to tell both you stubborn women that you're playing with fire. That's dangerous, remember?"

"How? In what way?" Surely nobody was going to start bashing heads because of something their grandpa or great-grandpa did a hundred years ago.

He started to answer, then swore and jerked the truck into a sharp turn that threw me against the door. He left the track and sped across the rock and brush strewn field, braking to a halt in front of a barbed wire fence. The fence was down for about six post lengths, nothing that seemed to warrant such a reckless dash across rough terrain.

He jumped out and surveyed the wreckage, lifting the strands of wire to look down their length. I got out too, and walked over.

"Damn it, don't touch anything," he snapped. "Get back in."

Furious, I stomped back to the truck and slammed the door behind me, convinced the only source of danger around here was Max Holman himself. He swung into the truck and took off across the downed fence.

"Look for cows," he said.

I didn't deign to answer, but found injured silence difficult to maintain while bouncing around like a jumping bean.

"There they are." He swung the truck toward a small group of cows and calves. "Can you drive this thing?"

"I doubt it," I answered stiffly.

"Then get out on foot. Circle around behind them a bit so they don't run the wrong way. When they're between us we'll move them back across the fence. All right? Do you understand?"

I gave him a withering look and climbed out. The last time I saw a cow was back in the days of visits to the kiddie zoo. They were not my favorite animal. However, I was prepared to go down under thundering hooves before letting Max Holman suspect I was frightened.

Circling behind the cows, I matched them stare for stare, glad, as I dodged clumps of cactus, that some flicker of sense had made me put on tennis shoes this morning rather than my usual sandals.

I reached the far side of the animals without mishap and heard the truck rev up. Max stuck his head out the window, whistling, shouting and banging the side of the cab with his hand. To my surprise, the cows jerked into movement, heading in the right direction. I stayed to the rear on my side as Max was on his, though he, of course, was riding in the truck while I was jogging on foot, shooing the dumb animals with my voice until they crossed through the downed fence.

Huffing, and still miffed, Max's brief, "Good," was hardly the praise I craved. He chased the cattle further away with the truck, then drove back to where I sat, leaning against a post to pick cactus needles from my Reeboks.

He drew on a pair of gloves—black, of course— stuck a few tools in his belt and began to issue orders.

"Grab that next post and hold it up." He wired and pounded the post he held until it stood firm. Then, "Straighten up the top strand and hold it as tight as you can."

I grabbed for the wire and caught a barb in the flesh of my thumb. I winced, but wouldn't give him the pleasure of hearing a "city girl" yell, or curse, for that matter. The stupid wire kept sliding through my sweaty hands, cutting jagged paths across my palms, but I wasn't going to let him know about that, either. So we proceeded down the ruined length of the fence.

"There." He gave a final smash to the top of a post. "That should hold 'til I get a chance to do it right. Come on, I'll have to take you back. I've got to get a horse and make sure there aren't any more cows in that pasture."

I climbed back in the truck. Pain snaked across my hands as I cupped them carefully in my lap. I rested my head against the seat and closed my eyes. They opened wide again when Max took one of my hands and turned it over to expose the cuts and scratches.

"Silly fool," he said. "Why didn't you say something? There's another pair of gloves in here." He turned back to his driving, but kept my hand in his, absently rubbing his thumb over the palm, which did nothing for the pain. For some reason the small show of sympathy brought tears to my eyes. I snatched my hand away.

"Sorry again," he said to my silence. "This is the third time in the last ten days that fence has been down. I was suspicious before, but this is definitely one time too many. There's a bit of sabotage going on, with the wells and the fences."

"And I gather Minnie doesn't believe you," I said, remembering the breakfast table conversation.

"Right. She thinks I'm an alarmist." He cast me a telling glance. "Along with some others I could mention."

I ignored the remark, honing in on the thought of sabotage. More headlines to play with. *Community Harasses Little Old Lady: Fears She'll Reveal Family Secrets.* Rather tame, but Roger could spice it up.

"Why would someone tear the fence down?" I asked. "If that's what you think they're doing."

He gave a hefty sigh. "I don't have proof. The wires haven't been obviously cut. I've got no solid evidence of tampering, just this gut feeling."

"What would be gained?"

"Discouragement. Make things tough for Minnie; run her off. She's grazing the cattle for the Enrights. It's in the contract that the cows remain open. If they get accidentally bred Minnie will lose a bundle of money."

"But you said it's the book everyone is worried about. What good will running her off do? She can write anywhere. And if someone did want to run her off—scare her—wouldn't they be a little less subtle? I mean, she doesn't even believe anything's happening."

"Could be. I hadn't thought of it that way. But there's still that feeling."

"I know. How accurate is your gut? Got any

references?"

He was not amused. He scanned the countryside, looking everywhere but at me. I hadn't the faintest idea what he really thought.

"You said there has been talk about Minnie. What kind of talk?" I asked, fishing for more usable information.

"Well, for one thing," he said with a quick grin and a wicked gleam in his eye, "they say Minnie plans to open Halfway Halt for business again, help out us poor country boys."

CHAPTER 5

I had to laugh. The thought of Minnie trying to run herd on a bunch of "girls" was too ludicrous for words. Or was it? She already had me dancing on eggshells.

"When folks heard that Lil's little sister planned to restore Halfway Halt, well, that was enough of a two plus two for them to add up to four. You can imagine the excitement. The church held battle meetings, the old men licked their lips and dredged up the ancient yarns for us young pups to savor. Lil Darrow was a town legend, anyone who hadn't heard of her before, soon did. Anticipation ran high, let me tell you."

Indulgent fondness replaced sarcasm as he warmed to his story, and I wondered how he fit in. What was Max's connection to these people, this community?

"And when Minnie arrived?"

"A major anticlimax. There was as much disappointment as disbelief when Minnie didn't pick up where Lil left off. The militant ladies refused to let loose of the bone, and sent the sheriff out to question her intentions. Things quieted some then. That was one of the early rumors; it's about died down. Until you showed up," he added blandly.

"Oh no," I groaned. "Is that why Potts wanted to save my soul? Did he think I was going to be the first filly in Minnie's stable?"

"Probably, but I don't think anybody else does. Not really. It's just the favorite joke in town."

But I remembered the sheriff and the others in the cafe. No wonder they eyed me strangely. I squirmed, not happy at being the butt of a stupid joke. Even Jim Enright had gotten a chuckle at my expense, I thought, remembering how amused he was when I said I was here for work. Max's grin didn't help.

I felt him watching me with those veiled, knowing eyes. Looking for my reaction to reality, no doubt. This was bound to be one of those small occasions of his that were so revealing of character. I bit my tongue, then said, "Minnie told me she hadn't been welcomed here, but I didn't realize they'd sicced the sheriff on her. How embarrassing."

"Yeah, and when she tried to interview the old-timers for her book it just gave them something more to get riled up about. Minnie's sister was in a position to know everything that went on in her day and to hear about all the events before her time as well, usually directly from the horse's mouth. Those were wild days even for Hijax. A lot went on that people figure is best forgotten, or if it were chronicled for posterity they'd rather it be by someone other than the sister of the town's madam. So they refused to talk with her, or socialize. Except for a few independent old guys like Helby and the Parson. And of course, Potts thinks he has to disguise his interest as proselytizing."

Helby, my talisman from the past. Such a

marvelous-looking old man. I was glad he was being decent to Minnie. Still, he hadn't been all that pleased to see me. He'd acted as if my presence were a nasty intrusion. Or like Potts, did he take me for a whore? A humiliating thought. I'd like to fry them all!

Max drove up the final incline and pulled to a stop between the house and barn. I started to open the door.

"Don't," Max said, and leaned across me to remove my hand from the handle. "It will hurt, let me."

I'd forgotten my sore palms. He was very close. The hollow beneath his cheekbone begged to be touched and a tiny scar etched the corner of his mouth with laser clarity. I breathed in the earthy scent of his sun-warmed skin. Our eyes met with a spark charged as much by challenge as attraction. The door clicked open and he drew away.

"Thanks," I said, "for telling me about Minnie. I…" But I couldn't think what I wanted to say, so left it, scooting out of the truck and into the house.

Minnie was in her office typing on the old Selectric. I'd have to try to talk her into a computer. She looked up and noticed my hands right away.

"Land, girl, what have you been doing?"

"We found some fence down and I helped fix it," I explained.

"You better clean those cuts out good. You should have worn gloves."

"I know, I know." I didn't need anyone else telling me how ignorant I was. But Minnie said nothing more, just fixed a basin of warm water and sat me at the kitchen table to soak while she puttered around the sink preparing lunch. I dabbled in the water letting it soothe my scraped skin. It seemed as good a time as any to bring up the subject.

"Max doesn't think you should be writing your

book," I said.

"What does he know about it?"

"He says there's talk around town, rumors and such. People are frightened about what you're going to write."

"Max's job is the outside work. He has no call worrying about anything else."

"He thinks it could be dangerous."

She made a disparaging sound, dried her fingers meticulously and headed towards her office. "Come in here now."

Reluctantly, I removed my throbbing hands from the bowl and followed her.

Minnie's office was strictly utilitarian. An unpleasant room that looked as if it had simply been cleared out and the furniture set at random; every year of abandonment showed. The tall ceiling dwarfed a roll top desk in the corner. A typewriter on a stand was next to it, with a well-sprung sofa against the adjacent wall. Two metal filing cabinets and a pile of boxes filled another corner. A white oak library table stood in the center of the room littered with books, magazines and newspapers. Minnie pulled a chair up to the table, motioning me to do the same.

I inspected the magazines with interest. All of a kind: *True West, Frontier Times, American West* and Sweeney Publishing's own *Western True Adventures*. The books were western history as well, some with familiar titles and others not. Minnie pulled a leather-bound scrapbook from under a pile of newspapers. Pushing other things aside, she cleared a space and opened the scrapbook between us.

Faded newspaper clippings jammed the crumbling manila pages along with pictures cut from various sources, and old photographs—mostly old photographs. Minnie turned the pages randomly, supporting each one with her hand before flipping it over.

"All I ever had in my life was my sister, Lil." Her voice drifted like moss in the heavy air, light and wispy. "Sometimes I called her Lilly, but she'd just laugh and say her name was never Lilly, only plain Lil.

"I never had a Ma, or Pa, or grannies, except in this book." Her fingers skipped lovingly over the pictures as if to reacquaint themselves with old friends. "When I was little, I'd sit on the floor and look through this book over and over, never got tired of it. 'Tell me about this one, Lil,' I'd say, 'tell me about Ma again.'" She turned the fragile pages back to the front of the book, and stopped at an old photo of a rough, grim-faced man with a girl seated rigidly at his side, her homely features stretched taut by tightly braided hair.

"That's Ma and Pa," Minnie said, fingertips tracing each stiff figure. "Pa bought this land in the eighteen-nineties; screwed some homesteader out of it, Lil said. He and Ma had a cabin out back by the dugout. Lil had plenty of chances to sell the place, but she hung on to it all those years...for me."

The soft whoosh of turning pages sent the musty odor of newsprint sifting through the air.

"This book is my life, Thea." Her simple words made me think of my family. Real flesh and blood, not crumbling photos on a page.

Minnie pointed to a smudged snapshot of three small ragamuffins. "These are my brothers, Jud, Shep and Austin. I never knew any of them. Lil was oldest. I came way at the end when Ma shouldn't have been having kids. Lil was already thirty."

"Aren't any of your brothers still living?"

"Don't guess so. They left home or ran away as

soon as possible, and nobody heard from them. Lil said it was good riddance; they were wild ones. This is my mother holding me."

I craned my neck trying to get a better look at the frail woman with scraggly hair holding a closely wrapped baby. The words "Ma and Minnie" had been written underneath.

"Ma died shortly after I was born, worn out by Pa, Lil said. How she hated him. Pa was never any good; a drinker and worse, according to Lil." She skipped over several pages and stopped at a sepia-toned picture of Halfway Halt.

"Mostly Lil told me the truth, I think," Minnie continued with a sigh. "She didn't paint any pretty pictures, anyway. No, I figure it was mostly the truth. Except for this." She tapped the slick surface. "Lil always called it a boarding house and I never had cause to believe otherwise. Pa built this house with gambling money, and lost it gambling. To a rich lady, Lil told me, who named it Halfway Halt and took in boarders. Pa sent Lil to work there when she was twelve."

Her own father? Twelve!

"Of course, now I know it was Jersey Roo who won the house...and who Lil went to work for. By the time Lil was twenty she'd bought the place back from Jersey and was supporting Ma and Pa. She was always a sharp one with money.

"After Lil died, I found Jersey's diaries in Lil's safe deposit box. When I read them I knew exactly what kind of place Halfway Halt had been. I didn't want to believe Lil was in the same business as that woman—couldn't imagine it—so I did some research. Didn't take any time at all. I found everything in the old Hijax newspapers."

"Oh, Minnie, how awful for you."

She shook her head as if it were nothing and patted my arm. "Heavens, girl, I'm over sixty."

But it had to have hurt. Hurt horribly. Her precious memories twisted and reshaped after so many years.

"It bothered me some," she admitted, "'til I figured it was like those women's libbers been saying—didn't have much truck with them 'til then. No, Lil did what she had to do in the best way she saw. She made a living, supported her folks and raised me like a mother. She wasn't like that wild woman, Jersey Roo."

A flurry of knocks on the front door took us both by surprise. We stared at each other and for the briefest moment I thought I saw a flash of fear cross Minnie's face.

The front door opened and a voice called in, "Hello. Anyone home?" Didn't anyone keep doors locked around here?

I didn't recognize the voice, but Minnie obviously did. An angry flush darkened her face, then drained and left her pale and rather sick-looking.

I followed her brisk footsteps out to the hallway. Sheriff Beesom stood on the porch, still holding the doorknob. When he saw Minnie he opened the door wider and stepped in.

"Hello. Hope you don't mind me opening the door; I didn't know if you could hear me or not in this big old pile." He removed his Smokey the Bear hat and ran a hand over his thinning hair.

Minnie nodded acceptance, but her mouth compressed into a thin line of disapproval. Nor did she offer a greeting. I remembered what Max had told me about the sheriff's first visit. Evidently Minnie wasn't about to forgive him for thinking she might be running a whorehouse.

The sheriff skirted Minnie's silence with ease. "Had

to drive out this way, so thought I'd just stop by and say howdy. See how things were going for you."

His glance moved from Minnie's stony face to mine. "I see you found your way out here okay; didn't think you'd have any trouble."

Minnie cast me a sharp, questioning look.

"I stopped at the hotel for iced tea yesterday, and the Sheriff was there," I explained quickly. I didn't want her to think I was somehow in cahoots with him.

Minnie stubbornly hadn't moved one foot from the door, but the sheriff sidestepped her easily and ambled across the entry.

"This is some old place, isn't it?" he said, peering first into the parlor and then the great room. "Miss Darrow has done a fine job fixing it up, now hasn't she?"

He chatted away as friendly as could be. And if, when he looked at me, there was a glimmer in his eye that showed his appreciation of the situation, I also sensed an air of quiet determination. This was not some rube lawman.

Finally he held his hands out to Minnie in comic supplication. "You wouldn't happen to have a cup of coffee would you, or even a big glass of water? I'm just dying of thirst, and I've got to drive clear out to old Harney Applegate's place yet."

For a minute I thought she might refuse, but when he moved as if to take matters in his own hands, she led the way to the kitchen herself, saying, "Yes, I think I have some coffee back here. Come along."

He motioned me to precede him down the hall. I didn't believe all this coming-to-say-howdy business any more than Minnie did. Obviously, he was here for a purpose, and I thought perhaps I should disappear discreetly and let them talk in private. But when I headed for the office, he called me back.

"You're not going to make me drink alone are you?"

"No, of course not."

Minnie had poured him a cup of coffee, which he in turn handed to me. He smiled at her blandly and held his hand out for another. Reluctantly, she poured it. He took a big appreciative gulp, and then turned to me.

"My apologies," he said. "I know we introduced ourselves yesterday, but I can't for the life of me remember what you name is."

Of course, we both knew I hadn't told him my name. All of a sudden it dawned on me that I was the one the sheriff had come out to talk to, not Minnie. Well, I didn't have any secrets.

"Thea Barlow, Sheriff."

"Hank, please call me Hank. You going to be spending some time here?"

"Don't tell him anything, Thea." Minnie jumped in like a bull dog. "What happened, Sheriff? The Women's League send you out here again? It's none of your business why Thea's here. You've got no right coming out here snooping around."

"It's all right, Minnie," I said with a laugh, beginning to enjoy myself now that the sheriff was showing the first signs of being uncomfortable. "I've got nothing to hide. I didn't come out here to begin work as a prostitute, if that's what you're wondering, Sheriff. Minnie's a client of mine, and also a friend. I'm an editor." I upped my job title a bit for effect. "The company I work for is going to publish a book Minnie is writing. I'm here to oversee the completion of a very worthwhile project."

"Whoa, now," the sheriff said. "You two have got me all wrong. I'm sorry I insulted you last time I came out, Miss Darrow, but I was just doing my job. I felt I had to answer those ladies fears. But nobody sent me out this time. Truly, I just stopped by to say hello and, well…It's not often a new good-lookin' woman shows up in these parts." He even managed a slight blush. He was either honest, or a consummate actor. Minnie seemed to thaw a bit, and topped off his coffee.

Cup in hand, he wandered the kitchen restlessly, looking out the back door, eyeing the paint and the old appliances. "I'd heard you were writing a book. I know it will be a big success. Just imagine, we're going to have a well known author among us." He paused in the doorway to the office. His inquisitive eyes swept the room thoroughly.

"Boy," he said. "That's some collection of books you got there." He stepped in.

There weren't *that* many books in there. I followed him, and Minnie pushed past me.

He was bent over the scrapbook, peering intently at the pictures, ready to turn the page. Minnie stepped up to the table and closed the book in his face.

He grinned at her sheepishly and said, "Sorry about that. Didn't mean to be nosy." He gave the room another quick inspection, then went through to the kitchen and placed his cup on the counter. "Thanks for the coffee, Miss Darrow. I'd better get back to work."

The three of us strolled into the hallway and Sheriff Beesom said, "You know, I've wanted to see the inside of this place ever since I was a kid. Is there a chance…? Could I possibly see the upstairs, where all the rooms were?"

"There's not much up there," Minnie said. He took her hesitancy for acquiescence, and bounded up the stairs two at a time, then waited politely at the top for further escort. We followed him up like a couple of lemmings.

"My room and a guest room is all that's finished up here." Minnie gestured to her closed door and my partially open one.

"Then these must have been the girl's rooms." With no further invitation he started down the right side of the stairwell and opened each door.

"There's nothing there," Minnie said. "I haven't done anything to them."

I was curious, too. There were a bunch of packing boxes in the first room, but the others were empty. Drab, dusty and empty, with no signs of any of the agony, ecstasy or melodrama that must have gone on in them. The four on the other side of the stairwell were the same.

I lingered a moment in the last room, oddly depressed. It seemed as if some kind of essence should have remained of the lives lived here. A pall crept over us. Silently we went back down the stairs. Even the sheriff seemed subdued.

At the door, the sheriff took Minnie's hand and said, "It must be very lonely living here. I'm glad you've got company." His words seemed utterly heartfelt and sincere.

On the other hand, it didn't take much reflection to realize that in a very short visit, while being completely ingratiating, and not asking any direct questions, the sheriff had probably found out everything he had wanted to know, and gotten a thorough look at every room in the house, as well.

I didn't know if Minnie was thinking the same thing or not, but when we were back in the office she offered apologies.

"I'm sorry you had to go through all that." She opened the scrapbook and began leafing through it again.

"After I found out the truth about Halfway Halt, I wondered some myself about all those boarding houses we lived in when I was young. Then I realized that all the time we lived in Iowa we were treated like respectable folks. After I finished school both Lil and I did bookkeeping for businesses in town and we had our little Canasta club friends. No, I'm sure that part of her life was finished when she left Wyoming."

I couldn't think of a thing to say. It wasn't easy to be glib about whorehouses anymore. All I could think of was a frightened twelve-year-old sent away from her family.

"This is one of my favorites," Minnie said. She had turned to a page that held a studio portrait. The faint mark of a long-gone cardboard frame still rimmed the picture. It showed a woman seated in a chair holding a bare-foot young child who stood in her lap. The woman was neither pretty nor homely. The bobbed, stiffly waved hair and plain dress gave her that ordinary look so common to pictures of the era. A faint smile played across her lips as she struggled to balance the still wobbly-legged child. "Me and Minnie" was written on the bottom edge of the picture.

"That's Lil and me," Minnie said unnecessarily. "Lil left Halfway Halt for good around nineteen thirty, or thereabouts. Pa had died by then and I was around two years old."

At least a year or more after this picture was taken, I thought.

"We look happy, don't we?"

"You certainly do."

She pushed the book away and turned to me. Her eyes had lost the far-away look.

"Well, that's the story, Thea. Lil was the one who got me interested in writing. The only thing she read

were magazines like *Western True Adventures*.
Devoured them, complaining all the while that she
knew better stories and urging me to write them.
Always steered me clear from events around this part
of the country, though. Claimed nothing interesting
ever happened here. Anyway, after she died and I got
over the first shock of finding out her...It took awhile,
but I could finally read Jersey Roo's diaries for what
they were, an interesting bit of history, and thought I
could make some money from them. Then when the
lease on this land came due I realized I could move
out here to the home place. I'd had some health
problems and thought, well, now was the time. I told
myself it was for the good of the book, research and
all, you know, but mostly I wanted to find..."

Her hand hovered helplessly above the scrapbook
for a moment, then she rose and fussed a bit,
straightened magazines and papers into neat piles.

"You know," she went on, her composure regained,
"there was a big scandal in Hijax before Lil left. Some
sheepherder camped outside of town got accused of
setting a fire that burned down the general store. They
hung him on next to no evidence. The courts didn't
hang the sheepherder, mind you, vigilantes did.
Locals. This was cattle country. It didn't take much to
condemn a sheepherder. Anyway, the lynching proved
to be a big embarrassment for the town of Hijax. The
range wars between the cattlemen and sheepmen had
been over for a long time, and nobody wanted to see
that kind of lawlessness start again. So of course they
had to find a scapegoat. My sister, Lil. The do-
gooders labeled Halfway Halt a hell-hole of
conspiracy and accused Lil of instigating the vigilante
action, egging the men on. They ran Lil out of town
yet didn't even try to find out who was in the lynch
mob. A handy cover-up. The more I read about it the

madder I got."

She settled back in her chair and pulled the scrapbook towards her, turning to the last page. An obituary notice was taped in the middle of a new, creamy sheet. Sympathy cards surrounded it, with more stuck loose in the page.

"Lil was a good honest woman. She had a hard life, but managed to turn it around for me. I want people to know that, particularly the snobs around here. I decided to add a couple of chapters to the book, complete the history of Halfway Halt. That's what I went to town for that day, to call you and tell you what I wanted to do, but when I picked up my mail I found this, Thea." She scrabbled in the piles of magazines and newspapers, returning them to their usual disarray, and found a creased and crumpled sheet of paper. She gave it to me.

The letters were spiky and dark: Go back where you came from, bitch. Your kind's not wanted in Hijax. We do worse things to whores than run them out of town. Get out. Now!

The words swam in front of my eyes. I felt like I was in a bad movie. "That's awful, Minnie. Did you show it to the sheriff?" No wonder she had sounded shaken when I talked to her.

"No. I—" Then to my horror, her face crumpled, cheeks sagging into furrows that circled her quivering lips. Her eyes filled with tears that were quickly blinked back and replaced with tiny hot flames.

"All those years I loved this place. This house, the town and all the people Lil told me about. These people are my family, Thea, but they don't want me here. All they see is the sister of a whore and they think I'm one too." She slammed the scrapbook shut, sending pieces of brittle paper puffing into the air.

She crumpled the crude note into a ball. "They're

not going to scare me off, Thea. Not the sheriff, not a bunch of nosy old ladies, or anybody else. This is my home. Danger," she muttered, shaking her fist like a miniature Cassandra calling down the Gods. "I'll show them danger!"

CHAPTER 6

"Danger," I said, surprised to hear my voice crack. "What do you mean by danger?" I'd barely whispered, but the words echoed hollowly against the walls. My eyes flickered around the ugly room, oppressed by the tall ceiling, unfinished and dingy. The room was unbearably stuffy.

Minnie was staring at me, as well she might. The old brothel was turning me into a blathering idiot.

"I didn't mean to frighten you," she said, placid now as pudding. "There's no real danger. I just meant that I wasn't going to let anyone—including Max and that damn sheriff—scare me off. I know small towns. I've lived in them all my life."

"Some pretty vicious crimes are being committed in small towns these days."

"Sure, if you're threatening to take away the farm or something. I'm just a pesky little gnat nipping at proud folks' ankles. They'll talk nasty behind my back and snub me in person. I don't care. It's just not fair that Lil had all the blame put on her."

What she said made sense, and I was beginning to think she was right. Max *was* an alarmist, for whatever reason. One thing remained clear: I needed to distance myself from these people. The manuscript was my job. And that's where I intended to focus my attention.

"I need to see the manuscript, Minnie, and also any photographs you plan to use. I don't have a problem adding the chapters about Lil, if that's what you want to do, but I'll have to see how it all fits together, then we can talk about it. And I plan to reap some publicity from this harassment, or whatever it is. I'd like to get started on that as soon as possible."

"Publicity?"

"Yes. Newspaper or magazine items. Maybe a write-up in *People*. Would you like that?"

"Well, I don't know," she said hesitantly. I could tell she'd never thought of that kind of thing, and she was mulling it over.

"I want to take the manuscript with me when I leave. How close to finished are you?"

"The first part needs some clean-up typing, and I'm still working on the last chapters. How long can you stay? Can you give me two days?"

Max chose that moment to storm in through the back entry.

"Lunch," Minnie said. "Two days?"

I nodded and followed her into the kitchen. Max stomped the dust from his feet and hurled his hat at the rack by the door. He missed. His look was as black as the hat.

He jerked his head at me, but addressed Minnie. "She tell you the fence was down again?"

Minnie nodded and retrieved the sandwich makings from the refrigerator. "Did you fix it?"

"Yes, and I didn't find a bull in the pasture, but who

knows how long the fence was down? If Enright's bulls get to those heifers, you stand to lose a lot of money."

"It's your job to see that they don't."

"You know damn well what I'm trying to say. No matter what you think, you're being sabotaged. Someone wants those heifers to get bred, they *want* your wells to run dry."

"What they want is *me* out of here. Right?" She threw the words at him like a fistful of stones. "How do I know it's not you, Max Holman? Tell me that. You've got a vested interest in getting me to leave this place, now, don't you?"

She turned back to her preparations, and wrenched open a large can of soup.

Dark color flooded Max's face and the tiny pulse I'd noticed before twitched back to life. I watched him make a visible effort to relax, ease out the anger. Curious. He'd had no compunction about yelling at me. Was all this admirable self-control in deference to Minnie's age, or a prudent concession to employee relations? Or could it be a simple case of not wanting to rock the boat for reasons unknown? And of course, I was dying to know what his vested interest was. But something else nagged at me, something concerning Max that I wanted to remember. I couldn't quite grasp the thought.

The basin of water still sat on the table. I dumped it and set out the luncheon things. Minnie brought the food and I took my place beside Max. The sandwiches were filled with last night's stringy dreadful in some new disguise, and the soup looked strangely unappetizing. How can you ruin canned soup?

Silence dragged on. I had to smile. The two of them looked like a pair of recalcitrant sixth graders. How Max managed to keep such a sour expression while wolfing down those awful sandwiches, I'll never know. I toyed with the idea of mediating; Little Suzy Insufferable offering lessons in communication to those in need. But no. I intended to keep my distance, stick to my job. If I could drum up some publicity, fine, but no entanglements.

I was hungry. I picked up half a sandwich and put it down again. Urged on by the bony specter of starvation, I said, "Minnie, why don't you let me cook dinner tonight?"

It took a moment, but then the tension broke. Her face blossomed into the dimpled softness I found so appealing.

"Oh, Thea, would you? I hate to cook. I'm used to TV dinners and a grocery store on the next corner. Can you make stuffed pork chops? I haven't had any in years."

Actually, I was thinking more along the lines of salmon fillets, but what the hey. What difference did it make?

Max's face lightened as well. Minnie leaned across the table, grinned and patted his hand. Really, was a pork chop all it took to erase the tight-lipped accusations and barely controlled fury that went before? I wondered.

"Max, take Thea to town for groceries. The wells can wait. We deserve a decent meal."

I would have preferred going on my own, but wasn't quite ready to face that awful road again. "All right," I said with a laugh. "I need to call the office, anyway. Did you say the closest phone is in town?"

"Not the closest. I'm welcome to use the Enright's phone anytime. They live five miles down the road in the other direction."

I didn't want a phone in someone's home; I needed more privacy. I wanted Roger to get started on the publicity. I should buy a camera, too, I thought. I wasn't sure exactly how these things were handled, but it wouldn't hurt to have pictures on hand if they were needed. The driving sense of direction felt wonderful. This was what I wanted, a project I could control, something to push to goal.

Once again I found myself in the front seat of the pickup with Max Holman. We were getting to be great buddies.

"The sheriff came to call this morning."

"Oh? What did he want? He's not still giving Minnie a bad time about running a house, is he?"

"He claimed it was just a friendly visit, but I think he was checking me out. Wanted to make sure I wasn't a tarnished dove in disguise. Minnie wasn't giving him an inch, but he seemed a decent sort, kind of a teddy bear, actually."

"Don't kid yourself. Sheriff is an elected position around here and he's held office for close to twenty years. Has his thumb firmly on everything, I'd bet."

"He doesn't look that old."

"He's not, he's just got a hell of a lot of relatives. There's a Beesom under every other rock in the county."

"What do you mean?"

"That's what keeps him voted in."

"You mean he doesn't do the job? Is he corrupt?"

He shrugged. "He's probably a good enough sheriff, but I'm sure he takes care of his own. Don't they all?" He paused then asked, "Did Minnie tell him about the fences getting cut?"

"No. She barely spoke to him."

"I'll probably have to tell him myself," he said, more to himself than to me.

Minnie wouldn't appreciate Max going over her head, but if he was really concerned about Minnie's property being damaged, maybe that was the best way to go. Someone should tell the sheriff about that nasty note, too. Was Max aware of it? I didn't think Minnie would ever go to the sheriff for anything less than murder. Maybe I could clue him in about the note. Minnie seemed so vulnerable, and so stubbornly determined not to ask for help.

I wondered what Max's opinion of the sheriff was based on, fact, or inbred cynicism? I suspected the latter. But really, I couldn't worry about it. Minnie had a right to do things her own way. I just wanted to get the manuscript and get out of here.

I must have been squirming with impatience. Max said, "Relax. That's something else about country life: you learn how to wait"

He was right. Right, at least, in that I couldn't fight the distance. If it took X amount of time to get to town, then X amount of time it would take, and letting my stomach knot with impatience wouldn't change anything. I decided to sit back and try to enjoy the ride.

Apparently, the trick to driving on the road was speed, hovering above the rocky roadbed rather than traveling on it. When I mentioned my observation he slowed some and even began pointing out things of interest, though I had a hard time picking out the deer from the sagebrush and rocks. If something didn't move, I couldn't see it.

My eyes needed to get their sea legs, Max told me, indifferent to his mixed metaphor. "You're not used to distance yet."

We jounced along and I pummeled him with questions. What did the cows eat? There wasn't any grass. Why were all the buttes and ridges the same height as if they'd been sliced off with a knife? Why weren't sage hens an endangered species when they were too dumb to get out of the way of the truck? Why did antelope crawl under the fences instead of jumping over them as the deer did? He seemed to have all the answers, at least they sounded sensible to me. An easy camaraderie soon lulled me into forgetting my earlier resolves about noninvolvement.

"What was Minnie talking about at lunch?" I asked. "What are your 'vested interests'?"

He had a disquieting way of sizing me up before he spoke, as if trying to calculate what effect his words would have.

"She's right," he said, and turned his eyes back to the road. "I'd head a list of people who'd benefit from her leaving Hijax."

"Why?"

"I want to buy her ranch; we have an agreement of sorts."

That was a surprise. "I didn't know she was going to sell."

"She might not."

Nothing Minnie had ever said to me indicated she planned to leave Halfway Halt. "But I thought she was going to make this her home."

"So did she. When I heard Enright lost the lease, I called her in Iowa to make an offer. She wasn't interested in selling then. In fact she was excited about coming *home* to Hijax. I tried to tell her, prepare her for the reception I knew she'd get, but hell, I didn't know what to say. I didn't even know her. Like all the kids who grew up around here I'd heard of Lil Darrow and Halfway Halt. Halloween wasn't Halloween without a bunch of us trying to break into the old place. Minnie never had a chance; the ostracism hit her hard."

My heart wrenched for her. I could still see her caressing the old photographs and her dreamy two-step into the past.

"When things were at their worst," Max went on, "about the time the sheriff paid his call on Minnie, I made another offer."

Incredulous, I swung my head to look at him. *How fortuitous for you, Max Holman.* I mean, really! No wonder Minnie was suspicious. Had he set her up? Kept the wheels of rumor whirling? Or as Minnie suggested, cut the fences, fouled the wells and done whatever it was they were worried about with the stupid cows?

He must have felt me staring at him. He turned those hooded gray eyes on me and cocked his head in an inquiry I ignored. But there was no outward sign of any difference that I could detect, no show of concern that perhaps he'd given himself away. Or did he think I was incredibly stupid? I concentrated on the scenery.

"Minnie's not a quitter," he said. "She turned the offer down, but didn't slam the door in my face. We kind of hit it off right from the start."

My snort of derision wasn't intended to be heard, but his ears were as sharp as his eyes.

He laughed. "We have our moments. She's crusty, but that's one of the things I like about her."

Yes, I thought, rather surprised, and recognizing for the first time that I, too, liked Minnie Darrow very much. There was a leavening tang to her personality that made the vulnerability even more poignant when it pierced her tough surface.

"I guess I felt sorry for her," he continued. "I knew what she was looking for…and that she wouldn't find it here. Not in this dammed town."

"And what was she looking for?"

"Her home. Her past. Roots, if you will," he said, each word gaining more bitterness than the one before. He shifted his weight uncomfortably, embarrassed, I thought, by revealing too much.

"Minnie and I are a lot alike," he added. "We're loners, but always looking for something more."

I wasn't sure what I wanted to reply to that, so avoided it. "What kind of agreement do you have?"

"Nothing official, a handshake deal."

"Code of the West, and all that?"

"Right." This time I got the super deluxe smile, the one he saved for special effect. And rightfully so. It was a powerful weapon, and sent my stomach into silly school girl flutters that made me feel like a marionette whose strings had been pulled.

"Since Enright was using the leased land for summer pasture," he went on, "Minnie thought the least she could do was let him continue, so she signed a grazing contract. Unfortunately, there's a bit more to grazing other people's stock than she expected. Enough at least, so that she needed to hire someone to keep an eye on things. I was at loose ends for the moment and agreed to help out for a month or so until she decided whether to stay or sell. In turn, I got first option to buy. I wanted some thinking time, and it was a good chance to get a close look at the property and the problems that go along with it."

As well as an excellent opportunity to manipulate Minnie into a most advantageous decision for him. Something she was not unaware of. Well, I wasn't ready to take him at face value, either.

So I stuck my foot in further. "Does Minnie really think you'd ruin her fences, or whatever? You didn't say much to defend yourself."

His heavy shoulders moved noncommittally. "Minnie likes to needle people. That flinty core keeps things interesting, but I try not to give satisfaction when she hits her mark. I get the idea she doesn't like men much; a typical old maid." He added blandly, "A lot like you."

Minnie wasn't the only one who liked to needle people. I, of course, rose to the bait.

"You want a reaction to 'typical', or to 'old maid'?"

"On second thought," he said, eyeing me appreciatively, "I guess you're not typical. How about old maid?"

"If you mean unmarried, yes, I'm an old maid. If you mean do I hate men—only selectively."

"Ouch. No attachments? I'd find that hard to believe."

"Not at the moment," I answered, promptly sinking into my own miserable thoughts. I hadn't heard the term 'old maid' in years, but suddenly now, it seemed depressingly apt. I'd shown no more talent for picking men than I had in choosing a career. To be fair, none of the men at college stood a chance of competing with my zeal to become the most amazing teacher in recorded history. And my last, most serious attachment, an engagement, really, with a fellow teacher had disintegrated in pace with my disenchantment for teaching poetry to sixth grade boys. Whatever I was looking for, I'd not found it yet.

I gazed out the window, moodily watching dusty, sage-strewn fields give way to wired-in lots scattered with rusting junk and weathered signs that advertised the approaching delights of Hijax, Wyoming. Max slowed as we passed the shabby Tastee-Freeze and its accompanying swarm of teenagers that heralded the outskirts of town.

"I was married once, a long time ago," he said, and pulled to a stop in front of the small drugstore. "I don't recommend it. You've got an hour and a half to explore our thriving metropolis while I pick up supplies. I'll meet you here, then we'll get the groceries and head out."

Before I knew it I was standing on the curb squinting into the sun watching the truck disappear around a corner.

How like Max to throw out bits of information, then not give me time to reply. Why did he want me to know he'd been married before? And why was I so certain he had a reason beyond the obvious one?

Well, I'm not going to worry about it now, I thought, glad to be out of the truck. I wanted to find a telephone and a camera. And now that I knew something about Minnie's background the prospect of investigating the town seemed more interesting.

Whirlwinds of dust danced up the street, swirling debris onto the sidewalks and against the already grimy clapboard buildings. I didn't see a phone booth on the street, so I decided to begin my exploration with the drugstore.

The store was small, but bright and cheery with an old-fashioned soda fountain along the back wall that sent a sugary scent of nostalgia drifting through the narrow aisles. A hot fudge sundae would be nice, I thought. I'd not eaten much of Minnie's lunch. But business first.

Magazines filled a rack under the front window, and a pay phone hung on the wall beyond a pile of newspapers. I headed towards it, smiling at two middle-aged women who occupied stools at the counter. Not much privacy. The women made no attempt to conceal their interest in my every move. I called Mother first for a trial run, testing how far my voice would carry and how far curiosity would push the two women.

As usual, Mother was delighted to hear from me, and relieved to hear that no, the West wasn't all that wild anymore, and no, I hadn't seen any Indians yet, and yes, I thought I'd met a cowboy.

Indulgent smiles from the soda fountain informed me that the ladies' committee had taken it in as well. I'd decided to find a different phone for my call to Roger when a group of teenagers filed through the door, providing a perfect screen with their loud voices and laughing demands for service. I turned my back and quickly dialed Roger's number.

Roger was delighted to hear from me, too, glad I'd arrived without any mishap for which he'd be sued.

I tried to push through his barrage of questions and commands, saying finally, "Be still, Roger. I've got an idea and need your advice." Me asking for help stunned him into silence. "This is a public phone, so I can't go into details, but I've got a great idea for publicity that..." I glanced over my shoulder to check on the two women, and nearly dropped the phone. Jim Enright stood not two feet from me, leaning casually against the wall with a welcoming smile on his face.

"Don't hurry," he mouthed. "I'll wait."

I grimaced self-consciously, wondering how he'd read the confused mixture of guilt, pleasure and alarm washing over my face. Thank goodness I'd looked around before blurting out anything more.

"So anyway, Roger," I said, with forced brightness, "I'll be in touch soon," and hung up before anyone could hear his annoyed sputtering.

"Hi." I turned to Jim. "I thought you were going to Cheyenne."

He was better looking than I remembered, and less formidable dressed in the local uniform: well-worn jeans and a plaid shirt with snap buttons and rolled up sleeves. His cornflower blue eyes were startling against the golden tan of his skin, and I couldn't detect a trace of Enright arrogance anywhere. Only pleasure.

"My meeting got called off," he said. "I was on my way to get some lunch when I saw you through the window. Will you join me?"

"Oh, you can probably talk me into a piece of pie or something." Little did he know.

"Come on then." He grabbed my hand. "I'll give you another tour. It doesn't take long in Hijax."

"Okay, but can you wait a minute? I want to buy a camera. I forgot to bring mine, and my…my parents will be disappointed if I don't bring back pictures." I sounded like a ten year old. He didn't seem to notice.

I chose a bright orange camera, the only color available, but it was inexpensive, had an automatic flash and looked easy to operate. It also had a carrying case with a long strap. I put it all together, slung it over my shoulder and hoped I looked like any casual tourist. Jim ushered me out and we sauntered along the cracked and crumbling sidewalk.

"Hi there, Jesse," he called into a small office as we passed, banging the screen door without slowing our pace.

"Yo Jim," came a disembodied voice.

We stopped at the corner and waited for a dust-covered Cadillac to sweep past. The car's grizzled driver raised his hand in salute and Jim waved back.

"Come on," he led me around the corner. "You can take a picture of the new high school. Not everything is old and shabby around here. Over there, next to the park, is the new courthouse, finished last year."

"Courthouse? You mean Hijax is a county seat?"

He grinned, tickled by my astonishment. "Yes. It's the only incorporated town in the county. The courthouse used to be in that old house on the corner. Took a lot of finagling to get the bond issue passed for a new one, but we did it."

"We? Sounds like you had a hand in the action."

"Yeah." His smile was rather sheepish, but pride shone through. "City Council. Hijax has been a sleepy cow town for over a hundred years, but we finally got some of the old duffers out of office, and were starting to bring in our share of energy dollars when the bottom fell out of the oil and coal market. There's a lot of potential in this town, though it probably doesn't look like much to you. When the next boom comes—and it will come—Hijax will be ready to grow. Hell, when that happens Wyoming's going back to the top. This state will put the U.S. in the driver's seat as far as energy control goes."

I laughed. He sounded like my dad. I couldn't resist teasing him.

"I think you're still campaigning," I said. "You and my father would make a good pair. He loves small town politics and is always running for something. What's next for you, Jim? Governor?"

He smiled noncommittally. "I guess soapboxes are second-nature to me. Granddad was one of the town founders and pretty much ran things to suit himself in the old days. Dad was about the same, though you'd never know it the way he acts now."

"He doesn't approve of politics?"

"He's old guard, as well as old and crotchety. The ranch is his baby, but the future doesn't lie in ranching. In the land, yes. Land will always be king, but not used as it is now, raising a handful of cattle on hundreds of acres. I don't want to hurt dad, or make light of the years he's put into the ranch, but times have changed and I have other interests, as well. He doesn't want to hear that."

"You're gone a lot then?"

"Yes, off and on. I've had to establish a broader base for my real estate business, as well as politics. I've got offices and residences in Cheyenne, Gillette, and Casper, as well as here."

My guess at governor didn't seem far off.

"But I'm here in Hijax a fair amount." He gave a rueful laugh. "And whenever I am, Dad fires any hired help we have, hoping to force me to stay. But enough of me," he said. "Let's get something to eat, and I want to hear how you like Wyoming so far."

"Wait," I said. "Let me get a picture of you in front of the courthouse." He posed with a show of impatience and a practiced smile.

"Hurry up. I'm starving," he said and walked out of focus before I could get a third shot.

He tucked my elbow closely to his side and led us back to Main Street and a tacky little restaurant whose dangling sign proclaimed Stirrup Cafe. Curls of peeling white paint gave the exterior an odd, tactile look of warmth, pleasantly reinforced by the aroma of apples and cinnamon that surrounded us when Jim opened the door.

As we entered, the soft clatter of silverware and conversation ceased. Then the nods and the "Hi, Jim's" and the "How're the roads out your way's" began, but all eyes were coldly fixed on me. I nodded and smiled at the dark-haired woman whom I recognized from the hotel. She sat with a man who could have been her husband. Jim and I slid across the ripped plastic seats of the next booth.

"Believe me, "Jim said, and reached across the table for my hand, "the food's great here."

I must have winced when he squeezed my fingers. He turned my hand over, gave a low whistle, and asked, "What have you been doing?"

"Fixing fence, believe it or not." I laughed, rather proud of my battle scars.

"I thought that was Holman's job."

"Yes, but he got stuck showing me around. I ended

up helping with some repairs."

Menus flopped down in front of us and I glanced up at the most beautiful girl I think I've ever seen.

"Coffee?" she asked, holding out the pot. Her blond hair looked natural and was caught up in a delightfully frowzy knot on top of her head. Skin-tight jeans and a crimson tank top revealed a figure any fool would reveal if they were lucky enough to possess one like it.

I sighed, feeling as if my twenty-eight years had doubled. "No coffee. Something cold, please."

She gave me a wide sympathetic grin, "Yeah, I know what you mean. It's hotter than fresh cow shit out there, isn't it? How about a half and half?"

She took my startled look for ignorance, which was all right with me.

"Half iced tea and half lemonade. It's got a nice bite to it." She poured coffee for Jim without asking.

"Great," I said. I liked her brash style. There was appreciation in Jim's eyes, too, as they followed her tantalizing behind until it disappeared through the kitchen door. He wasn't the only one. A spindly cowboy on his way to the cash register stopped dead in his tracks to do the same, then turned to us.

"Whoeee," he said with a silly grin on his face. "How ya doing, Jim?" He touched the brim of his hat to me, but didn't remove it. His words were aimed at Jim, but his eyes kept sliding my way.

"Get any rain out your place?" he asked.

"Not yet, Buck. How's it going out south?"

"Drouthy as hell." He turned a toothy leer on me and said, "Hey, I bet this here is Minnie's girl."

"Yep," Jim answered, matching his grin.

I was getting real tired of this.

"Thea, this is Buck Sanders. And Kim Kavenaugh," he added as the waitress placed my tall drink on the table.

The ribald smile on her exquisite face told me she'd heard their remarks.

She cast me a knowing look and cocked an eyebrow. "How's tricks?"

I might have appreciated her sly humor if it weren't aimed at me, and if I weren't now the center of attention. A couple in the front booth actually stood to get a better look, and a turkey-necked man with a greasy apron tied around his middle opened the swinging door from the kitchen to gawk.

"Look," I said with what I hoped was an air of nonchalance, "why don't we set the record straight." I addressed the two standing by the booth, Buck and Kim, but spoke loud enough for everyone to hear.

"Sorry to disappoint you, but I'm not some hen Minnie's imported for a chicken ranch. Minnie Darrow has no intentions of opening Halfway Halt for business; it's not her line and never has been."

Buck ducked his head, reddening with embarrassment. A spark of appreciation lit Kim's eyes before she threw back her head and let loose a raucous laugh, but I went right on. If any real trouble were brewing I meant to stop it.

"Believe it or not, Minnie wasn't aware of her sister's past until she began doing research on Halfway Halt. I'm Ms. Darrow's editor and I think you're all going to be proud of the book she's writing."

The silence was palpable, and the sea of hard, resentful eyes nearly stopped me. Even the cook had stopped to stare, leaning on the kitchen pass-through. The hotel lady half rose from her seat and craned her neck around to see me. Her mouth hung open and her eyebrows drew together in an intense frown.

I stuck my nose in the air and said, "I understand

there's a lot of speculation about Minnie's book. I can tell you it's simply a history of the early days of Halfway Halt when Jersey Roo was the madam. It's a fun book, a light-hearted look at the old days. Minnie does have Jersey's diaries but there's nothing in them that you people wouldn't know about anyway. Minnie has no intention of dragging Hijax, or anyone in Hijax, through the mud."

I felt a slight twinge of guilt, but it seemed more important to ease the obstinate anger smoldering around me.

"In fact, if anyone's really interested, I suggest they talk to Minnie herself." Stubbornly, I met the eyes of each one. "She'd like to get acquainted with more people and enjoys talking about her work."

One by one the stony faces turned away. Still looking embarrassed, Buck slunk off. But if everything I'd heard about small towns were true, the news would be out in a flash.

I hadn't glanced at Jim during my little spiel, but did so now. What I'd said was meant for his ears as well as for the others.

His words, "Go for it, Tiger," were comforting, and I relaxed a bit. Kim took our order with a bland look and left.

The dark-haired woman from the hotel quickly slid from her booth and approached ours. She was followed more slowly by her companion, who stood and fished change from his pocket.

"I'm so glad you spoke up," she said to me. "Please don't think everyone here in Hijax is rude and crude."

"Hi, Cora," Jim said. "Thea, this is Cora Mae Croderman and her husband Lamar. They own the hotel."

"Well, I think it's so exciting that Minnie's writing a book. I'd heard rumors of course, but, you know, one doesn't pay attention to every piece of gossip that crosses their ears. I had no idea she actually had Jersey Roo's diaries. Where on earth do you suppose she found them? I'd love to get a look at them. I can't imagine why I haven't gotten out to see the dear woman yet; I'm so interested in history. Isn't that true, Lamar?"

She didn't want, or wait, for an answer. The words rushed from her in an irrepressible stream. Her eyes flickered nervously between Jim and me and her husband. Lamar wasn't paying attention. He just stood there, his gaze wandering over the room, diligently probing between his teeth with a toothpick. He was a short man, and looked to be at least ten years older than his wife.

"I bet I could help Minnie with her research," she rattled on. "My family's lived here forever, haven't they Jim? Just like yours." Her hands began to flutter, as if they, too, wanted to stem the flow, but weren't sure how to go about it. "And I've got all kinds of pictures of Hijax in the old days. I keep track of the photo archives for the Historical Society, have for years. Is she using lots of pictures? I'd sure like to see what she has. Do you think she'd mind if I ran out to see her? It's a shame nobody's—"

Kim arrived and plopped plates of food in front of us. "For pete's sake, Cora, shut up," she said, and went back to the kitchen.

Cora's mouth clamped shut. Lamar Croderman turned and headed for the cash register. Cora's lips worked as if there were still words in there that wanted to come out. I couldn't decide whether the strained look on her face came from desperation or embarrassment. I took pity on her.

"I don't think Minnie needs any help with her work," I said, gently, "but I'm sure she'd like a visitor. It's really kind of you to offer. Minnie needs some friends."

A look of relief washed over her. "Yes," she said. "Minnie needs a friend." And with that, she hurried off to follow her husband out of the cafe.

Jim and I grinned at each other. "Don't mind them," he said. "Cora likes to think she's high society. Lamar was actually quite a catch when he came to town and started the bank. He married Cora and bought the hotel from her family."

I picked at my food and wished I hadn't ordered so much. My appetite had disappeared.

Jim said, "Minnie has quite a defender in you."

I answered lightly. "She's a company asset; I feel protective." Then added more seriously, "I'm glad you and your father are being kind to her; it means a lot to her."

"Dad knew her sister Lil when he was a kid. But it was my Grandpa who went round and round with her. Dad said he used to rave like a madman about having a whorehouse in the middle of his spread. He was a real rip-snorter, tried everything in the world to get that land away from her. I think Dad admired Lil for never giving in to him."

"And Lil eventually leased to your father."

"Yeah, but not until after my grandfather died. Lil didn't have anything against Dad; still, she wouldn't sell the place to him either."

"Did that bother him?"

"He always said not, but I never believed him. He's as much of a land baron as Grandpa was."

"And what about now?" I asked, curiosity leading me recklessly on. "How does he feel—how do *you* feel—about losing the lease after all these years? Won't it hurt your business?" I couldn't help thinking about all those broken fences.

"Hurt us?" His faced crinkled with laughter and he squeezed my hand with genuine amusement. "Hardly. The Darrow section is just a drop in the bucket compared to what we have. And I'm not bragging, because I didn't do it. Dad and his dad before him are the ones who put it all together."

"But what if Minnie sells to someone else?"

"The Darrow place is too small to be of any use by itself, not big enough to run more than a handful of cows."

"Why would Max want it?"

"Holman? Is that why he's hanging around Minnie's?"

I nodded, uneasily aware that perhaps I was talking out of school. Had Max expected me to keep his dealings with Minnie confidential? Well, it was too late now.

"Holman doesn't know any more about ranching than Minnie does," Jim said.

"But he grew up here."

"That doesn't make him a rancher." He gave me an indulgent smile. "And he hasn't lived around here since high school."

"He hasn't?"

"No." He seemed surprised I didn't know that. "He used to spend all his time right here in the Stirrup. His mother eked out a living hashing while Holman was in school. Smart enough kid, I guess, but it takes more than knowing how to ride a horse and being able to buy a section of land to set yourself up in business these days."

He pushed his empty plate away. I could tell he was getting bored with the subject, but I was bursting with questions. He reached out and ran a finger along my cheekbone. "If Minnie's as shrewd as her sister, she'll never sell to Holman; she'll sell where she can get the most money."

"She has an agreement with him."

"Verbal, I bet."

I nodded, not caring now what I revealed.

"Holman's dumber than I thought if he expects her to stick by that."

"What? I'm shocked. You mean a handshake deal is no longer hallowed in your glorious west?"

He released my hand reluctantly when Kim came to pick up our plates. If I'd expected to lighten the conversation I was mistaken.

He gave me a somber look and said, "Too bad it isn't, because I'd hate to see the results if Minnie dares to cross Max."

CHAPTER 7

I rushed down the street. Time had gotten away from me. I could see Max leaning against the front of the drugstore, one foot braced against the wall, smoking and talking to a heavy-set man who leaned, just as casually, against the fender of a parked car. When Max saw me, he nodded to the man and strolled my way.

He pushed his hat off his forehead and glanced pointedly at his watch. "You must have got along all right."

"Sorry I'm late," I said, catching my breath. "But I was asked to lunch, and—"

"Fast work."

"I met him yesterday at Minnie's."

"Him?" His eyebrows climbed.

"Jim Enright," I said, exasperated. "It's none of your business, you know."

"Enright." His face hardened and the gentle teasing changed to sarcasm. "My, you're really uptown, aren't you? Come on. The pickup's over here."

We had to walk past the heavy-set man who still lingered on the sidewalk. "That Minnie's girl, Max?" he called out. He scratched his gross belly and gave me a lewd wink. "Aren't you gonna introduce us?"

"Ease off, Krocker." Max's tone and look was enough to send the man scuttling off. None too gently, he grabbed my arm and guided me across the street.

"Thanks," I said, "but you don't have to defend my honor. I've taken care of it." Half running to keep up with his stride, I told him about the scene I'd created in the cafe.

"I wanted to quiet the talk and speculation. I told them what Minnie's book is about, and that she has Jersey Roo's diaries."

He jerked to a stop. "You told them *what*?"

"I told them there was nothing to worry about."

"You think that's all it takes?"

"Look, do you mind?" I shook my arm from his grip. "You weren't there. I'm not a complete imbecile. It's time *someone* met all this ugliness head-on instead of letting it fester." If he thought my comment pointed, I didn't care. "My experience has shown that fear is countered best through honesty and openness. Or do you have a better method?"

He gave me one of those fathomless looks. "Throwing kerosene on open flames is never my first choice."

His reaction—overreaction, to my mind—was puzzling. I mean, I didn't want to believe that Max was fueling the rumors about Minnie, but why else would he be so disturbed by my trying to smooth things over? Or did he really think there was that much danger in what Minnie was writing? I vowed again to keep my nose out of the whole stupid mess. But I couldn't help wondering if I had inadvertently been the one to cross Max. And if Jim were right, that the results wouldn't bare contemplation.

We rode to the grocery store in silence. Max tore Minnie's list in half and we each took a cart and made short work of the shopping. Then it was back to that awful road and the long ride home.

I eyed the dark clouds gathering in the sky and made a half hearted attempt at conversation. "It looks like rain." I sounded ridiculously like all the other Hijaxians with their incessant weather-speak.

Max shrugged. "We need a soaker, but it can cloud and clear for months without giving up a drop." He glared at the sky in turn. "Just like a politician. All promises, no delivery."

If he meant that for a jibe, I ignored it. A while later I came up with, "Why don't they do something about this road? Aren't the rocks hard on your tires?"

"It's better than no gravel at all. That's a lot of mud to plow to get to town."

Another lengthy pause.

"Ever driven in gumbo?" he asked.

"No. I don't even know what it is."

"The soil's loaded with bentonite around here, absorbs an amazing amount of water, swells with it and makes the ground slicker than—well, let's just say it makes driving damn difficult when it's good and wet. If you're caught in a rain storm you'll be glad for the rocks. The stretch of dirt from the main road to Minnie's house is a real bitch."

That exhausted our repertoire. By the time we reached Halfway Halt his earlier prediction proved true. It wasn't going to rain. The clouds had blown away, leaving the sky clear.

A car I hadn't seen before was parked in front of the house when we got there.

I voiced my curiosity. "I wonder who that is?"

"Don't recognize the car." We drove around in back

and I carried the groceries in while Max took care of the other supplies.

Voices were coming from the office, so I looked in. To my surprise, Cora Mae Croderman was perched on a chair pulled up to the oak table. Wow, fast work. She must have dumped off Lamar and headed right out here after she left the cafe.

"Hello there," I said.

Minnie looked up from the stack of old newspapers and magazines she was riffling through. "You're back. Thea, this is Cora Croderman," she said with a shy smile.

"Yes. I met Cora in town. It's good to see you again."

"Her family has lived in the area for over a hundred years. She's interested in my work."

"I certainly am," Cora said. "I just can't keep up with all of these magazines, but I'd like to read the articles Minnie's written."

Evidently, Cora hadn't told Minnie I had encouraged her to visit, and I was just as glad. She might not have welcomed my interference, and she seemed quite pleased to have company. She pulled some old copies of *Western True Adventures* from the pile and handed them to Cora.

"Here, you can take them home with you, if you like."

"I'd love to. Of course, I'm most fascinated with the work you're doing now. Imagine! A history of Halfway Halt. It must be fascinating."

She turned to me and said, "Minnie gave me a tour. Don't you think this is the most fascinating old place you've ever seen? You know, Minnie, I have a lot of pictures I'm sure you'd like to see. Are you using many in your book?"

"We're using some. Thea's going to make the final

pick."

"I'd love to see what you have."

Minnie handed her the cigar box. "Helby Enright brought these over. I haven't had a chance to look at them yet. I have a bunch more and some clippings you might be interested in." She went over to her desk and began to pull things from the drawers.

I stood behind Cora and peered over her shoulder as she removed the pictures from the box and began to shuffle through them.

"My, aren't these wonderful. I encourage everyone to donate their old photographs to the Historical Society. I've been in charge of the photo archives for years. Such rewarding work."

She kept up a running line of chatter, which I soon tuned out. I was more interested in how speedily she was going through the pile, as if she were looking for something in particular. Her fingers worked with the efficiency of a Las Vegas card dealer, quickly winnowing out the pictures relevant to Halfway Halt, and of those, only a few got more than the briefest glance. I saw several duplicates of things Minnie had in her scrapbook, and many others I'd take a closer look at later. Cora seemed most interested in interior shots of Halfway Halt, particularly if people were in them. The one she lingered over the longest showed several women clustered around Halfway's bar, mugging for the camera.

She came to the end of the pile. "Aren't these fun. Naughty me, I really like the ones that have the girls and their customers in them," she said and picked up a duplicate of the studio portrait of Lil with Minnie in her lap. This copy still had the gray cardboard frame around it, and the same inscription, "Minnie and Me," scrawled across the bottom. "And here's Lil," she said. "Isn't it sweet, but—"

"I have one like that in my scrapbook," Minnie interrupted. She plopped more pictures on the corner of the table, and pulled out her scrapbook.

"Scrapbook?" Cora said, immediately interested. "I'd love to see your scrapbook. Do you have some older pictures? Any of Jersey Roo?" She had lost interest in Helby's contributions. I gathered them up, put them back in the box.

Minnie opened her scrapbook and the two were soon engrossed. I left them to it and went back to the kitchen to finish putting away the groceries. I was getting tired of Cora Mae's rapaciousness, and wondered what her secret agenda was. It appeared obvious that she had one.

Thankfully, Cora refused an invitation to stay for dinner. We ate late, as no one wanted to give up the idea of stuffed pork chops, and lingered over coffee. I listened to Minnie and Max talking about the old days and people I didn't know, but my mind was never far from the manuscript.

"How did your work go this morning?" I asked her. "I'll be ready to help you out tomorrow in any way you like."

"Good. I got a lot done." She chuckled. "Helby told me a wonderful story about Parson Potts when he was here the other day. Max, did you ever hear about the time he got bit in the rear by a rattlesnake?"

"Sure." Max smiled. "But tell Thea. She'll appreciate it."

"Potts was a young man helping with the spring round-up. Evidently he squatted behind the wrong bush and got bit right on the cheek. He went running back to the camp with his pants flapping around his knees, cussing and yelling for somebody to help him. The rest of the men started laughing and arguing and laying bets as to the best way to put a tourniquet on his butt."

Minnie's face sparkled with animation and her voice deepened, taking on a change of cadence and syntax that weren't her own. The shade of Lil Darrow, I guessed.

"Potts was just a boilin' and finally grabbed a bottle of whiskey and a bull whip and took off for town on a horse. Time he got there he was roarin' drunk and stalked through town shaking his whip, screaming he'd lay low anybody who dared laugh at him. 'Course the folks didn't know what there was to laugh about, so they crowded around old Doc Jones' place to find out. All the Doc did was give him more whiskey, and when Potts came out and saw all them people standing around, he just went mad. Started lashin' the whip and chasin' folks down the street hollerin', 'So you think a bite in the ass is funny, do you?'"

Minnie rubbed her temple and gave a small laugh. "He still turns purple at the mention of a rattlesnake. I asked him about it last night."

"Ha!" I crowed. "I love it. Are you going to put it in your book?"

"I might."

Max looked up, sharply. "You're putting *that* story in your book? I thought you were using old stuff. That didn't happen in Jersey Roo's time."

Or in Lil's either, I guessed, but it was fun.

Minnie's voice was bland, but determined. "The book's a history of Halfway Halt. I'm including some of Lil's background and the events of her day."

Max glared at me and rose. "I'm going to turn in. Goodnight." He walked out.

"Goodnight," Minnie answered, unaware of—or unconcerned by—his abruptness.

I sighed. Naturally, Max thought I'd lied to him

about the book's contents, which in a way, I suppose I had. But how could I keep up with his thought processes? In town he was upset because I told people the book was about the old days and Jersey Roo's diaries. Now he was upset because more recent things would be included.

I helped Minnie clear the table, and then went into the office, prepared to sort through the pictures in Helby Enright's cigar box. I dumped them out on the table. I'd seen a duplicate of an exterior shot of Halfway Halt that was in better shape than Minnie's copy. I found it and set it aside for possible use.

I also liked the picture that had interested Cora the most. Minnie was in it, too. She sat on the brass footrail of the bar nearly hidden among the legs of the women. Older now than in the formal portrait, she had her chin in her hands and an impish grin on her face. Cigarettes dangled from the women's mouths; their shapeless, short-skirted dresses made them look hard and unlovely, at least to my eyes. But Minnie didn't seem to mind. She probably got a lot of attention. Strange surroundings for a little girl, but it didn't appear to have damaged her much.

I looked at the portrait again and examined the woman, Lil, closely, looking for…What? A trace of degeneracy, dissolution? Some stamp of her profession? But there was nothing. She looked like any ordinary young woman, just this side of homely. And the child on her lap looked like any other child. I dropped it back in the box along with some other discards.

"There you are," Minnie said, coming in from the kitchen. She wiped her hands on her apron and looked over my shoulder.

"Here's one of you." I handed her the one of the women at the bar, and another of her climbing on a chair to join a group of men seated around the flagstone fireplace.

She chuckled. "Yes, there's one of those in the scrapbook." She yawned. "I'm sorry, Thea. You're not having a very exciting time of it, for a vacation."

"Don't worry about me, Minnie. I'm enjoying myself. And that reminds me. I met Jim Enright in town this afternoon and he wants to take me to a dance tomorrow night. Said it would be a real "experience" for me. What do you think?"

"Wonderful, that's what you need. Takes me off the hook as far as entertainment goes. Well, I'm going to bed. Don't know why I've been feeling so tired, and I've got a lot of work to do tomorrow. Stay up as long as you like."

I was about ready for bed myself, and sifted quickly through the remaining pictures, miscellaneous shots of cattle, barns and unidentified people. One was stuck to the back of another and I picked them apart. A small portion of the image tore away, but not enough to destroy the snapshot. It showed a motley group of men clustered around an open vintage car. All the men wore scarves tied over their faces banditti fashion. Behind them, a man's body dangled from the gnarled branch of a cottonwood, hung by the neck. Could this have been the hanging Minnie was asking about? The car placed it in the right time period, and surely there couldn't have been that many hangings in those days. My eyes slid from the gruesome angle of the man's head to a young cowboy braced cockily against the car's long hood, his hat knocked back on his forehead and his legs covered with shaggy chaps. The others were straight out of central casting as well, one in a long hide coat, another with a floppy-brimmed hat.

The picture was definitely a keeper. I could hardly

wait to show Minnie. I put it with the others I'd set aside and tossed the rest back in the cigar box with my special pile on top.

When I finally got to bed, I slept restlessly, my dreams filled with masked men, pork chops and never-ending spaces in which I continually lost my way.

I jerked awake with a stiffened alertness that wasn't part of the dreams. Listening for the sound that had roused me, I heard a definite scratching and the dog's tiny whine. There was no mistake this time. I'd forgotten him again. The dog was probably starving, and had been waiting all day for me to seek him out.

When I opened my door and faced the dark hall I paused a moment, remembering last night's folly. But that had only been Max. And, as it turned out, I was the prowling stranger, not him. Besides, I could flip on the light if I wanted. But by the time I reached the stairs and the switch, my brief hesitation was forgotten and I made my way quickly to the kitchen served perfectly well by night vision.

The light in the fridge showed a portion of leftover chops and enough milk to spare the dog a bowl. I reached for the cupboard for a dish of some kind, then stopped, suddenly alert. Before I could lower my arm there was a rush of movement and the excruciating pain of a blow on my head. I felt myself falling, but could do nothing about it, not even prevent my forehead from banging the edge of the counter.

But I wasn't out. I heard the swing and slam of the back door. Moaning, I rolled onto my hands and knees, propelled by the sound of running footsteps, and pure anger. *Someone* had hit me and I damn well wanted to know who. My head whirled with nauseating dizziness. I pulled myself up, clinging to a chair and then the table, impelled by some crazy urge to chase the attacker.

Clutching my head in my hands, I staggered out the door into the night. Cold air sucked through my light gown with the shock of ice water and I started to run towards the front of the house. Each step jarred unbearably, but I couldn't seem to stop the forward motion. My feet took on a life of their own.

A hand grabbed my arm and whirled me around. I screamed, then heard Max's voice cry out roughly, "What are you doing out here?"

I must have fainted or collapsed, because next thing I knew I was being carried in Max's arms. He was half-running, my head flopping miserably over his arm.

"Stop. Stop, please," I gasped when I could. He slowed for the back steps, then quickly took me in the kitchen and sat me on a chair.

I grabbed my head again, sobbing angrily, "If I'd had a broken neck, you'd have killed me for sure."

His voice matched mine. "What in hell were you doing out there?" He snapped on the light and turned back to me. "I ought to wring your neck." He stopped abruptly, and leaned over to look at the top of my head. "You're bleeding," he said furiously, as if it were all my fault.

To my great humiliation, I started to cry. Racking sobs, tears streaming down my cheeks, nose running, the whole ugly bit. He gave me a baleful look, then disappeared down the hall. When he returned, he carried a towel, a washcloth and a handful of tissue. Handing me the tissue, he filled a pan with steaming water from the tap, and brought it to the table. I blew my nose and pulled myself together. Gently, he began to sop my head wound, working methodically, letting a lot of water dribble down my neck. I didn't care.

He gave my head a final pat with the towel, then

pressed my shoulder. "Better now?"

"Yes," I said. "Sorry."

"Forget it. Sometimes that's the only way to let go. Sorry if I sounded sore. I wasn't."

"I know. Sometimes it's the only way to let go." I managed a tart smile. The dazzler he turned on me changed quickly to a frown as he ran his fingers over my forehead.

"You've got a goose egg here, too. Just what were you doing?"

I tried to remember. "I heard the dog scratching on the door. At least, that's what I thought I heard. No, I *know* that's what I heard, and came down to feed him."

"What dog?"

I looked at him blankly. "A black and white one. Haven't you seen him? I gather he blew in about the same time I did. We're—uh—friends."

"I haven't seen him," he said doubtfully.

"He's not very brave; people like to kick him. Anyway, when I heard the dog scratching I felt terrible about ignoring him and came down to get him some food."

I struggled for the correct sequence of events. "There was a noise or something when I reached for the cupboard, but before I could do anything, I got hit."

"What hit you?"

"Why, whoever it was hit me."

"You mean a person hit you? Somebody was in here? Thea, why didn't you say something?"

"Say something? How could I?"

"Are you sure?"

"Of course I'm sure," I said indignantly. "I heard him go out the door and run away. That's why I went out. I wanted to see who it was."

"That was stupid."

"I'm sick of you calling me stupid. I was doing perfectly fine until you grabbed me like a maniac. And what were you doing out there, anyway? How do I know it wasn't you in the house prowling around?"

"And bopping you on the head?" Flickers of amusement played around his hard mouth. "Sorry again. My alibi: I woke and heard someone, or something, running towards the trees. You know, straight out that way." He pointed to the front of the house. "I took time to pull on these." He looked down at the jeans and boots which were all he wore, then groped for details. "I walked out towards the road, but nothing was there. I figured it was just a deer, and headed back to the bunkhouse. Then I saw you." He frowned. "Come to think of it, even half asleep, if I'd thought what ran by the bunkhouse sounded like a deer, I'd never have bothered to investigate."

He gazed at me thoughtfully. I plucked at my gown wondering why I'd even packed the threadbare thing, much less worn it. But I needn't have worried that the sight of my luscious body seen through a faded Mickey Mouse would cast Max into throes of uncontrollable passion. His thoughts were elsewhere.

I couldn't take my eyes off him. His hands and arms were deeply tanned up to the point where he rolled his sleeves, as was his neck down to a deep V on his chest. The rest of his muscular torso was quite pale, making it appear as if he wore a skin-colored shirt heavily embroidered with hair to the navel. Embroidery my fingers were itching to trace.

"I don't like this," he said, his mind more gainfully employed than mine. "People don't break and enter much around here." He glanced around the kitchen. Two purposeful strides took him to Minnie's office.

He snicked on the light.

I caught his urgency and rose to follow, reeling a bit with the sudden motion.

The office was a complete shambles. Drawers had been removed from the desk and the contents scattered on the floor. Minnie's scrapbook, papers, and the emptied cigar box were tossed carelessly on the sofa. Loose photographs were strewn across the table and floor.

"Oh, no!" I gasped. "The pictures!"

"Don't touch anything," he said and held me back.

We stood in the doorway and stared at the damage. Max put his arm across my shoulders. "Do you always prowl around at night?" he asked lazily. His eyes swept the room with the same intent concentration he used outdoors.

"Of course not. I told you. I came down to feed the dog."

"And last night?"

"I was the hungry one that time." I sounded defensive.

"Why didn't you turn any lights on?"

"You can see better without. If I'd turned on a light I'd have been blinded for as long as it took to do what I had in mind in the first place. Do you think I made this mess?"

His hand rose to the sore place on top of my head, fingered it lightly. "No. No, I guess I don't. Whoever it was probably used a flashlight to search with and as a weapon."

His arm dropped to my waist I could feel the warmth and strength of his fingers as they flexed, drawing me closer to his side. I was more than glad to lean on him.

"Do you think they were looking for something?" I said.

"You mean money? It looks more like malicious vandalism to me." His expression was grim. "Same thing with the fences and wells."

"Maybe Minnie will be able to tell if anything is missing." Max gave me a stricken look. "Minnie!" He raced for the stairs while I moved like a somnambulist behind him. He took them two at a time, knocked softly at her door and entered her room. I was halfway up the stairs when he reappeared.

"She's okay," he said, descending. "Sound asleep."

I shivered. Had he thought she might not be okay? "Are you sure? Why didn't she hear us?"

"Evidently a bomb wouldn't wake her if she sleeps with the bad ear up."

I'd forgotten about her ear. He took my arm and guided me back to the office, this time through the Victorian parlor. Nothing had been disturbed there.

"She's snoring like a threshing machine," he said. "I can't think of any reason to wake her now, can you? It'll be morning soon enough." Still clasping my elbow, he led me around the litter of pictures and papers on the office floor. But I couldn't stand the sight of Minnie's beloved scrapbook lying open, face down on the sofa with the pages all askew.

I picked it up along with the cigar box. Then I scooped up some of the pictures and put them back in the box, relieved to find that the photo of the masked men was among them.

"If it were vandalism, Max, wouldn't they have wrecked more than just the office? What if they were looking for something in particular?"

"What would they want?"

"Oh, no," I moaned, horrified with this new idea. "Minnie's manuscript!"

"Where did she keep it?"

"I don't know. She was working on it in here

today." I picked my way to her desk and looked helplessly at the mess on the floor. There wasn't anything that remotely resembled a manuscript. "It must have been here." I rifled through a stack of unused typing paper. Nothing. "It's gone, Max. Someone has stolen her manuscript. Do you suppose she has a copy?" With a sickening feeling, I saw my lovely project going down the drain. "Potts. I bet Potts stole it."

"Look, I don't think we should touch any of this. And why Potts? What about your friend Enright?"

"You know Potts would hate having things like that rattlesnake story revealed to the world, and who knows what else she's telling?" After another helpless look around, I threaded my way back through the debris and fought a strong urge to clean things up. But Max was right, it should be left for Minnie to see. I turned off the light.

The sight of the homely old refrigerator humming away as if nothing had happened, reminded me of my original errand. I got the leftover chop and poured some milk in a dish. Max eyed the meat with interest and followed me out the back door.

I held the chop out of his reach and continued my train of thought. "Your Parson Potts is a sanctimonious fool, as well as a violent man. Just the combination to kick off an irrational act."

Max sat on the step looking unconvinced, while I whistled softly for the dog. The thump of a tail sounded from under the porch, and the dog appeared, pulling himself ignominiously along on his belly.

Max laughed. "Now that's a sorry specimen, if I ever saw one."

"He is not." I set the food down and scratched the dog's ear. "Potts kicked him."

"You're hung up on Potts. I'd like to go back to my

original suggestion."

"You mean my *friend*, Jim Enright?"

"Exactly. Politicians aren't crazy about skeletons popping up unexpectedly."

"Actually, I said as much to Jim myself."

"Oh?"

I wasn't sure if his inflection implied approval or doubt. "He said there weren't any secrets around Hijax, and that many Wyoming politicians have colorful history in their background. Do you think that's true?"

He took his time answering. "I suppose so. I can't imagine anything happening within fifty miles of here that the whole town didn't know about the next day. And plenty of politicos boast about their granddaddy the horse thief," he admitted reluctantly. "But I don't believe for one minute that either one of the Enrights is happy about losing the lease on Minnie's land. I've thought all along that either Jim, or Helby himself, was cutting the fences and damaging the wells."

"Something for which you have no proof," I reminded him. "And if they were guilty of such a thing, why? To scare Minnie away?"

The dog finished the milk, wagged his tail in thanks, and crawled away with the bone. My head throbbed when I bent to pick up the dishes.

Max stood aside to let me pass, then held the door open and followed me in.

"Or to scare me away," he said, "hoping that if both Minnie and I left they'd have a chance to buy the land or at least get back the lease."

"Then why ransack her office?"

He leaned, half-sitting on the table and rubbed his face. I could hear the rasp of stubble across his palm.

"Hell, I don't know," he said. "But if anyone has something to hide, the Enrights do. They've been here forever."

"Potts has too, hasn't he?"

"But the Enrights had power. Big power; the breeding ground of corruption."

"Now who's being melodramatic?" I placed the dishes in the sink. "At least we know something about Potts' character," I insisted, not wanting to give up my pet theory. "I can't see Helby sneaking around cutting wires or hitting people on the head. He seems too dignified and…and fragile."

"Put your money on Potts, if you like. I'll stick with land hunger." He pushed away from the table and stretched, sending shimmers of light racing across his bare arms and chest.

Was he even aware that he was a half-naked man and I was a woman, and we were alone in a deserted bordello? Alone except for a sleeping Minnie and the wraiths of passions spent. And unspent.

He stepped close and cradled my face in his large hands. "Nothing makes much sense now. We can worry about it in the morning." He peered deeply into my eyes.

My breath quickened. I let myself drown in his gaze, ready to cling and twine. My eyelids drifted shut.

"No sign of concussion," he said, and tilted my head for a brisk wound inspection. "Looks okay, stopped bleeding. You going to be all right now?"

I swayed, grasping for composure. His hands still cupped my face and his fingertips massaged the tender flesh behind my ears. His eyes lingered warmly on my mouth. But now it was my turn, damn his hide.

I made a slight, but unmistakable, move away from his caressing fingers. "I'm fine," I said, letting a chill frost my words. "But it's time you left. I'll tell Minnie what's happened here and perhaps see you in the morning."

He dropped his hands and glowered. Muttering something it was probably just as well I didn't hear, he strode to the door.

Hand on the doorknob, he hesitated and looked back. "No more roaming around, okay?" He let his face soften into a megawatt smile that illuminated the dark sharp planes of his face with a wicked flash of brilliant teeth. Adonis bestowing gifts.

I didn't trust that smile. Too glorious to be sincere. And why was he just standing there?

"Go on up," he insisted when I didn't move. "I'll turn off the lights when you get upstairs."

I hesitated, wondering why I was suddenly wormy with suspicion. Because he'd nicked my womanly pride? Or was there something else? I turned and went quickly up to my room, closing the door with a solid thump for his benefit. Silently, I opened it again and stepped into the hall.

The downstairs lights flickered out. Enveloped in darkness, I listened for the slam of the door and the soft crunch of receding footsteps. Then I crept to Minnie's door. I wanted to hear for myself the steady rhythm of her snoring. Reassured, I scurried back to my room.

CHAPTER 8

I was waiting in the kitchen, coffee made, when Minnie came downstairs the next morning. She wore a nondescript house dress sprinkled with small flowers, and white anklets over her hose. The soft, loose flesh of her arms looked pale and inappropriate against the dress's cheeriness. I hated to add fuel to her morning grumpiness, but a blunt telling seemed the best course.

"Someone ransacked your office last night, Minnie."

She started when I spoke, her mouth pursed in surprise.

"Max and I."

"Max and you?" Her eyes hardened.

"Yes, I…Look, it's a long story, and I'll gladly give you all the details, but I'm worried that your manuscript might have been taken."

Like a startled deer, Minnie headed for the office with me trotting close behind. She hesitated at the threshold, gaped at the mess, and began to massage her temples in earnest, as if the sight had given her a sudden headache. I could hardly blame her. In the harsh light of morning the ravaged office seemed more threatening than it had the night before.

"My scrapbook," she said in a small dazed voice. She picked it up from the sofa where I'd left it and cradled it in her arms. "Helby's pictures." She dropped into a chair, her face ashen.

"I picked some of them up." I gestured at the photos still strewn across the table and floor, "but we thought we should leave things pretty much as they were for you to see." I paused, but could wait no longer. "Your manuscript, Minnie."

"What?"

"Your manuscript. It's not here. I'm afraid whoever did this stole it."

She shook her head, as if to clear the cobwebs, and massaged her temples. "Don't worry about the manuscript. Do you think I'm fool enough to keep it lying around where anyone could get at it?"

I felt as if a thousand pound weight had been lifted from my shoulders.

The back door slammed, and Max's voice drifted into the office.

"Got any coffee around here?"

Minnie rose to her feet. "I think it's time you two told me exactly what happened last night."

Max and I managed our explanations well enough, earning a number of raised eyebrows and pointed references to the *convenience* of our *chance meeting* in the middle of the night, which we studiously ignored.

Minnie did seem concerned about my getting hit over the head, and I briefly became Exhibit A while the two of them examined my wound.

"Maybe she should have had a stitch," Max

muttered doubtfully when I winced.

"No." Minnie probed with sharp fingers. "See? It'll go back. I've seen worse."

Thus was I delegated to the outer realms of martyrdom.

Minnie refused Max's offer to find a phone and report the break-in. "Don't you go telling that sheriff anything. What goes on out here is none of his business, nor yours either, Max Holman."

When the pickup roared out of the yard, she smoothed the flowered dress over her rotund middle and turned to me.

"All right, Thea, let's get to work."

"Max is right, Minnie. You really should report this to the sheriff, and everything else. The fences, windmills, the note. Everything."

"Do you think he'd believe me? I don't want anything to do with him." She snorted, but without her usual conviction.

"He'd believe the three of us. Besides, I was the one who got attacked."

She sighed. "I know, I know. I'll tell him in due time. Let's just get busy. First off, I want to fix the pages in my scrapbook. There are unpacked boxes upstairs in the far room on the left. Would you go up and see if you can find some of those gummed reinforcers for ring notebooks? Should be in a box of writing supplies. I'll start cleaning the office."

I don't know how long it took, half an hour, maybe more. There was a ton of stuff up there and I never did find any office supplies. When I went back downstairs Minnie was sitting at her desk with a smug look on her face. On her lap was a typing paper box filled with loose pages.

She waggled the box at me and chortled. "I told you not to worry about my book. I take very good care of it."

Relief at seeing the manuscript safely in hand overcame any annoyance I felt about being sent on a wild goose chase.

"You had it hidden. In here?"

"Never you mind, dear."

"Do you have a copy?"

"No, it always seemed too much of a bother."

"It's imperative that we have a copy, Minnie. Particularly if you think someone might be out to destroy it. Could you tell if anything is missing?" She had cleaned up most of the contents that had been dumped from her desk drawers.

"I don't think so, but you know more about the things Helby brought over." She handed me the cigar box and I began the process of sorting all over again.

"Look at this one, Minnie." I handed her the snapshot of the masked men and the hanging body. "We'll use that one for sure."

She sucked in her breath when she saw it, and said, "You bet we will."

I hadn't paid enough attention to the pictures last night to remember them all, but it seemed as if my pile of possibles was smaller than before and the big picture of Minnie and Lil wasn't here. I got down on my knees and looked under the sofa. "Ah, here's some more of them." I ran my hand as best I could under the broken springs that reached nearly to the floor, and retrieved three snapshots.

"He had a copy of that nice studio portrait of you and your sister, too. It still had the cardboard frame around it, but it's not here." I tried to peer through the darkness under the springs. "Have you got a flashlight?"

"Never mind," she said, sounding impatient. "We'll look for it later. And from now on I'll hide the pictures we want to use along with the manuscript."

"Good idea. Let me see what else I can find in your scrapbook." I sat at the table and straightened and smoothed out the manila pages as I leafed through them. I was looking mainly for early interior shots of Halfway Halt, and pulled some I thought would reproduce well, but all the pictures were fascinating, and I was easily distracted. Lil had done a thorough job of labeling and identifying most of the pictures, and, I couldn't help but note, sanitizing. There were no orgies, nothing at all suggestive of the true nature of the house. The contents had been carefully edited to protect the reputation of the owner, or to withstand close attention by a growing girl. Fascinating.

I turned to a page crammed with three rows of photos. One in particular caught my eye. A colorful group of cowboys complete with bandannas, a crazy assortment of hats and ill-fitting clothing.

There were a profusion of arrows and names written in the margins. I bent more closely to read them. I should have guessed that the fresh-faced young man in the showy chaps was the still-flamboyant Helby Enright. Looming behind him was a much older man with formidable gray handle-bar mustache labeled "Enright". Helby's father, most likely. I looked through the other names and found Potts and his father, and a large man named Beesom. One of the sheriff's many relatives? Then I stared at a figure in a long hide coat. My eyes flittered over another detail I hadn't noticed before—a touring car parked under the shade of a big old tree.

"Minnie," I said, excitement building like a crescendo. "Hand me the picture I gave you, the masked men."

I compared the two pictures. The arrangement was different—not everyone was in the same position—

but it was the same car, the same tree and the same men. Even with their faces hidden, the cowhide coat and ostentatious chaps were obvious identifiers, as were the hats with their brims and crowns creased and folded to individual tastes. A cowboy Rosetta stone with all ten names conveniently written in. Helby, Potts, their fathers, and six other men.

"Minnie, come look at this!"

She was as excited by the two pictures as I was. "By golly, Thea, I've got them. I can identify them all."

My mind was running more to headlines. *Author unmasks vigilante action.* Or maybe we could turn the whole incident into a book of its own, include interviews with Potts and Enright. Helby. My eyes were drawn to the hanging image, a bit blurred, as if still swinging, and the cocky youth who leaned against the car as if what they had done were nothing more than a prank. I couldn't imagine him involved in such a sordid affair.

"How old were they, Minnie? Helby and Potts?"

"I don't know. It was Nineteen Thirty. Thirteen, fourteen? Potts is younger, I think."

"And with their fathers? I can't imagine a father wanting his son to accompany him to witness, or participate in a…a lynching."

"I suppose they thought it an act of justice."

"But you said there was no evidence against the man they hung."

"That's right." She sounded as awe stricken as I about the implications of an incident that had suddenly become real for us. "That's what the paper said: there was nothing to connect the man to the incident at all. He was just a sheepherder passing through. That was enough to incriminate him."

Potts was as tall as Helby, but looked quite a bit younger and much more vulnerable with naked wrists dangling from too-short sleeves. "Why would a father want to bring a son along on such a venture?" But then why would a father send a young daughter to work in a whorehouse? I felt sick to my stomach.

"People grew up young in those days," Minnie said, as if reading my mind. "That's what my sister always said." We sat in silence, each contemplating our own thoughts.

"Could they still be prosecuted?" I wondered.

"I shouldn't think so. Isn't there a statue of limitation?"

"Not for murder."

The word vibrated between us, taking on an unexpected life of its own.

"Do you suppose this is what the townspeople were afraid you'd find out?" I asked. "Are any of the rest of these men still alive?"

"I can find out."

My mind was racing. For an uneasy moment I remembered how the sheriff had inspected this room and the others as well, and the interest he'd taken in the scrapbook. He'd even checked out the back door. I wondered how close a relative the man in the picture was.

I said, "Do you suppose whoever broke in wanted to find out what you knew?"

"Or if I was going to put anything about the hanging in my book? But they couldn't find the manuscript."

"Helby had to know the picture of the hanging was in the cigar box. Why would he give it to you if he was worried about you finding out the truth? Did he know you had this other picture?"

"He looked at my scrapbook, but I don't remember that he took any special note of this other picture."

"Maybe he didn't make a connection at the time, but remembered later and broke into the house to get the picture back. But then," I added with a sigh, "the fact remains that neither picture was taken. They're both still here."

"Unless he was so surprised when you came downstairs that he forgot to take them, or dropped them?"

We both had a hard time imagining Helby in such nefarious activities. "Maybe he had Jim do it for him," I suggested, doubtfully, but somehow that didn't seem to fit either of their personalities.

"That leaves Potts," I said. Minnie didn't want to think him involved any more than I wanted Helby to be the bad guy, but then, she hadn't witnessed Potts kicking the dog either. I for one thought the shoe fit him perfectly.

Minnie heaved a big sigh. "Or it could have been like the note, someone trying to scare me into running."

Or the fences and wells, with which she suspected Max might have had a hand. I too, began to rub my temples, and reminded myself that none of this was my concern.

"It's a problem for the sheriff, Minnie," I said, automatically. I hesitated, but of course, Minnie had had the same thought.

"Ha! His name's on there, too."

"But it could be some distant, far-removed cousin for all we know. Besides, he's the person in authority, and the sooner you tell him about it the better. Our concern is with the manuscript and I'll trust you to keep it and the pictures safe until we can get some copies made." And I can get out of this crazy place, I added to myself.

We worked straight through. Minnie at the typewriter, and me stretched out on the lumpy sofa reading. The manuscript was all I had hoped for, and

Jersey Roo a most delicious low-life.

By mid-afternoon I was ready for a walk, or some kind of exercise, and went outside. The dog soon joined me and we ran down the hill to the gravel road. I remembered seeing some bright orange wildflowers on the way to town yesterday, and wondered if I might find some closer to the house. It was a beautiful day, the sky squinting bright, and the air smelled of baking soil and wild, sweet clover.

We wandered through the sparse growth in the borrow pit beside the road, but I couldn't keep my mind off Minnie's book for long. Roger was going to love it. It might even turn out to be the first book he ever read all the way through. I was particularly pleased with the sly undercurrent of humor that Minnie used to keep any incipient sordidness at bay. My trust had been well placed. I wasn't sure how the later chapters concerning Lil would fit in, but figured the vigilante expose would at least keep them from being anticlimactic. If not, I'd use Jersey's portion and talk Minnie into doing Lil's story as a separate book. We had plenty of publicity tie-ins for both.

I saw the dust cloud of the approaching vehicle long before the car itself came in sight. The car barreled past, Cora Mae Croderman at the wheel. I waved. She either ignored me, or didn't see me. Her hands gripped the wheel and her eyes were fixed determinedly on the road ahead. I wondered where she was going. If she was headed for Minnie's, she was traveling much too fast to make the turnoff. I stared after her, but not even that woman's strange peccadilloes could distract me for long.

I whistled for the dog and began a slow walk back, thinking again what an excellent send off Minnie's book would be for my project. I could be proud of my first venture. And with some national publicity, it might do much better than expected for that type of book. Whether Minnie was finished with the last chapters or not, I would leave tomorrow with the finished portion in my hot little hands. I could hardly wait to show it to Uncle Charlie. I knew he'd love it.

I was glad I had a date that evening, because I couldn't have slept. And a country dance seemed a fitting finale to my western adventure. I planned to take the camera with me.

The Smoky Creek Community Hall was about nine miles outside of Hijax on another dusty county road. The board building, serviceable rather than beautiful, sat in the middle of a large bare pasture ringed by a sagging barbed-wire fence. If the signs outside were to be believed, it also served as meeting place for the American Legion, VFW, and the Four Square church.

The entire population of the Hijax community appeared to be crammed into the moderately-sized building.

Folding chairs rimmed the walls right up to the raised dais where Bobby Ray's Country Rhythm Boys thumped their hearts out. Babies propped in plastic seats set on the floor watched solemn-eyed as older youngsters surged in and out among the dancers, their shrieks drowned by the insistent beat of over-amplified country guitars and a heavy-handed drummer without much sense of rhythm.

Two long tables loaded with plastic wrapped plates and bowls stood at the far end of the hall, hemming in a bay area where the old-timers gathered, looking like a pride of restless, white-maned lions.

Jim paid our fee to a woman sitting at a card table at the top of the stairs by the door who in turn stamped the back of our hands with a bilious green mark from a rubber stamp pad.

Jim led me into the melee. "Care to two-step?" he

shouted, with a big grin on his face.

I'd dated an urban cowboy for awhile, so wasn't at a complete loss. That is, not as long as I concentrated on what my feet were supposed to be doing, which was nearly impossible with so many people to watch.

"Oops," I said, as I stumbled out of sync for the second time.

"Forgive me."

Jim smiled and held me closer, but I couldn't resist watching some of the wildly improbable couplings that danced by. Then I saw Max. He was dancing with Kim Kavenaugh, the gorgeous waitress from the Stirrup Cafe. His head was bent, intent on listening to what she was saying. Her shockingly beautiful face was alive with animation.

Lights shimmered through the golden strands of Kim's hair that brushed across Max's cheek. His eyes were nearly invisible under their heavy lids, and I recognized the small twitch at the corner of his mouth seconds before it broke into the flashing smile that, somehow, I felt belonged to me.

I lurched onto Jim's feet again, surprised by the surge of jealousy. Jealousy? How had that sneaked up on me?

"Whoops," I said, rather too brightly. "I'm afraid I'm giving you sore feet. You're a good dancer, but I don't seem to be in tune tonight." I was shaken by the unexpected burst of emotion, and didn't want to analyze it. Thankfully, the number ended and Jim's quick squeeze stopped my ridiculous chatter.

We stopped close to the old-timers staked out territory. I could see Parson Potts perched on a chair too small for him. Helby Enright stood in front of the smoke-grimed windows holding forth with a straight-faced tale that had the others wildly amused.

Jim led me around the lunch tables. *Into the lion's*

den, I thought grimly, as the talk and laughter stopped abruptly.

"Hi, dad," Jim said. "I think you've met Thea Barlow."

The old man nodded with the same crispness I had noted before. His face was calm, but the frosty eyes were alert and observant. The epitome of the strong, silent western man.

Potts lurched clumsily to his feet.

"Whoa, there," Helby said, and steadied the heavier man with a hand to the elbow. In that quick movement I thought I saw a flash of the self-confident youth who had leaned so carelessly against a car hood.

"How-do, Miss Barlow," Potts muttered. His hands seemed lost without something to clutch.

"We've met also," I said, dryly. My hand—consciously or unconsciously—rose to the sore spot on top of my head. Potts flushed, shuffled his feet nervously, and refused to meet my eyes. *Harmless, my foot*. He positively oozed guilt. Suspicions confirmed, I felt certain I knew who had raided Minnie's office.

Potts sidled away, mumbling something about getting a beer.

I looked back at the crowded dance floor, and wondered if I could find Max again. I wanted to tell him about Potts' reaction, but the band had struck up a country waltz and he was lost somewhere in the crowd.

"May I?" Helby asked, drawing my attention back. And before I really knew what was happening, the old man tossed a curt nod at Jim and took my hand in a surprisingly firm grasp. "Come along now," he said, and swung me onto the dance floor. "This is more my style."

He was barely taller than I, and loaded with old-world charm evident in the tilt of his head, the quirk of an uneven smile and the sparkle of appreciation that glimmered in the pale, icy eyes. In his day he'd surely been a lady-killer. An unfortunate expression. It brought an unwanted picture to mind of a body dangling from a tree, its features blurred as it swung out of focus.

I pushed the image away, willed it to disappear within the lovely swirling movements we took, swooping in large, lazy circles across the floor. Besides, I told myself, he'd been too young then to be anything but an observer, surely, dragged into an unsavory affair by an unfeeling father. I closed my mind to any further implications, caught up in the heady rhythmic steps that went on and on, and brought us breathlessly back to the place of beginning as the music ended. He was more short of breath than I, but just as delighted.

"Nothing like a pretty girl to make an old codger want to dance," he said. "My one dance of the evening, all I can manage now."

Jim took my elbow and shook his head ruefully at his father.

"You should take it easy, Dad."

"Go to hell, boy," he said with a cold dismissive glance, then addressed me. "Tell Minnie to bring you over sometime, and tell her I'll be by."

Jim's mouth was tight with anger and his fingers bit painfully into my arm.

"What's the matter?"

"That old man is stubborn as a jackass. The more the doc tells him to slow down, the worse he gets. Not that I mind him dancing with you, but he's got no more business whirling around out there like a kid than he does riding that outlaw horse of his." He stopped, gave me a sheepish grin and said, "Well, enough of that. I think you've made a conquest, though. Dad isn't like most Westerners. He doesn't issue invitations unless he really wants to see you."

"It can't be easy for someone like him to slow down. I like him, Jim. I'm just sorry I won't have a chance to know him better. I hear he was quite a...a heller when he was young." Actually, that was what I'd heard about Potts, not Helby, but didn't figure it mattered.

"To hear them tell it, they all were. A point of pride. Those were the good old days."

My just deserts, I suppose. Those who fish for information come up empty handed. I tried a more direct method.

"Then why are they so against Minnie and her book?"

He laughed. "Prostitutes don't count, I guess. Besides, she's an outsider. How are you two getting along? I've an idea Minnie can be as difficult as my father in her own way. How did you get to know her?"

"I bought a couple articles from her. I've been editing *Western True Adventures.* Are you familiar with the magazine?"

"Sure. I have to admit I don't read that kind of thing myself, but a lot of people in this part of the country do."

His answer didn't surprise me. Nostalgia wasn't Jim's thing. He was obviously a man of today, not yesterday. "Anyway," I went on, "in the process of buying articles and exchanging ideas for more to come, we corresponded and spoke occasionally on the phone."

"And got to know her pretty well, huh? Were you as surprised as we were when she decided to move out here? She ever tell you why she decided to do such a thing after so many years? Seems kind of strange to me."

"Oh, I don't know. People frequently start searching for their roots as they get older. I'm sure she didn't think of herself as an outsider; she just wanted to make some kind of connection with her past. Find her home and family."

"Yes, I suppose so," he said with cold austerity, and again I caught a resemblance to his father, some subtle flash of cattle baron inheritance that bespoke little tolerance for the peons of the world. But it was just a flash. Then his eyes softened and he smiled.

"You have a lot more tolerance for old people than I do," he said. "You even had Potts blushing like a school boy."

So, he had noticed, too. It wasn't just my imagination.

I started to answer, but couldn't compete with the Rhythm Boys who were struggling through the opening of a morose country ballad. Jim held out his arms to me and I turned to step into them, but Max was there.

"This one's mine," he said. "I can't compete with Enright—Helby, that is—but I'll do my best."

I smiled a quick smile of apology to Jim as I was whirled away again. He smiled back, and if he'd heard Max's dig, it didn't seem to bother him.

I looked up at the dark face, amazed to find myself a bit self-conscious about being in his arms. I couldn't remember what it was I wanted to tell him. He misread my scrutiny.

"I'm not much of a dancer. You looked pretty good out there with Helby."

"He makes it seem easy," I said, glad for something to talk about. "He's very imperial, isn't he? So...so mildly furious at being old."

"It's the mildness, not the fury, that's unusual.

Nothing happened around Hijax, good, bad, or indifferent, that Enright didn't have a hand in. He commanded a lot of respect. Still does. I guess the mellowing had to come."

We danced silently a minute, then Max said, "Mildly furious. You're pretty observant, or is it sensitive?"

"Observant sounds more flattering."

Jim danced past us, his arms wrapped around Kim Kavenaugh. We exchanged the customary arch smiles before we drifted apart once more in the crowd of dancers.

I wondered if Max minded his partner being appropriated by Jim, and saw him grimly follow their progress down the floor.

"And that," he said, "is probably part of his fury."

"What? What do you mean?" I asked, trying to reel in the threads of our conversation.

"Nothing." He pulled me closer.

But I was curious. "You mean Helby's fury? And Jim? Jim's part of his problem?"

He shrugged. "I get the impression that Helby doesn't like Jim much."

"What a terrible thing to say." I said it even while remembering the chilling exchange I'd witnessed a few minutes ago between the two of them. "Differences between father and son are pretty common, especially when there's such a difference in age."

"Generation gap and all that, huh?"

The condescension roused me. "I think it's more that you don't like Jim. Why not?"

He laughed and I could feel his hand tighten on my back, but I resisted.

"No, please. I'd really like to know."

He gave me that long considering look of his before he responded. "Sour grapes, I guess."

"What do you have to be sour about?"

He laughed again. "You're a nosy female."

I was, and didn't care, nor did I expect him to answer me. I gave in to the pressure on my back and relaxed against his chest, vibrantly aware of all the places where our bodies touched. He began to speak softly into my ear.

"All the usual reasons. The age-old conflicts between the haves and the have-nots. I was the poor boy with my nose pressed against the candy store window."

The music's dirge-like pace allowed minimal movement on our part, a slow sensuous swaying. It felt wonderful. So did the soft breath of his voice on my ear as he spoke between frequent pauses.

"I was an over-achiever, but no matter what I accomplished, I never got what I wanted most: to be a rich rancher's kid with a flashy pickup and a thousand dollar horse to haul around to rodeos. Instead, I waited tables and washed dishes at the Stirrup Cafe for my mother. When I finished school I lit out of here with a bad taste in my mouth and a determination not to come back until I could buy up a bigger parcel of land than Jim Enright could ever lay a hand to."

After an interminable pause I said, "Where did you go?"

"Denver. College. I had a scholarship to the School of Mines."

I tried to look at him, but his hand cupped the back of my head and with gentle pressure, he kept it where it was, tucked under his chin.

After another lengthy pause, I prodded, "And?"

"I started as an oil field geologist. When things were booming a buddy of mine and I formed our own company. We've been pretty lucky."

This time I resisted the pressure; I wanted to see his face.

"So now you've returned to the old hometown with a bundle and plan to buy up the county."

He relaxed his hold, and let me lean back against his arm.

"Not quite." he said. "That was a long time ago. I've grown up some since then."

For once I let myself bask in his smile, not worrying if he had an ulterior motive, or was trying to manipulate me. I just wanted to enjoy its warmth and give him some of mine. My feelings must have shown on my face. With a small, rough sound deep in his throat, he drew me back in his arms and executed a couple of whirls that didn't match any music the Rhythm Boys could come up with.

"No," he said, slowing his exuberance to a statelier pace, "believe it or not, I was working legitimately in the area, checking out some prospective oil leases at the courthouse in Hijax when I discovered the Darrow property might be up for grabs. I'm ashamed to admit that the thought of being an irritant in the middle of Enright's property had its attractions. Brought back all those old feelings I thought I'd gotten rid of a long time ago."

But I could tell he wasn't ashamed at all; he was delighted with the prospect of being a thorn in the Enright's side.

CHAPTER 9

When the music stopped we were caught in an impenetrable crush of bodies. Max turned me in the direction of the flow, guiding me from behind with his hands on my shoulders. We began to inch our way through the crowd.

"As we were saying," I tossed the words over my shoulder, congenitally unable to let anything die on the vine, "what if Minnie doesn't sell, decides to stay here herself?"

"She won't—"

"Here you are." Jim materialized in front of me. "I thought you'd skipped out on me."

"Heavens no," I said, denying a twinge of guilt. It seemed like ages since I'd last seen him. He maneuvered me out of Max's hands, and I caught an exchanged glance between the two men that left me chilled and silent; a primitive wave of communication that unhappily brought to mind Jim's earlier comment: "I'd hate to see the results if Max Holman gets crossed."

Max disappeared into the crowd and I felt suddenly tired and claustrophobic.

Jim put his arm around my shoulders. "You look like you're wilting. Had enough of the Wild West?"

I gave him a weak smile and nodded. He brushed strands of hair away from my damp forehead.

"What you need is something to drink." We were standing just to one side of the milling crowd that headed down the stairs toward fresh air. "There isn't a bar here, but they always have a cooler of pop and beer downstairs."

Private bottles passed freely among the adults, too, I noted. Everyone on the sidelines seemed to have a plastic glass in hand. "Beer would be fine." I needed a thirst-quencher.

Parson Potts ambled by and nodded to Jim. "Hi there, Parson," Jim said, and took his arm. "Why don't you keep Thea company while I get her something cold to drink? And how about a beer for you, too?" He took off down the stairs, and left Potts to stand awkwardly by my side. I didn't feel the least inclined to make things easy for him.

"How's Minnie?" he finally asked. His eyes slid away from direct contact.

"Fine."

"I...You know, I never thought I'd see that young'un again. That Minnie sure was a cute little thing. Everybody thought that worthless old woman would birth an idiot; never took care of nothing in her life, not even herself. If it hadn't been for Lil, don't know what would have become of Minnie." He ducked his head, then after a moment said, "It's good to see her."

I suspected there were limits to his friendship with Minnie, so I said, "Why didn't you bring her here tonight? She would have loved it."

When he turned his malevolent beady eyes on me, I wished he hadn't. With an abrupt movement, startling for its quickness, he left and disappeared down the stairs.

I was angry with myself for letting him bother me, and wished I'd told him that Minnie had come to town to report a break-in. I spied some empty chairs across the hall and made for them.

"How about a dance, Thea Barlow?"

It took me a moment to recognize the sheriff out of uniform. "Yes, of course. I'd be delighted, Sheriff."

"Hank." He guided me out on the dance floor.

"Hank. So you're off duty tonight," I said, making conversation.

"Yep, can't work all the time. But I'm always on call, particularly at these events. Things can get pretty rowdy now and then. How is Minnie? Everything all right out at her place?"

"Just fine." Not a lie, I told myself, more a social nicety. However, when it's the law you're talking to, it puts a different color on things. I hoped I didn't look as guilty as I felt. "Why do you ask?"

"No particular reason. There's been a lot of foolish talk going around about her. I don't want it to get out of hand."

He was a good dancer, light on his feet, with some tricky moves that kept me alert. He managed to keep his eye on the crowd and greet people while still being attentive to me and the music. I debated whether to tell him about Minnie's problems. She had been so adamant about both Max and I staying out of her affairs that I hated to go behind her back. She *had* promised to talk to the sheriff herself. Noninvolvement won out, at least for now. Which didn't mean I couldn't question him about other things I wanted to know.

"I understand your family has lived in Hijax for a long time."

"Now who told you that? Don't tell me I'm going to end up in Minnie's book, too."

"I doubt it. Unless," I said, teasing, "you had a bunch of nefarious relatives."

He laughed. "Relatives I've got. A slew of them, but not a horse thief in the lot, as far as I know. But then there was Great-uncle Dewey on my mom's side, a fast man with a branding iron, they say."

We bantered back and forth, thoroughly enjoying ourselves, but I got no useful information.

On one of our turns, I saw Cora Croderman dance by with her husband, Lamar. She seemed exuberant, full of herself, waving and throwing comments to all of her acquaintances. Lamar looked hot and uncomfortable, his usual lugubrious self. I doubted she got him out very often.

When the song ended, a couple of men hailed the sheriff, obviously wanting to talk. He kept his hand on my arm, but I shooed him off to tend to his flock with a promise of another dance later on. Again, I headed for the chairs. I felt rather inelegantly sweaty by this time.

It felt good to sit down, and I was content to watch the incredible mix of people swirling about. All ages, infant to elderly, hell-bent on a good time Saturday night.

Cora stood by the door now, alone and sipping from a plastic glass. Lamar must have made his escape. She wore a stylishly soft black skirt with a flower border along the hem, and a loose matching top. Her dark hair was meticulously combed into precise curls and whorls that framed her rather plain face, and looked as hard as cement. Still, she was an attractive older woman, and who was I to talk? I could feel my unruly hair springing away from the confines of the French braid that hung down my back.

Cora peered through the mass of dancers intently, as if she were hunting for someone. If she had glanced my way, I would have motioned her to join me, but she didn't, and soon drifted over to a group of friends. One of the men refreshed their glasses from a flask he took from his pocket. Cora took over the conversation with a lot of animation, but continued to scan the crowd. I wondered idly if she had something going on the side. Lamar wasn't my idea of a dreamboat.

Jim appeared with three bottles of beer and handed me one.

"Where's Potts?"

"Over there with your father," I said. "Jim, do you think anybody would mind if I took some pictures?" This would be my best chance to get shots of Helby and Potts.

"What for?" His glance swept the dance floor and the surging mass of kids running wild during the band's intermission.

"Local color."

He shook his head in disbelief. "Where's the camera? In the car?"

"Yes. I left it on the front seat. Thanks." I gave him my dishiest smile, and then went back to people-watching. I didn't see Max anywhere, but the sheriff was working his way around the edge of the floor. He stopped by Cora's group, spoke to them briefly, then went on.

A line began to form by the food tables and all the chairs were filling up. Except for the seats by me, of course, the pariah from Chicago. Solace came from an unexpected source when Kim Kavenaugh sauntered in my direction and sat down in the chair beside me, though I was amazed her jeans allowed that much action.

"Hi," she said. "Are you having a good time? These dances are crazy."

"Yes, they are. And yes, I'm having a good time."

"You were smart to wear a skirt. It's so damn hot in here, I think I'm getting crotch rash." Her laugh was infectious.

"Denim will do it to you," I agreed, welcoming her friendliness. She was totally unaffected, with an earthy frankness wildly incongruous with her cover girl looks.

It seemed incredible that anyone so gorgeous would bury herself in this place. "What on earth do you do in this town?"

"Shit, not much, let me tell you. But I'm only here summers now."

"College?"

"Yes."

"Where?"

"Brown."

"Brown!" To my shame, I couldn't hide my surprise.

She threw back her head with another outrageous laugh. "Right. And you better believe I suffered one hell of a culture shock that first year. But I like it now."

And I was willing to bet she gave the Eastern seaboard a run for its money as well. "Brown's a wonderful school."

She shrugged away the implied compliment. "Are the folks around here still giving you a hard time? I liked the way you handled yourself at the cafe yesterday. Guess we deserved it."

"It's not me that I care about, Kim. It's Minnie. Hers is a rather bitter example of the old Wolffian saw: You can't go home again. Minnie said goodbye to everything she knew to chase some dream of finding the family she never had. Now she's lonely, and more than a little frightened, I'd guess, though she'll never admit it. She gets hate mail, her fences are cut, her house broken into, and all she wants are a few friends."

"I didn't realize it was that bad." We both had our eyes on the white-haired group hemmed into the bay area. The sheriff had made his way there, and stood talking to Helby with what appeared to be a great deal of deference.

"Just look at them sitting over there," Kim said. "All tame and toothless. I hate to say it, but those old farts will never forget that Minnie is Lil Darrow's sister, even if she's lived in a convent the last fifty years.

"That's Tessa MacLean in the wheelchair. Years ago her husband died in the middle of winter. Left her with two little kids and pregnant with a third. She had to bury her husband, deliver her own baby, and get food for the table until the snows melted and she could get to town. And all of that before she was as old as I am. She's close to ninety now."

The bit of feminine fluff Kim referred to sat daintily on the edge of her chair, as if she were going to rise any moment. Prim and proper with her white hair and navy silk dress, she looked as if she'd done nothing more exciting in her life than tat an edge on a handkerchief.

"They're tough people," Kim went on. "Set in their ways. What seems like history to us is real close to them; their emotions are still invested."

Jim approached with my camera slung over his shoulder.

"Hi, Kim," he said. "Glad you're here. Join us for

some food?"

"Sure, but don't get any for me. I've got some coming."

He slipped the camera into his hand and held it out to me. "Here you go. I'll fill some plates."

"Wait a minute, Jim. Kim's been telling me some wonderful stories about—what's her name? Tessa? Tessa MacLean. Could you get a picture of her for me?" I asked, feeling suddenly shy about barging in on these people. "They know you. I'd love to have some of your father and Potts, too." I didn't mean to be devious, truly. Something else was at work. I was beginning to see these people as something other than stereotypes, or black and white photos.

Jim shrugged. "Always the past." He pointed an accusing finger at Kim. "Why don't you tell Thea some of the things you've been doing?" And proceeded to tell me himself. "She opened an employment agency in town this summer, the first one ever for Hijax. And last summer she started a senior center that's the prototype for four counties. There are a hell of a lot of things going on in this town and other places in Wyoming that are more important than all that Wild West stuff."

I smiled at Kim. "I am impressed. I thought you spent your summers working in the cafe."

"I like to fill in. My aunt and uncle run the place and it gives me a chance to see everybody in town. But if anybody should be tooting their own horn, it's you Jim. He—"

Jim interrupted Kim good-naturedly, "I'll go take your pictures, Thea, and get some food. I'm starving." He began weaving his way across the hall.

Kim said, "He's quite a guy; a tough businessman. A lot of people around here think he's a hotshot, but he just wants to be where the action is. I admire that.

He'll never be content to sit home playing nurse-maid to a bunch of cows, something his dad will never forgive him for."

I offered to share my beer with her and she poured half into an empty paper cup she found on a neighboring chair. I took a long swallow from the bottle.

"Helby fascinates me," I said. "He seems so...alone. So different." Cora had joined the group of old-timers now, and the sheriff had disappeared. She looked flushed, and had Helby off to one side, but he wouldn't let her monopolize him. He kept sidling back to the group, and didn't seem to be paying any attention to her. Which didn't bother Cora. I could see her mouth rattling on.

"Yeah, Helby's old aristocracy," Kim said. "Straight out of a tintype. Name counts for a lot around here."

"Yes, land and family. Jim said as much, too. It's rather like the Boston Brahmins; I'm just surprised to find it here in Wyoming."

"My family moved here from Nebraska thirty years ago, so we're not old family, but I did some oral history work awhile back and really enjoyed it. Interviewed Helby, Tessa, and a lot of others. Parson Potts, too. Now there's an interesting old bird for you. Have you met him?"

I nodded grimly.

"He inherited a pile and lost it all to wine, women and song, as they say. Then literally picked himself up from the gutter and reformed. Been an itinerant preacher for years, though I suspect it's just a mail order degree. He goes to all the little community churches in the boonies, and the folks like him better than the honest-to-God ministers in town."

I listened, and at the same time, watched Jim skillfully maneuver his father away from Cora Mae.

He put Helby, Potts and several others into a group behind the wheelchair and snapped their picture. By talking and laughing with them, and frequently gesturing back at me, he urged them into different poses. Ignored, Cora stood to one side for a moment, then with a final glare at Jim, wandered back into the crowd.

Kim emptied her cup. "A few years ago I wanted to do a paper on the same hanging that Minnie's been asking about. It was one of the last acts of violence between the cattle barons and the nesters, or sheepmen. An interesting piece of history, I thought, one deserving documentation. At the time there were three or four men still living who I suspected had an active part in the incident. But I couldn't get a word out of anybody. They saw the whole affair as a dirty splotch on Hijax's history. So I dropped it and went on to something else. I guess what I'm trying to say is that if the old-timers won't talk to local people about dicey events, there's not much chance they'll open up to an outsider." She stood and stretched. "But I'd be glad to go out and visit with Minnie, tell her what I know, which isn't much."

"I think she'd like that. Thanks."

Kim grinned, shook her legs, and tugged at the tight denim to ease it down her thighs. I followed her glance and saw Max making his way down the length of the dance floor, juggling two overfull plates of food.

Kim waved to get his attention. "Now there's the sexiest thing that's hit this town in years," she said. "Come to think of it, if Minnie wants to find out about the hanging, why doesn't she ask Max?"

"Max? Why Max?"

"Well, hell. It was Max's grandfather who got hung."

 CHAPTER 10

I spent the rest of the evening in a fog of confusion, my mind on nothing but Max. Why hadn't he told Minnie about his grandfather? Or told me? How did this relate to everything else that was happening: the fences, the wells, the break-in? Did Max know Minnie and I had identified the vigilantes, and did he know that Helby and Potts were included in their number? Was he out for a spot of revenge?

I didn't see Max again, though I looked for him, and I suppose my being so distracted was the reason why the camera got misplaced. Jim had kindly spent considerable time taking shots of all the old lions, and every other local character he spotted. I distinctly remember him handing me the camera, and feel quite sure I placed it on one of the chairs while we danced, but when next I looked, it had disappeared. Not much of a surprise for a Chicagoan, but I'd been led to believe such things rarely happened in Hijax, Wyoming.

We found the camera at the end of the evening

when we left the hall.

It was one of those black, black nights. The high-powered light on a pole by the corner of the building did little to illuminate the jumble of cars and pick-ups parked haphazardly around the lot. We headed around back, peering through the darkness for Jim's car, and in a puddle of light from a window saw my camera on the ground half-hidden by the bush, smashed into shards of high-tech plastic.

"What the hell?" Jim said. He picked up the biggest piece and turned it over in his hand. "Thea, I'm sorry. Wait here, I'll get the sheriff."

He was gone before I could stop him. The camera didn't matter, or even the pictures on it. I could always start over again. But who could have been so angered by Jim taking pictures for me? And why? If Helby or Potts didn't want their pictures taken, why allow it? Who else could have cared? Max? And what about Cora? What was her concern in all this, if any? I only knew it couldn't have been Jim. He'd been with me all the time after taking the pictures.

I gathered up the rest of the pieces and took them over to a trash barrel I could dimly see between two pickups. One of the trucks had nosed in at an angle, so there was more space between the two than usual. I dropped the camera pieces in the barrel with a clatter. As I turned away, something by the far front tire of the angled truck caught my eye. I leaned across the barrel to get a better look and saw the pale glimmer of a hand resting on the ground. I raced around the rear of the truck and nearly stumbled over the body in the darkness.

"Jim!" I yelled, and dropped to my knees by the still form. Heart attack? Passed out? This close I could smell the liquor. And see the dark skirt with the flower border. Cora.

"Jim," I called again. She was lying on her stomach, legs sprawled. I ran my hand up her back. There was no movement.

"Thea? Where are you?"

I jumped up and waved my arms, yelling, "Here. Come quick."

The sheriff was with him and had a flashlight. He ran the beam over Cora and knelt quickly beside her. The beam skewed away, arcing across the dark sky, when he placed the flashlight on the ground in order to turn her over. Jim and I hovered. I craned around, trying to see, but the sheriff's bulky shoulders hid her from our view.

"I know CPR," I said, prepared to help.

"No need," the sheriff said, swinging the beam of light on us. "She's dead."

Lamar was found in the hall's basement playing gin, and all the warm qualities of a close-knit community came into play for him.

The sheriff began the initial process of examining the body and taking notes. I stood numbly, taking it all in, not knowing what else to do. Max pushed through the crowd and stood next to me. He asked what happened, and I told him the little I knew. Jim stayed close to the sheriff, helping as needed until the ambulance, coroner, and sheriff's deputies finally arrived and the official procedures began in earnest.

Everyone was questioned, and the crowd buzzed with each new piece of information gleaned from whatever source. Practically everyone had seen Cora in the hall, but apparently no one saw her leave, or saw her in the parking area.

Max came by again to check on me, then left to take Kim home. People began to slowly drift away. The sheriff came up to me and put his hand on my shoulder.

"Are you all right?"

"Yes."

"I'm sorry this happened, Thea. Did they get your statement?"

I nodded. "What happened to her, Hank?"

"Can't tell for sure. They'll have to do an autopsy. There's a laceration on the right temple area, and some blood. Looks like she stumbled into the wing mirror on the truck. Didn't appear bad enough to me to kill her." He shrugged again. "It could have been the liquor, or her heart; we'll know in a couple of days."

Jim turned away from the men he had been talking to. "Do you need us for anything more, Hank?"

"No. You can take her home." He ran his hands across his face and through his hair. "Oh, by the way. Do you want to tell me about that camera?"

I had forgotten all about the camera. "No. It's not important."

I did tell Minnie about the camera the next morning. And about Max's grandfather, although not until Max left for work. At breakfast we had both filled her in on the awful events of the night before. Poor Cora.

"What an odd way to die. I guess the town will miss her. Who do you suppose will be in charge of all the history stuff she did? But, destroying the camera sounds like vandalism to me," Minnie said. "No one would care about the actual pictures you took. It was another message that they want me to keep my nose out of their business, and that I'm not wanted around here."

Her chin took on a determined hardness. "I'll have the manuscript finished by noon, Thea, and you can take it with you."

She was strangely silent about Max's grandfather.

"Minnie, why don't you come to Rapid City with

me? My Uncle Charlie would love to meet you, and
he'd see that you got back to Hijax whenever you
wanted." The more I thought about it, the better the
coupling sounded. The two could spend days talking
delightedly about the past. And Cora's death had me
spooked.

"Thank you, Thea, but no. Not this time. I'm not
going to run."

I could tell by the look on her face that arguing
would be useless. But it was a good idea, and I
planned to tell Charlie to look her up.

My own determination solidified along the lines of
withdrawal. Particularly concerning Max. I didn't
want to think about Max any more, or his grandfather,
or Helby, poor dead Cora, or any of the others. My
first instincts about noninvolvement were correct, and
with that I'd be on my way with a clear conscience.

Minnie was already at the typewriter. I went
upstairs, packed, tidied my lovely room, and tried to
deny the regret I felt at having to leave. And the
niggling worry.

I wandered outside, checked the dog's dish for food,
and whistled for him. I wanted a last look at the bleak,
beautiful countryside. I needed to see if the piercing
blue sky could burn away the image of Cora's dead
body from my mind.

I began to think the dog had given up on this less-
than-receptive household, when he appeared from out
of the barn, his front half crawling in humble
obeisance, while the back half danced with joy. Such
a ridiculous animal. And how was he going to fare
without me? I'd have to give Minnie a crash course on
pet ownership.

I followed the track that led to the fields behind the
house. The dog bounded after me with his great
tongue lolling and his nose leading him off on sniffing

detours. To my right rose a chalk hill; its steep but gentle contours offered a challenge within my grasp. I left the trail to investigate, and picked my way through clumps of prickly pear and tattered-looking yucca.

"Come on, dog, I'll race you to the top."

It was more difficult than I thought. The soil was loose and sandy, and crumbled out from under my feet. The dog, of course, raced right up with no difficulty and stood, king of the mountain. Then I too reached the top.

From here the bulk of Halfway Halt was reduced to insignificance. I turned my back on it. I wanted to see the incredible stretch of earth and sky meld into a barely distinguishable horizon. Only scattered windmills and lazy trails of fence snaked through the uncompromising terrain. Three days ago the sight would have filled me with anxiety. Today it gave me solace.

Ahead I could see a small glen filled with a strange mix of hardy pines and dead trees thrusting up their naked, gray branches in tortured whorls. Sun pierced through the tangled mass and bounced back in flashes of reflection as if the ground were littered with jewels.

The glen was farther away than I thought, but worth the hike. The dog bounded ahead and flushed a rabbit which took him off on another detour. I reached the dense stand of trees and walked among them. The ground was soft with sand and needles and, indeed, sprinkled with flashing crystals. Delighted, I picked one up and held it up to the sun. The crystals were big, flat diamond shapes, like those on a pack of cards, as richly layered as mica, but clear with rainbows caught inside.

I had no idea what they were, but it didn't matter. I soon gathered more than I could carry, and sat on a crumbly log with the hoard cradled in my lap. I grinned sheepishly at my impulsive greed.

The quiet was immense, made even more still by being filled with the soft sounds of squabbling birds, dog snuffles, and the buzz and whirl of tiny flying things. The solitude reached deep within me and filled me with a rich contentment I'd never known before.

Scattered back in the sun, the jewels' glassy look changed once more to brilliance. Oh, to live in a place like this, I thought. A cottage, or better yet, a hollow tree.

I tucked a crystal under my watchband, and propped a fat one in my bra at the vee of my blouse. All I needed was a crown, but the best I could manage was to balance a large crystal on my head. Stepping into a stream of sunlight, I twirled carefully, around and around, and wished I knew some Druidic song to chant.

A sound, or sense of presence, stopped me mid-turn, eyes searching. Nothing. Another half-turn and I saw Max, leaning against a tree-trunk, enjoying himself immensely.

Wildly embarrassed, I snapped, "What are you doing here?"

"I work here, remember?"

"Then why aren't you working instead of sneaking around spying on people?"

"I wasn't sneaking." He pushed away from the tree and came toward me. "I heard the dog and wanted to see who was around."

"You could have made more noise." I hated him catching me in that childish spectacle.

He took the crystal from my shirt, studied it a moment, then looked around the sun-dappled glen.

A sage-scented breeze brushed across my skin, but didn't erase the warmth from his fingers where they had lingered against my breast.

"I didn't find you foolish, you know," he said gently.

"I'll bet. Careening around like the Hag of May with garbage in my hair."

He laughed and helped disentangle the crystal from my hair.

"I understand how you feel, though. I've done it myself."

"Now *that* I'd like to see."

"Well, maybe not your bit out there, but when I was a kid...I always wanted to be a horse." He spoke hesitantly, as if recalling something pleasant he hadn't thought about for a long, long time.

"Some days when the weather was just right, and the wind ripped through me, and the earth smelled like...Well, I don't know, but the urge would hit, and I'd leap off the porch and gallop away whinnying and throwing my head. I was always getting the hell beat out of me for being frivolous."

Certainly nothing frivolous remained, I thought, pleased to have been allowed a glimpse behind his somber surface.

"Somehow," I said, "I can't see you as a little boy."

His eyes caught and held mine. "Somehow, I don't think you want to see anything but a cardboard cowboy."

His look was a challenge, one I wanted to accept, but didn't know if I dared. How much emotional energy was I willing to risk if I planned to leave this afternoon?

I dropped my eyes, fiddled with my watchband, and removed the last of my jewels. Avoiding the issue, I said, "What is this stuff, anyway?"

He answered easily, but didn't move away. "Selenite."

"Oh?"

"A crystal form of gypsum. It's all through this country."

My gaze met his again, and through no volition of my own, the question popped out. "Why didn't you tell me, or Minnie, that it was your grandfather the vigilantes hung?"

He turned away. "You didn't ask." He jerked some long wisps of weeds from the ground and began weaving them together as he leaned back against the tree.

"It's no secret," he said. "Everyone around here knows. I'm surprised Minnie hasn't found out." He gave me a hard look and went on rather defensively. "If she'd ever asked me, I'd have told her what I know. Which, believe me, isn't much. I'd just as soon forget about it. My mother was a baby when my grandfather was killed, and grandma never talked much about it. It was just one of those things I had to live with through school."

"What do you mean?"

"Kids." He gave a rueful laugh. "Woolie, they called me. Kept threatening to string me up."

"Woolie?"

"My grandfather was an itinerant sheepherder. Those were still fightin' words in his day."

"And in your day?"

"No, of course not. But the taint lingers. Hijax has always been cattle country."

"And how about your father? Was he a…a sheepman too?"

He sat on the ground now, his hands still plucking and plaiting. I sat on the rotten log.

He stopped his busy work and smiled at me. I melted into it, not caring whether he answered or not.

He said, "Don't make too much of all this, will you?

It's not that important. Weren't you ever a wallflower at the junior prom?"

I sat quietly under his gaze as he took thorough stock of me.

"No, I guess not," he said finally. "I've been gone from Hijax a long time. Coming home has been interesting. Pulled a lot of triggers I didn't know were there."

His pause was long but comfortable. I was content to wait, sure he would continue.

"My dad wasn't a sheepman. He wasn't much of anything as far as I can tell. Odd jobs, handyman. He left when I was just a kid."

"What happened to your grandmother after…"

"The night they hung grandpa, they slaughtered all his sheep as well. Left ninety head with their throats cut and bellies slit, lying in a puddle of blood a mile long, so the story goes. Grandma told mother the two of them were lucky to be alive. Claims they would have been killed, too, if she hadn't been off visiting friends that night. As it was, she and my mom were taken in by relatives over in Ten Sleep."

I couldn't imagine what it would be like to have such an exotic tale in your background. "Why did your mother come back to Hijax?"

"It wasn't until years later, and then just by chance. After my mother married, she and dad moved all over the state chasing work, and ended up here with the cafe. By then all the hate and fear was forgotten. Nobody ever bothered them. In fact, when Dad left Mom with a pile of debts, the whole town stood behind her. My problems were just kid stuff; I was an easy mark."

I don't know what reminded me of Minnie and her problems. Maybe I equated Max's dismal upbringing with Minnie's and Lil's. At any rate, I remembered what I had wanted to tell him last night.

"By the way," I said. "I got an interesting reaction from my suspect, Potts, last night, before the party was over and I found poor Cora. When I met him, my hand went up to my head," I mimicked the action, rubbing the sore spot I could still feel. "He practically fell to pieces, wouldn't look at me and left as quickly as he could."

Again, it took Max a long time to answer, as if he were concerned with more important things. "You sure he wasn't just being Potts? He's a strange one."

It was my turn to be defensive. "Of course I'm sure. He didn't come right out and say, 'How's your head?' or anything, but he certainly looked guilty as hell."

"But why? Why would he ransack Minnie's office?"

"Because of the hang..." I caught myself just in time. If Minnie was right, no one but the two of us, and possibly the person who raided her office, knew she had identified the vigilantes. And fortunately, some tiny remnant of common sense prevented me from blurting it out. But I couldn't help wondering what Max would do with the information. On the other hand, it was high time I got my nose out of places it didn't belong.

"Minnie thinks the ransacker was after her manuscript, but she keeps it well hidden." I ran my fingers through the sandy hot soil and kept my eyes on Max's strong hands as they worked the strands of grass.

"Maybe you're right." He echoed my sigh, but sounded totally unconvinced. Rising to his feet, he picked up a large flat crystal. With a few fast twists he secured it by both points with the braided grass, then pulled me up and tied the bracelet around my wrist with a neat knot.

"For the princess. Your friend is over there waiting

for you and I've wasted more time than necessary."

I turned and saw the dog a few yards away, sitting on his haunches, panting. I called and he slithered over, keeping a wary eye on Max.

Max shook his head. "As I said before, a sorry animal."

"But he has a frivolous heart. You should feel kin to him."

He gave me the full blast of his smile and pulled me into his arms. His kiss tasted of sun and salt and was utterly satisfying.

When finally we drew apart he said reluctantly, "I really do have to get this stretch of fence fixed, but I'd like to spend some time with you, alone. How about tonight? We could go to town. There's not much to do there, but we could find someplace where we could talk, get to know each other better before you have to leave."

"Mmmmm," I said, instead of telling him I planned to leave this afternoon. *Go home, you fool, you have work to do.* But the old, comfortable, pragmatic me was fast overridden by a strange new entity whose heart was going pitty-pat. What the hell, I thought, my emotions were already in a turmoil, why not let the pot boil a bit?

"You've changed your tune. I seem to recall—when first we met—you growling something like, 'Why don't you go back where you came from?'"

"Did I say that?"

"As a matter of fact, you did."

He nuzzled my neck. "I can't imagine why."

"Try." I pulled away, suddenly quite serious. "How did you know who I was? Why did you tell me to leave?"

"A bad day, I guess." His hands massaged my spine, making it hard to concentrate. "Minnie was giving me a hard time. I tried to point out, not for the first time, the consequences of her writing that damned book. If she'd just let herself settle into the community for a year or so, and get a chance to meet people without prying into their affairs, then maybe they'd be more receptive. She didn't want to listen. Told me you were coming, and I knew you'd be pushing for her to finish that book. I was ready to throw in the shovel and leave. Want me to eat my words?"

"That's not necessary."

"Why don't you come along with me while I finish the fence? No, wait. Will you do something for me? Would you drive over to Enright's and see if they have some wire stretchers I could borrow? I can get this done twice as fast with stretchers."

"How do I get there?"

"Turn right on the gravel when you come out of Minnie's drive. You can't miss it. About five or six miles, nice looking house, mailbox on the road."

"All right." I could use some thinking time. To stay or to go.

The dog and I watched Max walk down the fence line and disappear around a hill. Then we turned and headed for Halfway Halt. The words, once used by Max, "Why don't you go back where you came from?" ran through my mind like a nagging reprimand. Go back home. Yes, I thought, that's what I should do, get on with my goals, don't get distracted. Think of my career, my job. But instead, I was thinking how I could rearrange my plans. What difference would it make if I left tomorrow instead of this afternoon? None. I would still be going back to where I came from, just a little later than expected.

The words jarred something, stirred the dark pool of suspicion that lurked so close to the surface. The hate letter Minnie had received. Hadn't it begun with the

same words Max had said to me that first day on the
road? "Why don't you go back where you came
from?"

Coincidence? Yes. Yes, of course. The crude
language of the note wasn't Max's style. Besides,
practicality assured me, all I had to do was ask him
about it. Tonight. Yes, tonight, we'd talk. I would
allay all my suspicions, once and for all. And maybe
there would be more than talk.

CHAPTER 11

The Enright's house was quite new. A one-story affair, like those built all over the states and called ranch style, though I was beginning to discover that real ranch houses bore little resemblance to the suburban models. The real thing seemed to be either out-of-place mausoleums like Halfway Halt, or an uncontrolled sprawl of additions tacked onto any kind of beginning.

I parked in the driveway behind a truck, and chose the back entrance by the garage to knock on rather than the remote and unused-looking front door. It was the right choice. Jim opened the door almost immediately.

"Well, hello," he said, then led me through a spotless utility room and into the kitchen where Helby sat nursing a cup of coffee.

"Look who's here, Dad. Your charm is still intact. You invite her to come and see you, and boom, here she is." His cheerfulness seemed forced.

I sensed a strain, and wondered if I'd interrupted an

argument.

Helby rose. "It's more likely you that brought her here."

His austere face seemed to lighten and I thought he was glad to see me.

I said, "I hate to disillusion you both, but this is a business call, though no one said I couldn't enjoy myself while I was here."

"What can we do for you?" Jim asked as Helby poured a mug of hot coffee for me.

"Wire stretchers, whatever they might be. Max wondered if you had some and if he could borrow them."

Helby nodded. "I think they're in the pickup."

"No, I put them in the shop, Dad. I'll get them. What's Holman doing, anyway?"

"Fixing fence, obviously." Helby's voice was heavy with sarcasm.

"Yes," I added quickly, not wanting to get in the middle of another disagreement. "He seems to work from dawn to dusk fixing things that are broken."

"We could use some of that around here," Helby said pointedly.

Jim just gave me a wink, smiled at the old man, and went out the door.

Helby turned to me and asked, "Have you recovered from last night? You're not having a very good introduction to Wyoming. Jim says it was you who found Cora."

"Yes."

"I'm sorry for that. Sheriff said he wouldn't know what she died of until tomorrow, maybe not then." He shook his head sorrowfully. "Well, she was a foolish woman." And that apparently closed the case as far as he was concerned.

He brightened. "How's Minnie? Ornery as ever?"

"Yes," I said. "She's been working all morning. I feel quite slothful."

"She's quite a gal." He poured himself another cup of coffee. Mine was still in the sip and blow stage. Helby looked older today, dressed in faded jeans and a cotton shirt. He walked with the slight forward tilt of the aged which was more evident now without the loose vest.

"Everybody spoiled that Minnie like sin. Halfway Halt was lively in those days. You would have liked it," he added wickedly.

I laughed.

"That place was more than a whorehouse, you know. In fact, we most never thought of it that way. The big room, that was a place where you could put your feet on the table and spit on the floor if you wanted. Meet your friends and such like. Lil even let us young whippersnappers hang around. Of course, the women—the wives and such—never believed it was just meeting friends and talking. Maybe that was half the fun."

Jim came in saying, "You're all set, Thea. I put the stretchers in your car." He glanced at the clock. "I've got to get going. Hate to leave you, but I've got a meeting in town. Don't want to be late."

"Town again? You might have told me," Helby said. "What about those calves you were going to treat?"

"Dad, I told you. You keep forgetting." He dropped a light proprietary kiss on my cheek. "I'm going to get the vaccine while I'm in town."

"If you'd stop gallivantin' around the country and pay more attention to the ranch—"

"And if you hadn't fired the help. Ancient history, Dad, forget it. I'll doctor the calves tomorrow." He smiled at me. "Don't rush off on my account, Thea," he said, I think in way of apology. "Dad hasn't had any company in a long time."

"I'm in no hurry," I assured him as the door closed.

Helby sat with his head bowed over his coffee. We listened to the engine start, then retreat into the distance, accompanied by a larger rumble.

I looked up. "Is that thunder?"

"Yeah, but don't count on rain." He peered out the window.

"It sounds more business-like than usual."

"Maybe." He stared up at the clouds. "If it rains the calves won't get treated tomorrow, either. Does more damfool running to town." As if to accent his thoughts, two large drops of water splashed against the window.

"Well, someone has to take an interest in civic affairs," I offered rather apologetically. I wasn't sure what I should say, if anything, but plunged on regardless. It wasn't likely I'd learn to keep my mouth shut at this late date. "It takes a lot of hard work and intelligence to get elected to the state legislature. I think it's pretty terrific that Jim takes the time and effort to get involved." All I needed was a megaphone and some bunting.

"Maybe, but it's no way to run a ranch."

"I understand you did your share of civic duties when you were his age."

He smiled slyly. "We always made sure the right people got elected sheriff." He paused, shook his head. "I'm too old is all," he said. His voice faded on a note of bitter acquiescence. "Come on," he said, throwing off his depression. "Let's have some lunch, and watch it rain."

A big pot of chili sat on the stove's back burner. Helby ladled out two large crockery bowls full, handed me one, and grabbed a box of crackers. I followed him out to the front step, a concrete slab big enough for two metal chairs, and protected by overhanging eaves. Casual chatter satisfied both of us while we ate the thick, spicy soup, and sucked in great draughts of rain-sweetened air. The parched grass darkened with anticipation.

Helby's voice broke into the silence. "I've always been too old."

With a queer inner flip I thought of the cocky teenager, and the hanging body with the broken neck.

"Didn't marry until I was forty. Then it was five years before we had a baby that lived: Jim. My wife died when he was six."

The rain began to fall in fat, sluggish drops that splattered here and there, raising tiny haloes of dust.

"Didn't know nothing about raising kids." His voice was flat and dry, the emotions involved had been spent long ago. "Too damn old."

"Being a parent at any age is tough," I ventured. "Maybe you were expecting too much of yourself, wanted results that are difficult to achieve in this time, this age." I was groping.

"You mean what it took to be a man in the old days?"

I nodded. "Something like that."

He ran his hand over his chin, his eyes on the sky. "God knows, I didn't want Jim to be like me. I wanted him more...to be...I didn't know how."

I'd listened to enough bewildered parents to understand some of the agony he was trying to express.

"I guess no child ever lives up to what a parent expects or wants." I thought of my mother and her hunger for grandchildren, and Dad's wistful hints that I become more politically active. "But somehow we—

the children—manage to muddle through. Jim is intelligent and ambitious. And if those attributes tend to pull him away from the life you're used to, and want for him, still aren't they some of the qualities you hoped he would have? You mustn't think you were a failure."

I quailed under his frosty gaze. Certainly I had breached the boundaries of casual conversation. Perhaps he guessed my consternation, because he reached out and patted my hand.

"You're a comfort," he said, "if that's the right thing to say to a young...uh...swinger." But I got the feeling that I hadn't really convinced him of anything.

The rain teased, falling sporadically, just enough to cut the dust and raise a rich, loamy smell. It would take much more than this to make the road slick, but I wanted to reach Minnie's before that happened. I had stayed longer than I intended, and Max was waiting for the stretchers.

Helby walked me to the car and opened the door. "Tell Minnie to come over to see me sometime. There's a lot of things we need to talk about."

I wondered what he meant, and if the hanging was one of those things. Did he realize he could still be incriminated?

Back at Halfway, I parked my car close to the front porch, and ran through the drizzle, waving at the dog who sat in the open door of the barn, enjoying the rain as much as Helby and I had. I stepped out of my shoes in the hallway, not wanting to track up Minnie's polished floor. The falling barometer had robbed the house of every breath of air and left a musky smell that reeked of ancient molds.

"Minnie, I'm here," I called, and padded through the hall to the kitchen. I threw open a window and let in a gust of fresh air, then crossed to the office door.

Minnie was stretched out on the couch, a magazine
on her chest, sound asleep. She had either finished her
work on the manuscript, or decided to take a break. I
didn't disturb her, but went upstairs to change clothes.
If I was going to get caught in the rain when I took the
stretchers to Max, I wanted to be dressed for it.

In the process of exchanging cotton slacks for
heavier jeans, a noise from below startled me. I
hopped around off balance, jumpier than a school girl.
It was just Minnie stirring around, I thought, and
pulled a shirt on over my tank top, and brushed my
hair. The sudden humidity had turned it into an unruly
mass of curls.

Back downstairs, I peeked into the office again.
Minnie was still sleeping, but the magazine had fallen
to the floor, explaining the noise I'd heard. Still
uneasy for some reason, or remembering Cora,
perhaps, I stood in the door a moment until I saw the
upward heave of her chest, then returned to the
kitchen.

I'd seen a plastic raincoat and overshoes in the back
entry, and was sure Minnie wouldn't mind my using
them. With a lighthearted laugh, I realized that I'd
made my decision. The storm was a perfectly useful
excuse. Why should I drive to Rapid City in the rain
when I could leave just as easily in the morning? Yes,
I'd cook dinner for Minnie as a last treat, and leave
tomorrow. And I'd have that talk with Max.

I took chicken from the freezer to thaw. I could do
lemon chicken, and maybe even prepare a nice stir fry
for Minnie to fix the next day. Surely, if I had
everything chopped and ready in a bowl for her she
could swish it around in a pan with some left-over
chicken. On the other hand, it might be better to tell
Max what to do with it.

I had just checked the crisper for veggies when I

heard a series of sharp barks from outside. Curious, I went to the back door. The yips and howls sounded further off now. I stepped out into the warm drizzle and whistled for the dog. When he didn't appear and the yowls started again I ran around to the front of the house. The pitiful keening seemed to be coming from the road.

With thoughts of traps, or hit and run drivers, I jumped into my car and headed down the hill. The road was thoroughly wet by now and surprisingly slick. My foot poised halfway between the brake and the accelerator, not daring to do either as the car slithered crazily down the treacherous curve. Only luck kept me on the road, and allowed the turn onto the gravel at the bottom.

Then came the rain. As if a plug had been pulled, great driving sheets of water pounded against the windshield whipped by a wind that appeared out of nowhere. I inched the car forward. The wipers were useless in the flood, and the meager visibility out the passenger side window wouldn't help much if the dog were in the trees or bushes. A search seemed useless. I began to look for some way to turn around on the narrow road.

Luckily, I saw an old turn-off, fenced across now, but long enough for my purpose. I turned in and stopped, reluctant to abandon the animal in this lousy weather. Abandonment seemed to have been too much his lot in life as it was. The rain pounded and the wind rocked the little car with its force. I rolled the window down, risking a deluge on the chance that I could see better. I was instantly drenched, and could see nothing, but an unmistakable whiny cry reached my ears.

I quickly rolled the window back up, opened the door, and stepped out into a cross between Niagara

Falls and hurricane Andrew. I wished I hadn't run off without the raincoat, but it was too late now.

The effort of slamming the door against the wind put me off balance. My feet slid out from under me and I shot down the slippery verge into the ditch, landing painfully on my seat. At least from that vantage point I was able to see the dog huddled tightly against a fence post, a black and white bundle of misery. Only the tiniest tip of his tail acknowledged my presence.

He whimpered, but didn't move. I thought he was hurt, but when I tried to turn him, found he was tied around the neck, his head drawn unnaturally against the rough post.

In a fit of fury, I pulled and tugged at the speckled rag that bound him. The material was soaking wet, the knot wrenched tight by his struggles. Who would do such a thing! Frustrated, I took the blasted knot in my teeth, hoping the poor animal wasn't so frightened he would bite. I should have known better. He nuzzled my neck and licked the rain from my cheek as the musty reek of dog burned my nostrils. I shivered in the sudden cold. The storm had robbed the day's heat, dousing everything in ice water.

"It's all right, baby," I crooned. "I've almost got it." Finally, the knot loosened and began to separate in my fingers. I threw the rag in the mud and rubbed the dog's neck.

"Come on, let's get out of here." He wouldn't move. Whatever courage he had gained over the last few days had been beaten out of him. I'd have to carry him. I got a grip around his middle and lurched towards the car, slipping and falling to my knees with every third step. The dog finally decided he was in mortal danger, wriggled free, and crept beside me to the car. It was just as well, I would never had made it up the incline with him. As it was, I had to crawl hand and foot up the slimy ground.

Boosting the dog into the front seat, I plopped down beside him, little caring about the ruin we made of the rented car. I wiped my hands on my pants and wrung the water from my hair. The clammy drag of my clothes sent shivers coursing through my body.

I backed the car onto the gravel, and figured my best chance to get up the hill to Minnie's was to gain as much momentum as possible. So I gunned the motor and sped down the road, gauging my speed so I didn't need to slow for the turn. So far so good. Then the dog moaned and rolled on his back. I glanced down, and gasped at the bloody mass on his stomach. Without thinking, my foot jammed the brake, and all I could do was hang on as the car slid sideways off the hill and into the ditch, thankful we hadn't been higher up the hill.

I pulled the dog back onto the seat and examined his belly. It was a mess. Bloody weal's criss-crossed the tender skin. Not only had the dog been cruelly tied, someone had beat the poor thing with a whip or stick. Why would anyone dare do such a thing so close to the house? They must have known anyone in hearing distance would come running.

The thought hung there, practically visible, stabbing me with needles of apprehension. Had someone wanted *me* out of the house? Why?

Not stopping for answers, I scrambled out of the car, arms and legs propelling me like a cyclone up the hill. All I could think of was Minnie, asleep and vulnerable on the couch. An overwhelming sense of danger pushed me through whipping rain that cut icily to my skin. Wind snapped the treetops, and filled the air with wailing groans that blended with mounting rolls of thunder.

Thick gumbo mud clung to my shoes like cement weights, sending me into a nightmare struggle of slow-motion until I couldn't lift either foot and fell forward. My hands sank wrist deep into the mud.

I loosed my hands and pulled my feet from my hopelessly mired shoes. Barefoot, I staggered on, each step a sucking horror, the icy muck filled with sharp flakes of stone that bit into the tender skin between my toes.

I reached the top with screaming muscles, and lungs barely able to pull in enough air, then found better footing on patches of weeds and ran to the house, not sure why I was running, only wanting to reach Minnie.

My mud-caked feet slid on the polished floor of the hallway. Uncaring, I raced across the parlor carpet to the office.

"Minnie," I called, grabbing for the door frame. "Minnie!"

But Minnie was gone.

CHAPTER 12

Dazed, I walked through the office to the kitchen, then out the other entry into the hall. The bathroom door was open. Empty. Into the great room, hurrying again, I tried to stem a sense of rising panic. Up the stairs. I called her name, raced through the rooms.

Outside, I thought, and flew back down the stairs. She probably went outside for something, got caught in the rain, and was waiting in the barn for the downpour to stop.

I cringed when the shock of wind-blown rain hit, as if it were my first time out. The sky had turned a sickly yellow-green. The gnarled cottonwood popped and moaned, straining against the wind.

I ran directly to the barn, truly expecting to find Minnie standing patiently in the open door. She wasn't there. I looked everywhere, my bare feet partially protected by caked mud. Minnie's old Buick was parked in the shed, but she was nowhere in sight. I moved as quickly as possible, checked all the buildings, and even found myself stupidly lifting collapsed boards.

Max. Go get Max. I had enough sense to know I couldn't go that far barefoot. I took overshoes from the back entry, pulled them on over the mud, and set off in a peculiar gait that was all I had left, a kind of jogging on one foot, walking on the other. I followed the same path I'd used that morning and avoided the worst mud by treading as much as possible on the grass and weeds along the fence line.

Fortunately, the storm concentrated its energy on releasing tons of water rather than dangerous displays of lightning, but the going wasn't easy. By the time I reached the glen, exhaustion had set in, and I hardly wasted a glance on it. There was no magic left; the jewels had disappeared with the sun, and the dead trees, shorn of their dignity, gleamed obscenely in the scummy storm light. Finally I saw the pickup, and ran towards it, clutching the stitch in my side. The door shot open and Max stepped out, sensibly clad in a bright yellow slicker and a sodden hat.

I stumbled toward him.

"Thea!" He caught me in his arms. "What's wrong?"

"Minnie!" I clung to him, gasping for breath, relieved by his presence.

He gripped my arms and held me away from his shoulder to look at my face. "What happened?"

I began to shiver uncontrollably. "I'm not sure." The words tore at my throat like a rasp, fighting my lungs for air. "She's gone."

He shook me a little, as if he could tumble my words into a sensible pattern.

"What do you mean, gone?" He hauled the long stick, bolts and hand tools he'd been working with out of the cab, and threw them in the back of the truck.

I crawled inside, grappling with an inability to

express the menace I'd felt. "It was horrible. First she was asleep. Then someone beat the dog, whipped him, to get me out of the house. And…"

Max pulled an old flannel-lined jean jacket from behind the seat. "Here," he said roughly. He draped it around my shoulders and pulled me to him. He wiped my face dry with a greasy rag from the floor and sopped some of the water from my hair.

I recoiled from the acrid odor. "Don't you have a hanky?"

He glanced impatiently at the filthy rag and threw it back on the floor. "You're reviving. Hurry now, tell me what happened so I can understand."

He tucked me tightly to his side and reached under the jacket to rub warmth into my back with his strong hands. I warmed to his touch and forced myself to concentrate.

I began slowly, starting with the trip to Enrights, step by step, trying not to leave anything out.

"That hill, Max, it was horrible. When I realized someone must have beaten the dog to get me out of the house, I tried to run up the hill, but it kept pulling me back."

"It's all right." His hands had lost their impersonal touch. One softly stroked my spine, the other kneaded the base of my neck, and when he spoke his voice was husky. "When you reached the house?"

"Minnie wasn't there."

"You looked?"

"Everywhere. In all the rooms."

"Could someone have come by and picked her up? Like Helby or Potts?"

"You mean while I was looking for the dog?" Could they have? "I don't think there was time. If they came from Enright's direction they would have passed me. No, wait. There weren't any car tracks on the hill other than mine and, believe me, no one could have duplicated the ones I made."

He set me aside, gently, and asked, "You okay now? We better get back." He started the motor. "Did you look outside?"

"Yes, everywhere. And, oh dear, I left the dog in my car. I didn't shut the door, so he might have crawled away somewhere. Do you suppose he's all right?"

"He's probably holed up some place where he feels safe."

Our progress was dreadfully slow. The tires dug deeply into the mud, strained for every inch of ground they gained, or slithered wildly off-track. Max swore and I found myself trying to urge the truck along its path with body language. Tension began to build again. My stomach tightened.

The rain beat on the truck and nearly hid the house from our sight. It was only three o'clock, but it looked like twilight. I wished I'd left some lights on. We pulled up by the back door and shot out of the truck like springs to race through the torrent.

Max kicked off his overshoes at the kitchen door, but I couldn't be bothered with such niceties, and hurried to Minnie's office, calling her name.

"You see," I said. "She's gone. Somebody got her."

"Who?"

"How should I know?" My voice sounded shrill. "Whoever beat the dog, whatever madman is running around out there." I began to shiver again.

"Stop that," Max said. "You don't even know if there was a man." He shoved me none-too-gently into a chair and pulled off the overshoes.

"Whoa!" he said, staring at my mud-caked feet and pants legs. He pulled me up and directed me toward the bathroom.

"Clean that mud off and change your clothes, you're

soaking wet." When I just stood there, numbly clutching my shaking body, he said, rudely, "Move. Do you want to look like a mud ball the rest of your life?"

I stalked into the bathroom and slammed the door. Who in hell did he think he was anyway? I'd have hysterics if I damned well pleased.

I tore at my ruined clothes, revived by anger. What did I know about Max Holman anyway? He could have staged this whole scene himself. Who was to say he was fixing fence all the time I was gone? He could have come back here and done anything he wanted. I'd caught him sneaking around that first night, hadn't I? A sudden sense of silence sent me racing for the door.

"Don't you dare leave this house without me," I yelled.

"All right," he yelled back. "But hurry." After a moment he cracked the door and tossed in shirt, jeans, and shoes, urging me to hurry again.

I tried, but my fingers had become strangely inefficient trying to peel the sodden jeans from my legs. I could hear Max banging cupboard doors in the kitchen, looking there for Minnie. And he called me stupid. Then the thought of why. The possibility of something being stuffed...

Quickly, I stuck my feet under the faucet in the tub, but the mud was incredibly stubborn. Tiny globs of the stuff clung persistently in the strangest places. Finally I gave up and rubbed off what I could with a towel and began to dress.

"She's not in the house," Max said through the door. "I've looked everywhere, even through the trap to the attic."

I stuck my head out again. "You didn't get any underwear."

"For crissakes!" he erupted.

"You are the most unpleasant person I've ever met!"

He grinned. "Sorry. This is a little out of my line."

"I'll bet," I shot back. I wondered what he made of my packed suitcase.

Finally dressed, I joined Max and said, "I searched the barn loft, in the shed where her car is parked, every place I could think of. And I called out, too."

"Well, I'll check them again. I don't know what else to do, Thea."

We went silently to the back entry. Max shrugged back into his yellow slicker and handed me the light plastic raincoat that hung from another hook.

"Minnie's?" I asked. He nodded dourly, and I'm sure we were both thinking the same thing. If Minnie had gone out, she would have worn the coat herself.

He picked up a flashlight, and I followed him out the door, pausing under the minimal shelter of the cottonwood to button the flopping ends of the coat. I twisted away from the wind and found myself staring at the humpy bulk of the old dugout.

"Max, wait," I called, halting his steps towards the barn. "I didn't look in the dugout." I hurried across the rain-slicked grass and down the crude wooden stairs. An inch of water puddled the ground in front of the door.

"Watch out!" Max called, as he slid down the stairs behind me, knocking me into the door. He took my arm and gave me a concerned look. "Are you all right?"

"Yes," I said with a reassuring smile. "Don't worry, I'm fine." And I was. No more hysterics. I'd had my first and last case of nervous shock, if I had anything to say about it. What if Minnie had needed me, what good would I have possibly been?

Lizards be damned, I thought, and pushed on the door. It didn't budge. Max lent his shoulder to the task and the door wobbled partially open, then stuck.

"Here." Max gave me the flashlight and I scraped through the narrow opening.

A rush of fetid, fungal air overpowered me. The flashlight beam swung across dark mossy strands hanging from the earthen ceiling and rickety shelves laced with webs. Then the light glanced the floor and picked out Minnie's recumbent form lying still behind the door.

"Max! She's here!" I dropped the light and eased her away from the door so he could push his way through. Her skin felt cool and damp, and I thought I heard a soft gasp of breath from her lips.

"Let's get her out of here, " Max said, and gathered her up in his arms.

I shoved the door open as far as possible and steadied Max from behind as he struggled up the slick stairs with his awkward burden. Then I ran ahead to open doors and get some blankets.

"Just put her on the floor while I get the truck," he said.

I made a pallet and he laid her on it. I wrapped another blanket around her. Her face was as gray as putty and looked oddly misshapened, though I couldn't see any bruises.

"What happened to her?" I asked, more to fill the silence than anything.

"I don't know, but I'm getting her to the hospital as quickly as I can."

"Are there any wounds, or broken bones?"

"No," he said sharply.

I glanced up quickly, but his face was shadowed by his hat. How was he so sure? I hadn't seen him examine her in any way.

"Get a couple more blankets," he said.

I stood, mired once more in a flood of suspicion. Why hadn't he bothered to look her over? Because he already knew? Or wanted to hide something from me? Had he really been working in the field all afternoon?

Max raised his head and stared at me; his mouth hardened into a grim line as he slowly got to his feet. My hand flew to my throat. I stepped back, but stood my ground. Under the circumstances, I considered Minnie's well-being my responsibility.

He glared at me, eyes narrowed and coldly reptilian. Wordlessly, he strode from the room. I dropped to Minnie's side as I listened to his steps recede up the staircase. I checked again for the faint heartbeat, and pulled the blanket away from her arms and hands, looking for cuts, bruises, anything unusual. When he returned, I was tucking the cover back around her. He kept his distance; he was only a dark, shadowed figure in the fading light. My heart thudded miserably even though I'd detected nothing further amiss with Minnie.

He dropped the extra blankets by my feet, and went out.

The angry mesh of gears rent the air as he slammed them back and forth, rocking the truck through the mud.

Then he was back. He brushed past me as if I didn't exist. Water shedding from his slicker spread in rivulets onto the floor. He threw an extra blanket over his shoulder, gathered Minnie up in his arms, pallet and all, and headed out again.

I followed, shielding her face from the rain and helped to settle her on the deep seat. Her feet would have to lie on Max's lap, which was just as well. "Keep her head down and her feet up in case of shock," I said.

He tried to move me away to close the truck door, but I stopped him. "I'm going with you."

"No you're not."

"Oh, but I am."

"There's no room."

"I'll sit on the floor."

"With your head under the dash?" He lifted me out of the way, kicked the door shut and pulled me into a fierce full-bodied kiss that held more anger than passion. My initial startled response turned quickly to struggle. His arms tightened, then just as roughly, he put me from him.

"Catch," he said with a bitter grimace, and flung the blanket from his shoulder at me. "If I kill her you can turn me in."

The blanket covered my head. I struggled with it, instinctively trying to keep the ends from falling into the sodden mess I stood in. If I'd just thrown the damned thing down I might have been able to catch up with him before the tires caught and the truck skidded out of the yard.

I stomped into the house, and after a moment to calm down, was surprised, or perhaps comforted, to find I was more furious than apprehensive. Did I really think Minnie was in danger from Max? No, I didn't. But reason demanded caution. I just hated being bested by him. Hated being stuck here with nothing to do. How long would it take him? Forty minutes or more to get to town, and how long would he stay at the hospital? An hour? Another forty minutes to get back here. If he came back. Surely he wouldn't leave me waiting in suspense. I'd kill him if he did.

Pacing aimlessly, I kicked at the clumps of mud I'd scattered throughout the house. I felt helpless. How could people stand to live like this? Totally isolated.

My car was useless, mired in the mud at the bottom of the hill. I could take Minnie's car, though the chances of getting any vehicle without four-wheel drive out of the yard and down to the graveled road were slim. If I could get to Enright's I could at least telephone the hospital and tell them Max was bringing Minnie. How long would it take me to walk to Enright's? Probably longer than it would take Max to get to town. I was stuck here, completely useless, stewing in my own juices.

Making coffee is a comfortable ritual, and I made the most of it, banging the pot around, making a lot of noise. While the coffee perked, I looked for Minnie's car keys on the off chance that if Max didn't return soon, and it stopped raining, I might want to give her car a try. I went to the office. The magazine that had fallen from Minnie's chest while she lay on the couch was on the floor. I picked it up and tossed it on the table. One of her shoes was also on the floor by the end of the couch. I picked it up, too, and absently slapped the worn brown loafer against my palm.

Funny I hadn't noticed she'd lost a shoe, but in the confusion I supposed it wasn't surprising. But why, I wondered, had she gone to the dugout with only one shoe on? She must have been in an awful hurry. And why go to the dugout, anyway? My mind spun back to those hours, trying to arrange them, fit things together.

When I returned from the Enrights, Minnie was sleeping on the couch. Right? I had gone upstairs, changed my clothes and come back down. No, wait, I thought, remembering the crazy one-footed dance I'd gone through putting on my jeans. I had heard something, a loud enough sound to startle me, and assumed it was the magazine falling off her chest, but would a magazine have made that much racket? Maybe not. Could someone else have been in the house and made his escape while I was upstairs?

I poured a cup of coffee and paced some more, hunting for a logical scenario. Perhaps the same person who broke into the house the other night had returned, for whatever reason, and—

"The manuscript," I yelped. Minnie had been working on the manuscript from the time she got up this morning. I ran into the office and looked through her desk; it wasn't there. I knew she had a hiding place for it somewhere, but would she have bothered to hide her work if she was just taking a break? And if she had finished working on the manuscript wouldn't she have left it out, ready to give to me when I left? She had no way of knowing I'd changed my plans. I hadn't wanted to bother her when I went out for my walk, nor had I disturbed her when I'd gone to the Enrights for the stretchers.

She could have finished her work early, and not knowing where I was, put it in safe-keeping until I was ready to leave, particularly if she wanted to take a nap. So it was possible that the manuscript hadn't been within ready reach of an intruder. I began a systematic search through the house. But there was no way of knowing if I had simply failed to find the secret place, or if someone else had taken it. Eventually, I gave up in frustration and, with nerves jumping, returned to my coffee and contemplation.

I began again and started with the premise that someone had been in the house taking advantage of a sleeping Minnie for his own purposes, perhaps searching for whatever he hadn't found during his first attempt. Once again he gets stopped by my arrival, hides, then escapes when I go upstairs. He might well have seen the dog in the barn, just as I had, and made the most of a chance to get me out of the house. He'd tied the dog, whipped him until he made enough racket to bring me running, leaving Minnie alone again.

The man had returned—that meant he had not gotten what he was after—Minnie wakes and catches him. In the ensuing struggle she loses her shoe, breaks away, and runs for the nearest hiding place, the dugout. Then what? She faints? No, there was something much more wrong with her than a faint. He could have struck her some way that didn't leave an obvious mark.

An obvious mark. Cause of death. What had Hank said about Cora? There was a slight bruise on the side of her head. Could she have been killed by a blow? Even if it didn't leave much of a mark? That would make it murder. I could still see Cora flipping through Minnie's pictures, searching for something. Could she have been killed for some reason connected to Minnie?

I didn't know enough about Cora to even contemplate why someone might want to kill her. My mind whirled. There were too many questions and not enough answers. Cora could have gotten that bruise when she fell. The only certain thing was that what had happened to Minnie today couldn't have been done by Cora.

But Minnie could have been struck. Something had been wrong with her face, though I couldn't quite put my finger on it. Or maybe her assailant thought he killed her and had thrown her in the dugout, or thrown her in, thinking she'd be dead by the time she was found. Either choice seemed grisly, but entirely possible. And had the intruder, or had he not, found the manuscript and our little pile of photographs?

Or, I thought, recognizing a distinct possibility, was I building a mountain of melodrama out of a shoe that could have been dropped to relieve a bunion?

CHAPTER 13

I wished Max were here. I needed someone to bounce ideas off. And what about Max? Could he have done this? I flopped down on the couch and attempted to erase all my feelings about him (ambivalent as they were) and face the situation with cold-blooded clarity. Max was the one who had sent me away from the house in the first place. Certainly he had the time to accomplish everything I'd envisioned and been waiting at the pickup when I got there. Why he would harm Minnie was another question. He seemed to be genuinely fond of her. If he didn't want the story of his grandfather's hanging revived, well, he was in a better position than most to simply plead his case with Minnie. And if she printed the story anyway, the discomfort, embarrassment, invasion of privacy, or whatever it was that concerned him, didn't seem of great enough consequence to warrant attempted murder, or even assault.

How badly did Max want her land? And wouldn't he stand a better chance of getting it with her alive?

This brought up the question of wills, and if Minnie had one, and who would inherit if she did or didn't. Too many imponderables. The bottom line seemed to be that I just couldn't imagine Max dumping someone in the hopes they would die. No, I thought, rather grimly, if Max wanted someone dead, they'd be dead.

On the other hand I had no difficulty at all visualizing Potts throwing Minnie around, or anyone else for that matter. Regardless of his age, he was certainly strong enough; he had easily lifted me off my feet at our first encounter. And I could actually see him flailing the dog with the zeal of a Penitente.

I tried not to be blinded by my prejudice. Jim too, had the time and opportunity. Only Helby seemed to be in the clear. Jim could have stopped here on his way to town, or not gone to his meeting at all. But there hadn't been any car tracks on Minnie's road when I'd returned from the Enrights. Surely I would have noticed them. I cursed myself for not being more observant. The thought of someone prowling around on foot in this country where everyone was so dependent on vehicles was chilling. And where was that person now?

That thought sent me scurrying off on a security check. I also collected an assortment of possible weapons which I stashed in various places throughout the rooms I used.

The drone of the approaching pickup sent me racing to the back door. The rain had stopped. I peered into the darkness and watched the lights swing around the side of the house. Max trudged heavy-footed to the house. He pulled his overshoes off on the back steps and I unlocked the door.

His eyes swept across me coldly and he headed for the coffee pot. "This coffee all right?" His voice echoed the tiredness that was evident on his face; the heavy lines of his mouth cut furrows through new stubble.

"Fresh enough," I said, then, half-dreading the answer, "Well, how is she?"

"Okay." He looked up. "Sorry, I should have said when I first came in. At least she's still alive. She—"

"Thank goodness," I interrupted. Relief washed the tension away, and with it came a flood of words. "Someone must have been in the house, Max. I found Minnie's shoe in the office." Max shook his head, but I rushed on. "I think they meant to kill her; that's why she was thrown in the dugout, in the hope we wouldn't find her."

"Nobody touched her, Thea. She had a stroke."

I stopped mid-breath. "A stroke?"

"Yes, I've been trying to tell you."

"But who tied the dog?"

"I don't know. He might have been in the road, chasing a car or something. You'd be surprised how many people don't like dogs."

"What about the shoe?" I asked, snatching it up from the counter where I'd placed it and waved it under his nose. "Would she go out to the dugout with only one shoe on?"

"Look, I don't know." His voice was weary, on the verge of impatience.

I paused thoughtfully and answered my own question. "After a stroke you often lose control of your feet. Her shoe could have fallen off without her realizing it. But Max," I said, waving the shoe again, "why go to the dugout at a time like that? For a can of beans?"

"Maybe she had the stroke in the dugout."

"Then why only one shoe?"

"Thea, I don't know. All I can tell you is that Minnie had a stroke and there were no other injuries.

The doctor examined her thoroughly to be sure she didn't have a concussion or broken bones from the fall. There was nothing. If you'd just quit waving that damned shoe around and tell me what you're getting at, maybe I can help."

I told him the different scenarios I'd developed and the reasoning behind them.

"It could have happened any of those ways," he admitted when I had finished. "But the fact remains that Minnie wasn't bodily injured. She had a stroke. A stroke can happen to anybody at any time."

I didn't bother him with my brief worries about Cora's death. More and more I felt like a victim of my own imagination. I remembered Minnie's earlier reference to some health problems, and how she constantly rubbed her temples. Perhaps that had been an indication of an impending stroke.

Max went on, "There is no evidence that another person was involved. I also agree that there are enough coincidences or strange incidents to warrant a certain amount of uneasiness. But until there's something more concrete, or Minnie herself is able to tell us—"

"How stupid of me," I groaned. "And how callous I've been. Tell me about Minnie's condition. Is she conscious? How much damage has been done? What's the doctor's prognosis?"

"She was in a serious state of shock when we got there, and of course they wouldn't let me see her, but the doctor said she was drifting in and out of consciousness. Her right side is paralyzed and she can't speak. He said that was common for stroke patients and not necessarily permanent. Right now we're simply to hope she has no more strokes."

I felt dreadful. Here I'd been fretting about stupid mysteries while Minnie's life was in crisis, all her options reshuffled through no choice of her own. What would become of her now? Whether the damage caused by the stroke was major or minor she had surely been given another shove into the depths of loneliness. Who would take care of her? I staggered under the sudden weight of responsibility, but didn't hesitate. I couldn't leave now. Not until I knew how she would be taken care of.

We settled into a spell of gloomy silence that I finally broke with one of those inane bon mots, that for all their stupidity provide speakers with some small comfort. "There's so much that can be done now; rehabilitation and such."

Max had the good sense to say nothing. He put down his coffee cup and picked up the flashlight from the counter. "There's one thing that still bothers me." He headed for the door.

"What? Where are you going?"

"Your favorite place. The dugout. Want to come along?"

"Of course."

We stepped out into darkness foully rank with a saturation that had reached deeply and found all the rotting things that nourish the earth. I squished along beside Max, hanging on to his arm to negotiate the narrow steps. The old wooden door had soaked up rain like a sponge and it took our combined effort to get it open.

Max swung the flashlight beam into the corners and across the shelves we'd paid little attention to earlier. A sadiron, a broken pickle crock, empty glass jars. The light flickered to the far corner, then back.

"Wait, Max. Put the light back in the corner."

He swung the beam and my eyes lit on a familiar shape hidden on a bottom shelf behind the door.

"It's a typing paper box." I grabbed it and removed

the lid. The pictures were there as well. "It's Minnie's manuscript. This is where she hid it."

Now that we knew why Minnie had gone to the dugout, everything fell in place. Minnie had finished the manuscript, and decided to hide it, for whatever reason. Maybe she was already feeling ill, and I wasn't around to entrust her work to. Feeling woozy, or whatever, she had rested on the sofa. She could have been sleeping, or already felled by the stroke when I returned from the Enrights. When I went chasing after the dog, she had either roused from sleep and suffered the first effects of the stroke, or made enough of a recovery from the already received trauma to struggle after the thing she valued most, her manuscript. Perhaps she was afraid that if anything happened to her I'd never be able to find the manuscript. But the effort was too much and she collapsed for good inside the dugout.

It all sounded terribly logical, and perhaps it was the anti-climactic-ness of it that made a part of me continue to struggle with this simple explanation.

I was beat, worn to a frazzle. I couldn't deal with the problem any more, or with the nagging inner imp that kept reminding me that everything Max had told me could be a lie. For all I knew Minnie might be lying in a ditch somewhere dead. But to what purpose? I was numb with speculation. Finally, with me clutching Minnie's manuscript, Max and I stumbled off to our separate beds, having reached some kind of unspoken agreement that neither one of us was in any kind of mental state to begin unraveling the many uncertainties that lay between us.

I slept late. The bedside clock showed nine-thirty when I bounded out of bed, slow to realize that Minnie wouldn't be there to taunt me about late-risers. Max wasn't around either, though he'd left a pot of still-warm coffee on the stove and his breakfast dishes in the sink. I took a long hot shower, washed my hair, and finally got rid of every trace of yesterday's mud.

Back downstairs, I sat at the kitchen table and began a mental list of things to be done. Most important was Minnie's welfare. I should bring some of her personal things to the hospital, and depending on the doctor's report, I might need to go through her papers for insurance information. If she needed extensive rehabilitation care, there were agencies to consult. Everything depended on how incapacitated she was, and for how long. The problems seemed enormous. As far as I knew, she had no relatives that should be contacted.

Max came in and plunked two enormous clumps of mud on the kitchen table. It took a few minutes to recognize them as the shoes I'd left mired in the hill.

"I see you finally made it up," he said with a trace of his old mocking humor.

He looked vigorously alive, but as inscrutable as ever. I couldn't imagine that those arms had held me, those lips had…He seemed like a stranger. Just as well, I thought with a pang.

"Did you find out anything more about Minnie?"

"No. If you weren't up, I was going to Enright's to phone the hospital. Now you can do it. I've about got that well put back together. When I'm finished we can go to town and see her, if you'd like."

"Yes, I'd like to."

He shrugged. "I guess we're the closest to family she has."

"We'll have to manage all the arrangements. Who's going to take care of her, Max?"

"I don't know. Let's see what the doctor says, before we worry about that." He gave me a reassuring smile. "I got your car unstuck; it's at the bottom of the hill, and a mess. You left the door open. The dog is in the barn pretending he's invisible; I put out some food and water for him. I'll take you to your car when you're ready to go."

First I got some choice tidbits from the refrigerator and we took them to the barn for the dog. He was timidly eager to see us and more than happy with the extra treats. Max had put salve on his belly and it seemed to be healing properly.

I took towels to cover my car's wet seat and managed to drive to Jim's house with no mishaps. By picking my way carefully to the entry by the garage door, I avoided most of the puddles, but still gathered a fair amount of persistent muck on my shoes. I was running through shoes like a track star, and needed to replace Minnie's overshoes as well. Perhaps I could buy her another pair in town.

When nobody answered my knock, I opened the door and stepped into the utility room. Under the circumstances, I felt certain they wouldn't mind my using the phone even if they weren't home.

"Hello," I shouted through the open doorway into the kitchen. "Anyone home?" I grabbed an old rag from the wastebasket by the door and wiped the mud from my shoes. I was ready to shout again when I looked up and saw Jim standing a few feet away, staring at me.

"What are you doing?" he asked with a curious kind of sharpness.

"Wiping my feet," I answered with a smile, and threw the rag back on the trash. Was he a little miffed, or maybe surprised, that I'd walked in on my own? "I knocked, but nobody answered. I need to use the phone, if I may?"

"Of course." He held out his hand to draw me in. Even though he smiled, there was something quizzical in his look that made me feel gauche, or a little rude.

Finally he asked, "Is anything the matter?"

With some chagrin, it dawned on me that the strain and worry of yesterday must be plainly evident on my face. I wished I'd taken time to put some makeup on, or done something more with my hair. Oh well, so much for city chic. I was fast becoming resigned to my fate as a slob.

"Yes," I answered, "all sorts of things are the matter. Minnie had a stroke last night."

"Minnie? A stroke!"

"Yes. Max and I found her in the dugout, and lucky we did, or she would have died."

"I'm sorry, Thea, you must have had a hell of a night. I can't believe something like this has happened to you again." He put his arm around my shoulders and I must say I sopped up the sympathy like a sponge. It was nice to lean on someone. "Dad's going to be terribly upset."

"I need to call the hospital and find out how she's doing."

"Of course." He showed me where the telephone was and went down the hall to get Helby.

The nurse was very helpful and I was also able to speak to the doctor. By the time I was through talking with them, Jim was back with his father. Helby did indeed look distressed.

"How is she?" he asked. He appeared diminished: stooped and very tired.

"She's as good as can be expected," I said, repeating what I'd been told. "And barring any further episodes, they expect her to continue improving. But her right side is paralyzed and she can't speak."

"Never?" Helby croaked.

"They can't tell at this point. But, I know patients frequently regain some use…And there's speech therapy…"

Helby shook his head and sat heavily in a chair. "Too old," he muttered. "Too old."

"Who knows?" I forced some brightness into my voice. "Minnie might be one of those who make a complete recovery. She's certainly stubborn enough."

He gave me a frosty smile and nodded reassuringly, but his eyes were bleak, as if he really knew better. "One by one they go," he said and turned his gaze to the window.

I couldn't stand to see him so defeated. I wanted to shake him, force him into his fancy clothes and kingly arrogance.

"Look, why don't you go see her?" I said. "I'm sure she'd like that."

"Will they let us?" Jim asked, watching his father with troubled eyes.

"I think so. Max and I are going in soon. Well," I said hesitantly. There didn't seem much else to say. "I should get back. Thanks for letting me use your phone."

"Anytime," Jim said and walked me to my car. "Let us know if there's anything we can do to help, and don't take it too hard. I'll bring Dad in to town. He'll feel better for visiting her." He put his hands on my shoulders and softened the tension at the base of my neck with his long fingers. His eyes were intent on me, a worried frown on his face. "Are you sure you're okay?"

I smiled, truly grateful for his concern. "I'm fine. Please don't worry."

The hospital was a small, neat affair, all on one level, another repository of pride for Hijax and the surrounding community. The young and pretty head nurse greeted Max by name, a fact I was quick to note, along with the way his appreciative eye followed the swing of the close-fitting uniform as we followed her down the hall.

Minnie's room was dim and smelled of all the frightening unknown things that hospitals always smell of. I approached her bed with trepidation, feeling like an intruder who might be taken for a curiosity seeker. She seemed so small under the light covering, her face lax and strangely foreign. I wished I was back in Chicago, had never come here, or become more than just a voice over the telephone or a name that signed impersonal letters. How could so much change in a few day's time, and light friendship so quickly become a bond of human responsibility?

On the other side of the bed, Max reached out and enfolded Minnie's hand in his callused fingers. Her eyes fluttered open and came shockingly to life when she saw us. It was as if all her useless body's energy had concentrated in the only remaining outlet. Unimpaired intelligence lit her soft brown irises as they flicked from Max to me, over and over again, her mouth moving in a desperate attempt to form words. We stepped closer, drawn by the strength of her struggle, certain that success would follow such valiant desire. But it didn't. She couldn't speak and began to flail around, her breathing more rapid.

"Max," I cried in alarm, and he ran for the nurse.

I took Minnie's air-clutching left hand in both of mine and started a soothing babble. "It's all right, it's all right. Don't worry. We're taking care of everything. You're going to be all right, it just takes time. Don't worry." I repeated the words until she relaxed and closed her eyes briefly. When she opened them again they were filled with tears. I was at a loss; what comfort could I offer her?

At least she was watching me more calmly now. I gave her one of those bright, idiotic hospital smiles. "I brought some things you might need, a robe, slippers, and look," I fished in the bag I held, "I even brought your shoe. Isn't it lucky I found it in the office? You'll need it when you're ready to go home."

Fortunately, at this point Max returned with the nurse, or I'd surely have gone on to say it was the most darling shoe in the world, or something equally intelligent. Instead I clamped my mouth shut and gave up my place to Max's nurse friend and her blood pressure apparatus.

I took the bag of Minnie's things, and the shoe, over to the locker like closet. The clothes she had been wearing yesterday hung neatly from hooks, and the loafer's mate lay on its side with both white socks stuffed in it. I placed the shoe I held beside the other, straightened the pair, and methodically removed one anklet to put in the other shoe. As I hunched there staring at them, I could hear Max questioning the nurse.

"She can't speak at all?"

"No."

"Can she write?"

"No. Her left side is functional, but she can't handle it well yet. Give her a chance, Max."

"Well, how in hell can she tell you what she needs?"

I listened disconnectedly to the rising level of exasperation in his voice, noted it, but remained staring at those shoes. There was something...

"We're anticipating her needs for now," the nurse said. "We'll get some communication going soon. And I think you've stayed long enough. She needs to rest."

I took the shoe Minnie had worn to the hospital and turned it slowly over and over in my hand, wondering. "Max," I said.

"Max," I said again. He stood by the bed, staring

remotely at Minnie's inert figure, his face darkly fierce with an expression I knew could mean many things: anger, concern, frustration and even, sometimes, something much softer.

The nurse held Minnie's wrist and counted her pulse. I took the shoe and both socks, caught Max's attention and motioned him to follow me into the hallway.

I handed him the shoe. "Look." He turned it much as I had, then gave me a puzzled look.

"What about it?"

"There's no mud, Max."

CHAPTER 14

"When I came back from Enright's that first time—
when Minnie was *there,* on the couch sleeping, or
whatever—I stopped at the front door to take my
shoes off because I didn't want to track. I admit they
weren't caked like the ones I've ruined since, but they
were muddy."

"Someone here could have cleaned it off," he said
doubtfully.

"But what about the socks?" I held them up,
misshapen from wear, but quite brightly white. "If she
walked to the dugout missing a shoe, at least one of
these socks should show soil or at least a stain of
some kind."

"But."

"Like it or not, Max, someone must have carried
Minnie to the dugout and left her there to die."

He gave me a piercing glance, then stalked back
into the room. I followed.

The nurse was still, or once again, at her pulse-
taking. Max had no qualms about interrupting her. He

waved the socks in front of her. "These were in the closet over there. Did anyone wash them?"

The nurse stopped counting, but kept her fingers on the limp wrist. "No. We don't do anything with the clothes except remove them. Everything should be in her closet."

He rubbed his face and returned the socks and shoes to the closet.

"Is she all right?" I whispered to the nurse, noting that the pulse counting was still going on. She nodded.

"Look," Max said. "We've got to talk to her. Will you help me—"

The nurse cut him off with a firm no and added, "You really must go."

He was insistent. "But I've got to—"

"If you don't leave, Max, I'll have you thrown out."

I took his arm and pulled him out the door. "Giving Minnie another stroke isn't going to help."

"But if we could ask a couple of questions, all she'd need to do is nod or shake her head."

"The doctor doesn't want her to get excited. Maybe by tonight, or in the morning they'll let us try to talk to her." Then I thought of something else. I opened the door to Minnie's room and beckoned to the nurse. "Has anyone else been here to see her?"

"Parson Potts came by this morning, but I didn't let him see her."

"Anyone else?" Max asked.

"About an hour ago Jim and Helby Enright were here. Jim didn't go in, but the doctor let Helby see her for a few minutes. Thought it might calm her, but she got very upset. They had to ask him to leave. I doubt any other visitors will be allowed, except you two, who are acting as family."

"Thanks," Max said, and walked me quickly down the hall.

"Potts was here, Max. What do you think he wanted?"

"I don't know what to think, but there are a couple of simple things we can do right now. You talk to the nurse, or the director, or whoever you need to, and request that no visitors be allowed. I'm going to run over and see the sheriff and tell him everything. We should have done it a long time ago. Whether we're right or wrong, at least we can get Minnie some protection. The sheriff's office is next to the courthouse. I'll walk; you can bring the truck when you're finished here."

The hospital agreed to the no visitors plan without any arguments or demands for detailed explanations. I ducked in to see Minnie once more before I left. She appeared to be resting easily. I didn't disturb her.

I practiced with the truck's floorboard gearshift a bit before I turned on the motor. Hopefully, it wouldn't be that different from driving a stick shift car. I was lucky to have the whole parking lot to practice in. The gears were tight. I needed both hands to shift into first, but finally got onto the street, and headed for the courthouse.

I wanted to be sure Max told Hank everything about Potts. I didn't want my suspicions whitewashed to any degree. I managed to park the truck without mishap and found the office.

"Max?" the girl at the desk said. "Max who?"

"Max Holman. He came to talk to the sheriff."

"Nobody's been here in the last hour. Besides, the sheriff's not here, anyhow."

"But…" Uncertainty gripped me. Where was Max? Maybe he had run into Hank on his way to the courthouse and they were talking over coffee, or something.

It seemed easier to walk the block and a half to main

street rather than wrestle with the truck. Maybe Max had seen Potts and was checking up on him. Potts and the Enrights were probably still in town. Funny that Helby's visit had upset Minnie so much. And how had Potts found out so quickly that Minnie was in the hospital? Did the grapevine work that efficiently?

I stuck my head in the Stirrup Cafe. Max wasn't there. He wasn't in the drugstore, either, nor was anyone else I knew, which was fine by me. I certainly didn't want to run into Potts. The thought of him prowling around Halfway Halt hunting for Minnie's manuscript made me shiver.

"Oh, no!" I thought, jerked to a halt. Minnie's book.

Minnie always kept it carefully hidden, but where had I left it? I had taken it upstairs with me last night, but what had I done with it before I flopped into bed? Was it on the floor by my bed, or had I pushed it under the bed? One way or the other it was easy prey for anyone who might happen by the house. How could I have been so careless? I broke into a run, heading for the pickup. I had to get Minnie's manuscript. If anything happened to it I'd never be able to face her.

I left a message for Max with the girl in the sheriff's office, telling him I'd had to return to Minnie's and would be back as soon as possible, and set off in the pickup. Other than a few bad moments of jerking and stalling before I got going, driving the powerful truck gave me a rare sense of exhilaration. However, my confidence faded when I came to Minnie's hill. It still looked greasy and was crisscrossed with a wide variety of deeply plowed tracks. I wasted no time, parked the truck on the road, and walked up the hill.

Having learned a bit about mud by now, I stuck to the far edge of the borrow pit and walked on the heavy mat of weeds and pine needles. I couldn't believe I had actually run up that hill yesterday, straight through the gumbo. As it was, I had to stop half way up to catch my breath.

Even though the sun shown brightly now and a warm breeze caressed my skin, something of yesterday's storm-tossed urgency remained and I didn't linger, but hurried on to the house. I ran lightly up the stairs to my room without the least prescience to warn me of what was waiting, until I was upon him. His hulking figure filled the room. I stopped, breathless, speechless, and nearly lifeless. Potts!

We stood for a static moment like a game of frozen statues. My leg muscles quivered, then leaped to obey a pounding adrenaline surge. I stepped back, prepared to whirl out and away. The movement sparked Potts. He lunged for me; his large hands clamped onto my shoulders.

"What are you doing here?" he roared, and shook me like an old rag. "Where's that book?" Fire and brimstone lit his rheumy eyes. I screamed, a great tearing sound that ripped through all my vital organs and filled the room with skull-bursting vibrations.

His grip loosened. I jerked away, caromed against the wall and flew out the door and down the stairs.

"Wait!" he yelled, hard on my heels.

As if I would wait. I'd left the front door open, and was out in a flash, with his heavy tread thundering down the stairs behind me. If I could just reach the pickup. Surely I could outrun a seventy-year-old man. But I hadn't counted on the dog. He appeared from nowhere, eager for this new game, and bounced around my legs. I tripped over him, barely saving myself from a fall.

"Get away," I gasped. "Go! Please, baby, go." He bounded from one side of me to the other, blocked my way down the hill, and forced me in the direction of the trees. I risked a glance over my shoulder. Potts. If only he'd yell. His voice would scare off the dog. But he didn't yell. My legs tangled with the dog's again. Staggering, I managed to spin away from a fall. If I could make it to the trees…And angle back to the road…I raised my eyes to scout a path, and saw a vision from heaven. I ran right into his arms.

"Jim," I gasped. "Thank God you're here!" I buried my nose in his chest and wrapped my arms around his body.

"What in hell are you doing, Potts?" he said angrily over my shoulder. The name brought me alive again. I whirled in Jim's arms.

"He tried to murder Minnie, Jim." I gulped for air. "And I'm next on his list."

My words stopped Potts as if pole-axed. His great body heaved with fatigue, and his usually florid face had turned pasty from the uncommon effort.

"Murder Minnie?" Jim asked, incredulously. "What are you talking about? What is this, Potts?" he demanded, and tightened his arms around me.

Potts glared as if I were some evil succubus who had bested him, but only for the moment. I caught a flash of the dog slinking off toward the barn. He'd recognized his old enemy.

"All right, Potts, let's have it," Jim commanded, making a threatening movement towards him.

The old man drew his eyes from me, glanced dismissively at Jim, and then turned away. His lifeblood seemed to drain from him.

"No." He shook his head like a wounded bull. "I…No." The words were slurred, uncertain, as if he hadn't heard the question, didn't know the subject. His glance swung back to me, but its power had disappeared and was replaced with something that looked, surprisingly enough, like reproach. He shambled towards the back of Hallway Halt, his arms cumbersome weights that dragged his shoulders into a slump of defeat.

We watched, mesmerized as he disappeared behind the house, and heard the hesitant cough of a motor starting up.

"Jim, don't let him get away," I said, as the old man drove by us and down the road. "We've got to stop him."

Jim held me back. "He won't go far." There was a note of quiet sympathy in his voice as we watched the truck disappear. Then he looked down at me, his face grave. "Those were pretty rough accusations you were throwing around. Why don't you tell me about it?"

"Of course," I said wearily, as we began to walk down the hill. "There's so much you don't know." I began with the night of the break-in, when Potts hit me on the head, and went carefully over the rest in sequence.

"By the way," I said, interrupting my story, "Thanks so much for being the cavalry to the rescue. I was terrified."

He shrugged. "I was on my way home when I saw Holman's truck parked on the road. I got out to see what the problem was about the time you let out that blood-curdling scream. So I ran up through the trees."

"I must say, I'm glad you did." I went on with my story. "Potts must have come to see Minnie, but when he found her asleep he decided to hunt for the manuscript again, then I returned." I told him about the dog, how I'd found him tied, careful to eliminate as much sentiment and melodrama as possible, so as not to damage my credibility. And I included all the details, as much for his benefit as mine—my difficulties getting the rag untied from around the dog's neck, the slow-motion run up this very hill—so he'd have a clear conception of the amount of time I was away from the house.

He listened seriously, with none of the signs of impatience that my explanations always seemed to rouse in Max. We reached the bottom of the hill. His truck was parked in front of mine.

I ended the tale with the damning evidence of Minnie's un-muddy shoes and socks. "When Potts returned to the house, Minnie must have caught him and either the fright of finding him hunting through her things, or something else he did, brought on the stroke. So he dumped her in the dugout, hoping she'd never be found."

"What about Holman?" he asked. "How does he fit in to all this?"

"Max? Well, I think he's convinced now that someone had to have carried Minnie to the dugout, but is still dubious as to why anyone would go to such extremes."

Jim kind of huffed an agreement to that. "Where is Max now?"

"In town." I added urgently, "You do see, don't you, that it's not so much who did it or why, but that Minnie remain safe? And I just don't think that...that *murderer,* Potts, should be allowed to run loose."

"Minnie isn't dead, so he can't be a murderer."

"That's a technicality, and I intend to see that he's held responsible for the attempt. How do you know Potts won't disappear?"

Jim laughed and ruffled my hair. "You're a real tiger."

"Someone needs to protect Minnie. The doctor doesn't hold out much hope that she'll ever speak again. She might never be able to defend herself."

"You've got a point. But you saw Potts, he hasn't any juice left. The man hasn't been out of the county in twenty years. He'll go to town, or he'll hole up at home, but believe me, I know that old bugger, he won't go far."

I turned toward the truck, then stopped. "I haven't a brain left," I said with disgust. "I nearly forgot what I came for. I've got to run back to the house."

He motioned to his pickup. "Get in, I'll drive you."

I did and we roared up the hill, plowing one more set of tracks. Jim waited in the truck while I went in. After a moment's scare, I found the manuscript box under my dropped nightgown, a bit of sloppiness that had saved it from a quick discovery. Looking for something to carry it in, I retrieved a paper bag from the closet, dumped some anonymous purchases on the floor, and dropped in the manuscript, box and all.

Jim waited at the bottom of the stairs. I smiled at him. "Did you see the dog? He was about the end of me, but I hope he wasn't too badly scared. He's been having a rather tough time of things." I pulled the door closed behind us, and wondered if I should make some kind of provision for the silly critter. "Where is he, anyway?"

"Off somewhere, I suppose." Jim grinned. "With you in my arms, I wasn't about to pay much attention to the dog, now was I?"

I whistled, but really wasn't as interested in the dog as I was in getting back to town. "Let's go. I must admit he's not the smartest animal I've ever known. He'll show up sooner or later."

We climbed back in the truck, but something nagged at me. Some elusive thought I couldn't grab onto, stirred by something I'd just said or thought about. What was it?

"What's wrong?" Jim asked, making me jump.

I laughed. "Just one of those thoughts that keep slipping away. If I don't worry about it maybe it will come back, but it seemed important. Something to do with the dog," I mused. "Ah, well, it probably doesn't matter."

"Look," he said, as we headed toward Max's truck. "You've done enough running around the country alone. Why don't you come with me? I picked up some antibiotic in town to treat the calves, and it needs to be refrigerated. We'll call the sheriff from my place and he'll send someone after Potts. You can check on Minnie, too, if you want. Then I'll bring you back here and follow you to town. Okay?"

He turned towards his place before I actually agreed, but it would take less time to go along with him than to argue.

"What in hell was Holman thinking about, letting you come out here by yourself, anyway?"

"He didn't know." But my mind was chasing after that elusive thought that hovered on the edge of acknowledgment, only to dart out of reach again. I knew I should stop chasing it.

I felt Jim's eyes on me, but when I turned to offer him a reassuring smile, his glance was back on the road. He looked rather strung out, biting his cheek, his forehead creased in a frown. I was glad he wasn't taking this as casually as he wanted me to believe.

"Thought of anything yet?" he asked.

"No, whatever it is won't come through. What will they do to him, Jim?"

"Who?"

"Potts. Will they arrest him on the strength of what I say?"

He shrugged. "Who knows?" We turned into Enright's drive, and went around behind the house toward a beautiful old stone and board barn about half a mile from the house. To one side of the barn was a large complex of corrals, boxed and gated into compartments as complicated as a maze. Within them I could see the slow movement of cattle. The calves, most likely. The other out-buildings were painted and had none of the look of imminent disintegration that dominated Minnie's place. Beyond the barn were the familiar humpy rolls of chalky hills and barren meadows. Off to the left a scraggly clump of trees showed severe signs of char, some old disaster that must have been frighteningly close to the buildings. However, green dominated the whole area now, and lent a general air of tough prosperity. I could easily picture Helby as its creator.

We skidded to a stop in front of the barn. "Where's your dad?" I asked as Jim stepped from the truck. My idle question jerked him around as if he'd been struck. My heart jumped, and I caught my breath. *What's going on here?*

"What?" Jim's face was hard and strained.

"Where's Helby?" I repeated. No, I thought, please don't let Helby be mixed up in this. Not that wonderful old man.

"In town." Jim's usually friendly eyes turned watchful, searched my face. "He wanted to see Minnie again."

"Oh." But my brain was as busy as a computer, searching and sorting facts into nice little piles. As far as I could see it was still Potts all the way. Could Helby be working with Potts? They were both implicated in the long-ago hanging. Or did Jim have reason to suspect his father was deeply involved?

At least by now Max had seen the sheriff, and the hospital watch was on. Minnie should be safe. I wondered if I should try to ease Jim's suspicions about his dad, or just leave well enough alone. In case they weren't merely suspicions.

Jim relaxed, seemingly finding something

benevolent in my face. "Come on," he said, and gently handed me out of the truck.

The barn was cool and dim, welcome after the sun's searing brightness. The great sliding door at the far end was also open and I could see a cluster of milling calves. From a far stall came the sound of a horse chomping and snuffling his hay.

The first stall had been turned into storage space, with shelves and a small, ancient refrigerator against the wall. An old chest of drawers sat along one side, taking up most of the space. Miscellaneous tools, liniment bottles, rags and an opened tin of Bailey's Bag Balm covered the top of the scarred chest. Jim handed me the sack of medicine and motioned me into the stall, then he pulled open one of the heavy drawers, blocking the entrance.

"My doctor kit," he said.

The drawer was filled with more bottles, syringes, boxes of cotton, and villainous looking pills large enough for an elephant. I put the bag of vaccine in the refrigerator. Harsh, medicinal smells mingled with the strong warm barn odors. My stomach clenched.

"What's wrong with the calves?" I asked to relieve the leaden silence. I felt nauseous.

"Pinkeye."

The horse's steady chomping beat against my ears and the heat seemed to enfold me in cloying layers. "I need some air," I said, and motioned for him to let me by. Instead he opened the drawer further, and rummaged in the contents.

His voice sounded bodiless in the weighted atmosphere. "You remembered, didn't you," he said, not looking at me, still hunting something in the drawer. "Back there in the pickup, when you asked about dad. You had remembered; I could tell by your face."

His unmistakable menace froze me to the side of the stall, my fingers scrabbling at the rough splintery wood. My brain seemed numb, unable to decipher his meaning.

My words, when they came, were sluggish. "What?...Remembered what?"

He turned to me then, the words ripped from his mouth with a viciousness that twisted his face into a grotesque mask. "Don't play innocent with me," he yelled. "You know damned well what I'm talking about. I knew this morning when I saw you wipe your shoe that it was just a matter of time before you recognized that piece of rag."

"The rag," I said, stunned. Yes, that was the thought I'd been trying to connect with. The dog, and that awful rag he'd been tied with, that I'd sunk my teeth into, gray and sodden, but distinctively spotted with red squares. And the piece torn from it, that I'd found in Jim's house.

"Yeah, the rag," he spat out, then began to mutter almost to himself. "You and that damned dog. The only thing to connect me. I knew you'd remember. 'Helby,' you said," he raised his voice in biting mockery. "'Where's Helby?' you said. You were going to run to him, weren't you? As if he would save you." He grabbed a bottle out of the drawer and slammed it on top of the dresser. "You almost caught me when you came dashing into Minnie's, but I heard your car coming. You thought she was asleep on the couch, didn't you?" He smiled, almost as if he wanted me to share the joke. "I hid in the parlor, and left when you went upstairs. The dog was in the barn and so was the rag. I knew the perfect way to get little Miss Softie out of the house." He grinned and reached out a hand as if to caress my face. I recoiled and he laughed.

"What did you do to Minnie?"

"Nothing. Believe me, Thea, I didn't want any of this to happen. But she wouldn't listen to reason. She lied to me."

He paused and looked off into space. When he spoke again it was to himself, to something he replayed in his mind. "I didn't mean it to happen. I didn't want...I hardly touched her and she just collapsed." He stared at the floor, shoulders slumped. I held my breath. Minutes seemed to pass.

Maybe I moved. Something broke the spell.

He jerked upright. "Minnie. I thought she'd fainted, then right away I knew it was a heart attack or something. It was you coming back so quickly that shook me. Otherwise I would have revived her, or taken her to the hospital. Instead I dropped her on the sofa with the magazine, and hid in the parlor until you went upstairs. I didn't mean for it to happen that way. I got pushed into all of this."

I almost believed him. "Where was your car, Jim? Why did you hide your car?"

"I didn't *hide* it. It was a last minute decision to stop in. I'd gone past her drive, so I took an old back road, and parked there."

"Right. And you just happened to beat the dog within an inch of his life to get me out of the house so you could dump Minnie in the dugout. You wanted her to die."

"I thought she was dead."

"Then you would have been better off to let me find her. No one would have known you had been around. It won't wash, Jim," I said wearily.

He pulled a large wad of dirty cotton from the drawer. When he lifted the cotton, I saw a picture lying in the bottom of the drawer. I leaned forward in surprise and stared at it. It was the studio portrait that showed Minnie standing on her sister Lil's lap. One corner of the gray cardboard frame was bent and nearly broken off. It was the picture missing from Helby's cigar box collection, or another just like it.

"You? You broke into Minnie's house? Hit me over the head? Why?"

He gave me a strange look and I thought he wasn't going to answer. He said, "I thought I'd seen all of dad's pictures." He picked the picture up with a contemptuous look. "When I saw this, I knew why the bitch had come to Hijax. You know too, don't you? You're going to tell the world, make us a laughing stock, ruin my career, and all for a no-good whore."

He tucked the picture inside his shirt, tore off a piece of cotton and grabbed the brown bottle. With a sweep of his arm he spilled everything else back into the drawer and slammed it shut. I braced myself against the rough slats of the stall and watched for my chance.

His glittering eyes never left my face. His lips curled in a small smile, and he twisted the cap off the bottle. Fear identified the cloying fumes for me. How else would I have known chloroform?

I jumped for the side of the stall, frantically climbing the slats. A futile effort. One sinewy arm reached out and grabbed me back in a hold that caught hair, shirt and arm in a painful twist. I cried out. He smashed me against the boards, holding me effectively with one arm.

"Too bad, Thea." His free hand manipulated the bottle and cotton to soak the pad. His voice droned on, but I hardly noticed. "Like I said, I knew it was just a matter of time, so I followed you out of town. I didn't know that stupid fool, Potts, would play right into my hands. You and that damned dog. I should have killed him when I had the chance. I thought you'd guess when the dumb bitch ran yipping at the first sight of me, but you're stupid, too."

The pressure increased on my throat, and his words drifted away on the sickening fumes. I remember a giddy moment of one-upmanship, thinking foolishly that the dog was male, a bastard, not a bitch. So who was stupid now...

CHAPTER 15

I came to slowly. My stomach churned with nausea. My mouth was stuffed with something unspeakable, and bound with a rag that cut the corners of my mouth. Bile burned up my throat and brought a flash of panic. I swallowed, and swallowed again; tiny, nearly imperceptible movements, all I could manage around the awful stuffing. My eyes stung with the effort as I willed my stomach to accept the regurgitated matter. I refused, absolutely refused to die here, ignominiously suffocating in my own vomit. Not without a fight, I told myself, swallowing, swallowing. I lay still then, trying to relax and quiet the churning. Concentrating on the simple act of breathing, I pulled air through my nose in short rhythmical bursts. I would not think of my stomach, or of my mouth, and I wasn't going to cry, heaven forbid, or my nose would stuff up and I couldn't—no, I wasn't going to think about that either. Just breathe. In and out.

Finally a calmness took over and terror for a

moment was beaten back. Max would be proud of me. The thought warmed me while I became aware of other aches and pains that shot through my body whenever I moved.

I lay on my side. My arms were behind my back, tied at the wrist, and my legs bound at the ankles. I twisted my feet and the bonds seemed to loosen a bit. Rolling on my stomach, I bent my legs, and wondered if I was agile enough to grab my feet, and if I could, would I be able to loosen the rope that way. There was only one way to find out I bowed backward, grabbed and felt my fingers slide off the heel of my sneakers. My shoulders screamed with agony at the effort, and I had to stop and control my breathing again. But I'd felt a give at the heel of my shoe. If I could kick my shoes off, maybe I could work my feet out of the rope.

While I worked at rubbing my feet together, I tried to figure out where on earth I was. A dim patch of daylight showed through an uneven opening above me. Everything else was black even to my eyes, accustomed to darkness.

We had been in the barn, Jim's barn. Was I close by, or had he hauled me off somewhere? Jim! He was right. I'd been incredibly stupid, so willing to believe in his goodness, simply because he seemed to like me. Yet he was the one who had left Minnie to die, had beaten the dog…

I ran my hands along the surface I was lying on. Ground, earth, hard packed, uneven, but unmistakably earth. Could it be some part of the barn? I couldn't see walls, or anything else, for that matter. The floor felt damp, or was it just cool? The air had a musty fungal smell, not like the barn, more like the dugout.

I stopped worrying at my shoe, and scrunched cautiously along the floor until my feet hit a barrier I put my tied hands to the wall and felt the cool, crumbly surface trickle through my fingers. More earth. A spark of hysteria raced through my body. A pit! I wasn't in any kind of a building. I'd been thrown in some kind of a hole. Buried! I jerked my hands away from the rocky protuberance they clung to, reeling with visions of lizards, snakes, spiders, feeling them around me waiting to drop, crawl, creep. Feathery tendrils seem to brush across my face. A scream filled my skull, tearing at my blocked throat. I gagged and gagged, writhing in a desperate struggle for breath.

I must have blacked out, for when next I became aware of anything, I was lying motionless, sucking in air with labored breaths. The ache in my drawn back shoulders had become a constant, a permanent fact of existence that could almost be dismissed while I basked in the comfort of Max's voice. Max! I jerked to alertness.

It wasn't an hallucination, the voices were real, reverberating down into the hole as if from a distance.

"Where is she, Enright?" It was Max, harsh and angry, one step from explosion.

"How should I know?" Jim answered.

"Look, you bastard, I followed your tracks from where Thea parked our truck. I want to know what happened."

"*Our* pickup. Isn't that cozy. She your whore now? Get your hands off me." Icy contempt laced Jim's voice. Nothing would more easily put Max in a rage.

I kicked frantically, trying to make a noise that could be heard, but the murky darkness swallowed my pounding and moaning. I went back to rubbing my ankle against the heel of my shoe. Urgency did the trick, and my heel popped free from the canvas shoe. I flopped and kicked and shook it free, then began to work on the other foot.

Jim's fury seemed to have been shaken from him. "All right, all right," he said. "I did see her. She went to get something from the house and found Potts in there. Scared her to death for some reason. I ran him off and she left."

"How did she leave, Enright, how? The pickup's still there."

"I should know? She was standing by the truck when I left. I thought she went back to town."

"Thought, hell! You left her like that with Potts around?"

No Max, no, I thought. Please don't fight. Look for me. But I heard the sharp crack of fist against bone and feared the explosion was on.

I had to warn him; Max didn't realize how dangerous Jim was.

Jim's voice broke into a shocking shrillness. "Hit me again, Holman, and you won't live to find her."

Again I tried to shout, but the resulting muffled groan choked me into silence. If only I could get rid of the gag. I scraped my cheeks against the rough ground and tossed my head. The knot slid tantalizingly up and down, but was not loose enough to be pried from my open mouth.

None of my thuds against the earthen floor could compete with the sounds that filtered down to my ears from outside. Fist struck against flesh, followed by pain-filled explosions of breath. My eyes remained glued to the opening about ten feet above me, but not a flicker of shadow, or movement, crossed the scrap of light.

"What happened to her?" Max grunted in barely audible gasps. "Tell me."

Jim's answer, "Never," was followed by a sickening fleshy crack, and then another. Then dead silence.

For a breathless second I listened. Nothing. Once more I began threshing and flailing, until suddenly, my other shoe flew off and one foot slid out of the binding. I lurched to my feet and collapsed against the wall, heaving for air. The faint sound of an engine sputtered into life and moved away. Tears stung my eyes. Max had left me.

The stupid oaf! A rush of fury washed out fear and a rising tide of panic. *Stupid macho posing!* If he'd taken time to look around he might possibly have found me, but no! He and Jim had been aching for a showdown. Well, it was a cinch no one was going to rescue me. If I wanted out of this damned hole I'd have to do it myself.

Filled with fire—or false courage—whatever the body manufactures from senseless rage, I cautiously began to walk off the parameters of my prison. The wall face was rocky and uneven, but by keeping close to it, and testing each step, I fought the terror of a yawning drop-off lurking somewhere in the darkness. It soon became more difficult to keep my shoulder to the wall, and took me a moment to realize it was because the wall had taken a decidedly outward slant, and another moment to recognize the advantage that offered.

If this portion of the pit sloped outwards all the way to the opening, instead of being upright, I might be able to climb, or scooch, my way up. The uneven surface provided plenty of footholds. If my hands hadn't been tied behind my back, it would have been a relatively simple scramble. First I tried a sideways approach, thinking I could use my hands, even behind my back, to some advantage. I rose the first small distance from the ground, found another foothold and slid up another measure, but then was unable to move my inside leg into position again. Making an attempt rocked me off balance and I fell to the ground. Pain shot through my shoulders and ribs, but the little success spurred me on. I got back on my feet and attacked the wall again. Head on, this time, lying flat on my belly against the surface, legs splayed. By turning my torso, one of my hands could try for a slight amount of leverage. Slight was right. Mostly my hands flopped uselessly, but my chin proved surprisingly agile.

The pain was unthinkable. Dirt, rocks and roots scraped away layers of flesh and cloth with each sliding move. Yet every inch gained urged me further on.

Another push on a foothold sent a tearing pain along my cheek. The reflexive twist of my head nearly sent me plummeting, but the root that tore my cheek caught the gag and held me clinging to my perch. When my heart stopped pounding, I realized that the momentary weight of my body had pulled the cloth gag away from the corners of my mouth. I set to work ducking, bobbing, grimacing, trying to pull the sodden mass over my bottom lip, and chin, until finally it fell limply around my neck. Instantly, my tongue and jaws pushed the repulsive wad of stuffing from my mouth. With it came everything I'd eaten since the beginning of time. The revolting stuff slid down my neck and front. I didn't care.

I rested my cheek on the earthen wall as if it were a satin pillow and filled my lungs with great gulps of glorious air. With my mouth freed, everything seemed easier. Even the fear of falling was gone. If I fell, I thought blithely, I'd just start all over again. But did I dare try a scream? Was anybody up there to hear? More importantly: where was Jim?

The opening glimmered just a short way above my head. With my goal so close, I didn't want to risk the chance of discovery by the wrong person. A few more pushes and I could inspect the rim. To the left of a rough slab of rock was a smooth, stable looking, weedy edge held together with a tangle of roots. Could I inch my way over there, or would I have to try exiting over the rock slab? I debated the angles involved, weighed the pros and cons, knowing all the while that nothing short of an operable elevator would change my direction. I was just passing time, afraid of what awaited me outside. My chin rested on a clump of sod, the toes of one foot scrabbled for a precarious hold, while the arch of the other foot rested on something rather sharp, braced for a painful push off. Well, I thought, I couldn't just hang there forever.

The next move put my head through the opening. Light forced my eyes shut. I clung with my chin on the slightly jutting edge of rock while my left foot searched desperately for purchase. My arms floundered helplessly behind me, an aching mass of electrified numbness. I pushed with my toes and scraped my neck and breast painfully across the rock's edge. Another hoist gouged flesh from ribs and hip bones, until I was far enough out to flop over onto the rim's edge. Out! At least my center of gravity was clear, and I needn't worry about falling back in.

I tried to wriggle further, but couldn't move. I lay exhausted, breathing in short sharp gasps that were more like sobs. Max, I thought, eyes still closed against the sun. In a minute I'd scoot free, jump to my feet and go find Max.

My cheek rested against the hot stone and I squinted, letting the light gradually sift through my lashes until I could open my eyes and see. Fences, animals. In a flash, I recognized the back of Enright's barn and the maze of corrals. Awkwardly, I flopped my head over, scraping my chin across the rock until my other cheek rested on the stone. My stomach lurched. Jim sat propped against a pile of blackened logs, chin on chest and hands dangling between his knees.

Unconscious? I couldn't tell. I tried to pull myself forward, working to get my right knee up on the pit's grassy edge.

"Don't move," Jim said, without looking up. The harsh voice rasped along my spine like a saw.

I stopped immediately, unable to take my eyes from his still form. He was about twenty feet away, with a sagging barbed wire fence between us. From what I could see of his bowed head, he was in pretty bad shape. A large cut across his forehead had bled freely, and still oozed between clots.

In fact, I thought, spirits quickening, he looked completely done in. Besides, to get to me, he'd have to cross the fence. I moved discreetly, inching my knee up on the rim beside the rock. My other foot, still dangling down in the pit, scrabbled frantically for a firm hold.

"I said, don't move." Jim snapped.

I obeyed, but not as willingly this time. I left my knee on the rim, ready for the final push out when the chance came. "Please Jim," I croaked. My tongue felt too big for my mouth and the words sounded blurred and muzzy. "Let me get my legs out. It hurts."

He raised his head. The full view of his face was horrible, streaked with blood, the upper lip swollen into a malignant grimace. Mr. Hyde revealed.

He chuckled as if he'd read my thoughts and found them amusing. "Go ahead," he said, "but I'm just going to shove you in again. Only this time, I'll get the rocks thrown in so you'll stay put." He jerked his head, indicating something behind me.

At his first word I shoved and wiggled, flopping

around like a gaffed fish until I could roll away from the hole. Once free, I got a better look at my surroundings. A three-strand barbed-wire fence circled the area encompassing the gaping hole and a natural nest of reddish rocks that rose behind it. It would be an easy task to pry, or roll a boulder either into the hole or over its opening. I shivered and scooted further away, both from Jim and his hell hole.

I leaned against a rock, and we eyed each other warily, gathering strength. Except I didn't seem to have any left to gather. It was incredibly hot. Sweat licked across my abraded skin with pinpricks of pain. My mouth felt like a wool blanket and I couldn't seem to generate enough saliva to swallow. My resources were drained. Every nerve ending whanged with the agony of my pulled-back shoulders. Yet, somehow I had to prepare for another attack. Stave off disaster. No *way* was I going back in that hole.

Dazed with pain, I stared at my legs and wondered if they'd work when I needed them. My jeans were caked with sooty grime and my bare feet were dark with blood and dirt. I looked worse than Jim. A bra strap had broken and my camp shirt was a thing of the past, the buttons torn off and one side hanging in shreds. Every inch of exposed, and unexposed, skin was scraped raw and bleeding.

I groaned. "Why can't we just stop, Jim? It's so silly, nobody's really hurt—or dead yet," I amended giddily. It seemed a sane thing to do. Reasonable. I could actually see us, dusting ourselves off, going our separate ways, everything forgiven and forgotten.

"It's gone too far for that, Thea. I made my move, and now I've got to finish it. Minnie had no business coming out here in the first place. We made good use of Lil's land for sixty years; why should we give it up to some old woman," he spat out the words as an epithet, "who wants to play at ranching, or would sell to any dry-farmer trash who came along with a wad of money in his pocket? But she wouldn't take a hint. None of this would have happened if she'd just gone back to the sticks where she came from."

"So it was you who cut the fences, and damaged the wells to scare her off." I couldn't keep the contempt out of my voice. "And that nasty note left in her mailbox? I would have expected more from you."

"That was Cora's work."

"Cora?" So Cora was mixed up in this. "What did Cora have to do with it?"

"She didn't want anybody but herself nosing around in the town's history; she thought she could run Minnie off with a few threats." He made a disparaging sound. "Then Cora saw that picture. She knew right away what it meant. She told me, but I didn't believe her. I had to see it for myself. I still have a key to Halfway Halt, so it was easy to get in."

My thoughts had been so focused on survival that I found it difficult to pick up the pieces of everything that had happened before. But I remembered fast. I knew this land business wasn't the real issue. But what had they seen in that picture of Minnie and Lil that none of the rest of us, including Minnie, herself, had caught?

"What about that picture, Jim? Why did you steal it?"

He ignored my question. Bracing himself against the pile of logs, he rose to his feet and flexed his arms and legs methodically, one after the other.

I was scared. I had to keep him talking, and there was something else I had to know. "Did you kill Cora?"

"I pushed her. She was drunk. She said she wouldn't tell any one, but I didn't trust her. We met out in the parking lot I wouldn't have done anything if she hadn't shot off her mouth." His voice rose, gaining strength. "It was her fault. She was drunk. I just pushed her and she hit her head against the truck's side mirror. Dropped like a rock."

He leaned against a fence post. When he spoke again it was in the soft cultured tones of the old Jim, the one I thought I knew.

"I really liked you, Thea. For a while there I actually thought we might..."

I turned him off, unable to listen to what he was saying. I knew it was only a matter of minutes before he came for me. As unobtrusively as possible, I studied the fence, my biggest obstacle. It was ill-tended, the posts knocked askew and the wires limp. In one place they sagged nearly to the ground. Could I jump it?

Jim pushed away from the fence post, and my heart began a dull thudding. A fly buzzed lazily around my face.

He gestured to the gaping hole, "You wanted to see the coal burnout pit. How do you like it so far?"

I didn't answer.

"I've lost my touch. Cora and Minnie practically dropped at my feet. I didn't have to do anything. I should have known you'd be different. But you have to go. You do see that, don't you? I can't back out of any of this, now."

I tucked my legs under me and hoped I could rise to my feet when the time came.

He started toward me, walking slowly, stopping to stretch his neck, rub his arms, warming the muscles he planned to extend. Or maybe he just wanted to frighten me. He appeared quite confident that there would be no trouble from that quarter. He might be right, I thought grimly, but not from lack of effort.

He had to cross the barbed wire fence; that would be my chance. And it would be a chance only if I could get to the section of the fence where the wire sagged close enough to the ground for me to get across. My heart raced and I shifted my legs, heartened by muscle twitches indicating there was some life left in them. A pulse drummed in my head. Behind me, one of my useless hands grabbed a rock. What I thought I could do with it I'll never know, but its solid feel gave me a sense of security.

Jim's eyes never left my face. He stepped on the bottom strands of wire and held the top one up to duck under. When he did, I lurched to my feet and staggered into a run. I heard him laugh and within seconds his hands dropped heavily on my tortured shoulders.

"Sorry, sweetheart. I wish there were a better way." He twisted me around and pushed me back towards the hole. "Potts will be the perfect scapegoat for your disappearance. You made a pretty convincing case against him; even Holman will have to back me up if there's no other evidence."

He grinned, pleased with himself, and leaned forward as if to nuzzle my neck. Instinctively, I jerked my head up, trying to clip him under the chin. The blow glanced off his jaw but took him by surprise. His hands dropped. I lashed out with my knees and feet, the only weapons I had. I missed his groin, but caused enough damage that he gasped and doubled over. I kicked again, wishing I wore jackboots, reveling in the chance to inflict pain rather than receive it, so intent I lost precious moments before I realized I was free.

I turned and darted down the fence line. Without arms for balance, every rock, every pebble, was a threat; a dead branch to jump spelled imminent disaster. Would I be able to cross the fence? I heard his pounding feet and heavy breathing close behind, but ran on until he caught my tied hands, and yanked me to a halt.

Pain shot through my shoulder blades and brought a shriek from my throat that ripped through the stillness like a knife through canvas. He dragged me back towards the hole, muttering words I was too terrified to hear, dragging me back to that horrible darkness.

I struggled blindly, flailing, kicking, my head still filled with the dreadful knell of pounding feet. Then other hands seized me and threw me to the ground.

Max!

He twisted Jim around and landed a blow on the side of his jaw. Jim staggered, then lunged at Max, his face contorted with rage at the unsuspected attack. Momentarily stunned, I gasped for breath and tried to scoot away from their surging feet.

Jim struck with a flurry of blows that took all of Max's strength to meet. I watched as he fought for breath, ducking and dodging. How far had he run before jumping in two-fisted?

I staggered to my feet. I knew I'd have to help, but my legs were about as stable as trembling reeds. Everything swam fuzzy-edged in front of me. The sound of fist against flesh and exploding breath beat against my ears.

Max landed another blow and I felt a shocking surge of pleasure when the cut over Jim's eye opened again and blood leaked down his face. But still he pressed, backing Max steadily.

The hole! I tried to scream, but nothing came out. "Max," I finally croaked, painfully trying to gather more volume. "Don't back up. There's a hole!"

He surged forward like a cornered grizzly, into a raging, vicious battle. Blood flew, splattering the bleached ground with startling color. Jim flung himself sideways to dodge a knee. Something flew through the air and cartwheeled across the ground: the picture that Jim had tucked into his shirt. A crack to the jaw rocked Jim back on his heels.

Max leapt and followed him to the ground, pummeling him relentlessly until he appeared to be senseless, then raised him by the shoulders as if to slam his head against the rocks.

"No," I cried, backing away from this final blow. "No, Max, no." I sank down to the ground. My legs refused to hold me any longer.

Max raised his face to me, a grim frightening mask, as if he'd forgotten my existence. He let the limp form fall carelessly to the ground. He rose and came to me, wiping the sweat and blood from his face with the back of his hands. His lungs reaching for air filled the sudden stillness with a ragged aftermath to violence.

Fatigue etched his face and slowed his movements. I watched helplessly and wondered if the ferocity I'd just witnessed was the same kind of monstrous cancer that had lurked so close to the surface of Jim's charm.

Wordlessly, he took a jackknife from his pocket and kneeled, turning me to reach my hands. He pried loose the rock I still gripped in my paralyzed fingers and threw it across the lot with a vicious snap. His hands trembled as he sawed through the rope.

There was no way I could suppress the groan when my hands were freed and my shoulders rolled back into place. Max swore under his breath and massaged my abused muscles, pushing the pain around with strong fingers, spreading it out until the stinging, razor darts diminished to a manageable ache.

Then he sank down beside me, drew me into his arms and buried his face in my neck, seeking a release of his own. I recognized his reaction and took comfort from it.

After a brief moment, he held me away and smoothed the hair from my face. "Are you all right?" he asked, much too solemn.

"All right!" I countered, in my own hoarse voice. "Battered, bruised, tied, thrown in a pit, and you calmly ask if I'm all right? Well, I'm not; I hurt like hell." He managed a small smile, the tiniest turning of one corner. "But, I would have hurt a lot more if you hadn't come along when you did and, frankly, I'm rather enjoying this bit." I snuggled more closely against his heavy chest.

He wasn't deterred. "What's this?" His fingers pulled at the rag that hung around my neck. I looked at it blankly. I'd actually forgotten the ghastly thing.

"He gagged me, but you ought to know I'm not easy to shut up. I got rid of the thing on my way out of the pit." My attempt at lightness didn't work very well. His mouth hardened and a pulse jumped to life in the stiff line of his jaw.

"That bastard."

"No, Max." I put my fingers on the pulse, tried to smooth it away. "There's been enough of that already. It's over."

He glanced over his shoulder to where Jim was lying, but I had no desire to look at him again.

"I didn't think you'd ever come back, Max."

"You knew I was here?"

"Yes, and I tried to make enough noise to attract your attention, but couldn't."

"You can thank that damfool dog for bringing me back. I actually believed Jim when he said he didn't know where you were. So I went back to Minnie's. I thought I'd missed you somewhere. Then I saw the dog cut through the fields. I knew what a fool he was for you. I decided I'd better check where he was going, and followed him here. Heard you scream...I thought Jim was mixed up in this somehow; still, I didn't think he'd hurt you." He stared at his hands, slowly balling them into fists. "I honestly didn't think he'd hurt you."

"Forget it, Max. I handed myself to him on a platter. I was so sure Potts was the villain."

He kissed me then, with a thoroughness that I definitely was not too tired to appreciate; in fact, I didn't even care that I hadn't been able to coax a smile from him. There would be plenty of time for that.

Something jumped on me. I yelped, and pulled away from Max. The wiggling mass of dog trod all over us, even daring to lollop Max's rough cheek in his happiness.

"Whoa," Max said, trying to escape the wet tongue and beating tail. "Call your hound off." Then added, "I guess I owe you one, Sport."

"Jim beat him, Max. And at the house, I thought the dog was running away from Potts, but it was Jim."

When I spoke Jim's name, Max turned to check on him, then jumped to his feet with a sharp expletive. Jim was gone. "I should have known the dog wouldn't show while Jim was here," he said. "Come on, let's go." But we were too late. The sound of a vehicle roaring out of the drive hit our ears.

Max set off at a trot.

"Wait," I called, and limped off to where I'd seen the picture of Minnie and Lil land. I retrieved it, but the soles of my bare feet could stand no more. I felt like I was walking on a bed of hot coals, and was not one of the chosen.

Max glared at my feet. "Where are your shoes?" For the first time he seemed to take in my appearance, disgusting filth, grime, torn clothes and all. "You know, woman," he said. "I'm having one hell of a time keeping you clean."

He offered me his back. "Hop on. Let's get out of here." He carried me piggyback up through the rocks, weeds and cactus, past the barn and to the house. We entered cautiously, but it was empty.

While Max grabbed the phone and put the sheriff on the lookout for Jim, I tied my broken bra strap with a knot and tucked the shredded ends of shirt underneath it. I couldn't find anything that would stay on my feet, so Max again rode me on his back out to the truck, which he'd left on the road while he followed the dog.

"You could use some rapid transit around here," I said, trying not to choke him with my death's grip around his neck.

"Ooof," was all he said. I wasn't that much of a featherweight.

While we drove—or rather flew—to town, I filled him in on everything that had happened, starting with my reasons for borrowing his pickup, and leaving town without him.

"And I'm no better off now than I was then, Max. I left Minnie's manuscript in Jim's truck. We'll probably never see it, or the pictures, again."

"What pictures?"

"The ones we were going to use in the book. We had a snapshot that identified the members of the vigilante gang who hung your grandfather. Both Parson Potts and Helby Enright were in it And some relative of Sheriff Beesom."

I thought about the companion picture that had become so much more personal now, more than just an exploitable relic of the wild west. A depiction of the grandfather Max had never known, the father that his mother had never known. Not something you'd want to keep in the family album.

I guess I wanted, needed, him to know that I had intended to publish the picture without consulting him. "There was a photo of the hanging, too, Max, that we were going to use. It showed the body." I felt small, but relieved.

Bit by bit, I had gained a better perspective of the manuscript's importance to my life. There were other things in the world more significant than the advancement of my career, such as Minnie's health and safety, and yes, my own as well.

Max lit a cigarette, one of the few I'd seen him smoke, and gave me another one of those long considering glances, before he returned his attention to the road. All he said was, "I was worried when I couldn't find you, or the truck."

"I looked for you," I said, as glad as he to change the subject. "Why weren't you at the sheriff's office?"

"I caught him on his way to the courthouse, and told him what we thought had happened to Minnie. He put an official watch on her, but we wasted time trying to find Potts. He must have already gone to the country."

"Yes, I know only too well. I caught him searching Halfway Halt for Minnie's manuscript. He said as much when he grabbed me." I clutched my side, which was beginning to ache unbearably.

"It wasn't hard to convince Hank to put a guard on Minnie. He was worried about a lot of things. He'd just been told that Cora had more than a casual stumble against that truck mirror. Her skull was fractured at the temple. She died from a brain hemorrhage."

"Jim did it, Max. He told me. They had an argument and he said he just pushed her; but he must have really slammed her against it."

"But why?"

"I don't know. It has something to do with that

picture of Lil and Minnie. He was afraid she was going to tell people about it. But I don't understand. It was Jim who broke into the house the other night, too. Cora had seen the picture first and told Jim about it."

I had stuck the portrait under the belt of my jeans, the only place I had to carry anything. It was in pretty disgusting shape by now.

Max glanced at it. "Yeah, I saw that in her scrapbook."

"But this belonged to Helby. Obviously, Lil gave it to him, but he didn't keep it with his other old pictures."

"I don't suppose he would. It's not the kind of thing you'd keep along with keepsakes of your wife and family."

"Mmmm," I agreed. "His other pictures of Hallway Halt were in the box, too. But what's wrong with it?" The inked inscription, "Me and Minnie," was smeared a bit from the sweat on my belly. I tried to smooth the cardboard frame back into shape. The studio's name was embossed on a lower corner: Wick's Photographs, Clearfield, Iowa, 1932.

"Max," I said, peering more closely at the raised print. "The little girl in this picture can't be Minnie!"

CHAPTER 16

"What do you mean, it can't be Minnie?" Max said. "It's got 'Me and Minnie' written all over it."

"This picture was taken in Iowa in nineteen thirty-two. Minnie was already two years old. This child is much younger."

"Are you sure?"

"About her exact age? No. But I am sure that the little Minnie in all those pictures taken in Halfway Halt is older than this little girl."

Max slowed as we entered Hijax, and turned the truck towards the hospital.

"Do you think he told her, Max? Do you think Jim told her that she wasn't really Minnie? And the shock brought on the stroke?"

"Or maybe Minnie's really Minnie, and this other kid is somebody else?" Max pulled in to the small hospital's emergency entrance. He took the picture from me and inspected it closely.

I said, "It's one of Minnie's favorite pictures. I'm sure Lil told Minnie it was a picture of her. I'll bet that's why the frame was removed. Lil cleaned up everything else in the scrapbook. She arranged the past the way she wanted Minnie to see it." But who was the other child?

"Well, hang on to this, Thea, but for now we've got other things to see to."

The long ride had stiffened every muscle I owned. I could no longer tell which part of me hurt more than the other. Max danced with impatience, but insisted I be admitted to emergency. Any protest I was forming dissolved at the look of shocked concern on the nurse's face when she saw me. Max didn't look so great, either, but a quick trip to the rest room did wonders for him. He returned with a clean face and hands that looked relatively normal, except for darkening bruises on cheek and jaw, and knuckles that appeared to have fought with a buzz saw.

"Don't let her out of your sight," Max ordered the nurse. Then he took me by the shoulders. "Look, we don't know where Jim is, or what he has in mind, or even how desperate he is. Please be careful, and stay in your room. I'll be back as soon as I can and tell you what's going on. Okay?"

I nodded, and dropped thankfully into the wheelchair the nurse held for me. I would have agreed to anything at that point. Max turned down the corridor and spoke briefly to a uniformed man who sat in a chair outside of Minnie's room. The nurse wheeled me in the opposite direction. Potts stood by the nurse's station. His mouth dropped at sight of me, and I couldn't tell if he was horrified or delighted by my condition.

The nurse answered my agitated questions with quick assurance. Minnie was being carefully watched, and doing as well as could be expected. And then I remembered that Potts wasn't the person I had to worry about any more; it was Jim.

The doctor taped my cracked ribs, and I was clucked over, cleaned and painted to a fare-thee-well, then put in a room across the hall from Minnie. The nurse was a real sweetheart and even helped me wash my hair. I began to feel like a passable human being, and wondered what Roger would think when he got the bill for this little escapade.

I was too restless to stay in bed. If there was such a thing as a hospital gown that didn't open to the wind, this place didn't have one. I found a second gown in the stand beside my bed and put it on in the opposite direction so I was covered both north and south, or was it east and west? I wanted to see Minnie.

The guard had my name as an allowed visitor, and let me in without an argument. She looked much as she had earlier. Had it really been just this morning when I last saw her? It seemed as if days had passed since then, so much had happened. Not only to me, but to Minnie as well. The search for her roots had turned into a tragic loss of identity. Who was she really? And due to my carelessness, or stupidity, or whatever you wanted to call it, all the hard work she had done on her book was as good as down the drain. What would happen to her now?

She opened her eyes briefly and looked at me, but I couldn't tell if there was recognition there, and I might well have imagined the slight pressure from her fingers. I patted her hand and left her to sleep.

Potts still stood vigil at the end of the corridor by the nurse's station. He looked unnaturally timid and self-conscious. I don't know what impulse sent me down the hall, but I didn't think I'd be breaking Max's edict as long as I kept the guard in sight.

Potts cringed when I approached, and I found it hard to imagine that I'd once found him frightening. He held his hat in front of him and twisted it around and around in his swollen fingers.

"How...how's Minnie?" he asked in a low rumble. "They won't let me see her."

I repeated what the doctor and nurse had told me. He'd probably heard it himself, but I had nothing more to offer.

He looked so abject, so broken; an old lion whose claws had been pulled. I couldn't stand it. "I think I owe you an apology, Parson. I accused you of a lot of things you didn't do, and called you a murderer." That, surely, had been the final blow to his ego. "I should have known there was nothing to fear from a...a man of the cloth."

"I wouldn't have hurt you!"

"True, but you certainly frightened me." I said dryly. "And when I met you at the dance, you acted so guilty I thought..." But I was too tired to go into all the details. He would hear it all soon enough.

Dark color flooded his face. "I'd just found out you weren't a...a...Folks around town been saying Minnie was going to start up the old business, and I thought you..."

I waited patiently, struggling not to smile, but if I could apologize, so could this old duck.

"Well, I found out you weren't. And...and I'm sorry I thought so," was the best he could manage.

It was good enough for me, but I couldn't resist grinding a bit. "You can't blame me for being frightened when I found you in my room."

"Don't know what happened." He shook his head, and the words rumbled out of his great barrel chest. "Somehow the Devil got to me, but I wasn't going to steal Minnie's book," he insisted. "I just needed to know what she'd written about me, so's I could prepare. And pray," he said, regaining some of his accustomed force.

I had a few qualms about putting his steps back on the paths of righteousness; still, it was nice to see some of the starch return.

"There's people around here what depend on me," he said. "I can't let them down."

Strangely enough, I believed him. "I don't think anything in Minnie's book will destroy people's belief in you. They've known you for a long time."

However, there were limits to my altruism. I wasn't about to tell him I feared Minnie's book would never see the light of day. Everything depended now upon how much of a recovery Minnie made, and what she chose to do with the information she had. And, of course, if I ever got the manuscript back.

I had turned to go back to my room when, with another great rumbling, Potts cleared his throat. "About that camera, Miss."

So that had been his piece of work.

"I didn't know what you was planning. I didn't want no pictures of me in a book without knowing what was going to be said. Have a bit of trouble with my temper, now and then." He shrugged, as if that explained everything. "Be glad to buy you another."

"That won't be necessary," I said, and walked away.

"You look much better," Max said when he returned.

"Good, but you're going to have to rustle me up some clothes, as they say in the vernacular. I'm not staying here all night."

"The stores are closed."

"If there's a Laundromat, you can wash my jeans, and surely one of the gas stations sells T-shirts. Anything will do. Now, tell me, what did you find out?"

"Not much. Deputies have gone out into the

country, looking for Jim, but they're not real hopeful about finding him. He could be anywhere."

The nurse came in and said, "Helby Enright's in the lobby. He wants to see both of you." She handed me a striped cotton robe.

"Oh, Max, does he know about Jim?" I asked, as we hurried out to meet him. "I feel so sorry for him."

Parson Potts was gone. Helby was the only person in the waiting room. Once more, he wore the fawn trousers, a blond shirt with a black silk scarf tied loosely around his neck, a rich leather vest, and high-heeled cowboy boots. He held the high-crowned hat at his side. I smiled and extended my hand. He took it, and looked me over much as Max had, to see if I were suitably in a piece. I was glad he hadn't seen me earlier.

"I'm sorry," he said simply.

"And I'm…"

"I assure you, my son will be caught and charged with assault and battery. Both on your account, and Minnie's." He squeezed my fingers lightly, offering me the comfort I wanted to give him. He didn't know about Cora yet. He held himself with a great deal of reserve but still managed to convey that he had lived his life, knew what it contained, and what he had wrought. He didn't need sympathy.

He turned to Max. "I owe you a debt, young man, you and yours. Your grandfather was hung for a deed I committed, and wasn't man enough to own up to. I watched him swing, and told myself it didn't matter because he was sheepherding trash." He stood ramrod straight and spoke unflinchingly. "I was a snot-nosed kid then, fourteen years old, full of myself and the man I was going to become. But I always knew I did wrong. It never left me."

Max raised a hand as if to stop the old man, then

changed his mind and listened quietly.

"I started the fire that burned down the general store. Had some kind of grudge against the man who owned it. Can't even remember what it was now. The only person I told was Lil Darrow. She understood and took pity on me, knew how a young man could be carried away by what was going on around him. I just want you to know I never felt right about what happened to your grandfather. And I'm sorry for the sorrow that was caused."

"Thank you for telling me," Max said, matching the old man's dignity with a gravity of his own. "That was a long time ago. I never knew my grandfather, but I'll gladly accept your words for his sake."

"That hanging's still on the books. I'll go along with whatever you want to do about it."

"I think you've paid a big enough price," Max said. "My only concern now is for Minnie."

"Jim's debt. We'll take care of anything she needs." The two men exchanged the crisp nods that seemed as useful to Westerners as *aloha* is to Hawaiians, and the matter was settled.

Helby stopped to inquire about Minnie, and Max and I went back to my room so he could pick up my jeans for the Laundromat.

"You handled Helby very well, Max," I said. "It would have been terribly easy for you to be condescending or cruel. I'm proud of you. Could he really still be brought to trial?"

"I don't know. I think it's up to the district attorney to decide what cases can be legitimately brought to trial. Helby, and Potts, for that matter, were just two of ten, and I doubt if either one of them actually handled the rope. Charging a man in his seventies, or more, for a crime committed when he was fourteen boggles the mind. Would he be tried as an adult or juvenile?"

"You're right; I doubt if any court would want to mess with it."

Helby had waited to leave until Max and I returned to the lobby. We walked out together. The night air was soft, stirred by the constant breeze that rattled the leaves of the lilac hedge that bordered the parking lot. The path around the side of the building was narrow, so Helby walked briskly ahead. Max and I followed.

Helby stepped first into the open lot. We were a few feet behind him, unseen by the man who waited. He spoke just as we passed through the opening, too late to back away.

"Dad," Jim said. He held a rifle which he raised when he saw Max and me, but he continued to speak, otherwise unconcerned by our presence. "Why didn't you tell me, Dad? Why didn't you warn me?"

"I'm sorry, boy, but I thought it was something that would just have to eat at me 'til I died. That hanging—"

"Hanging!" Jim roared, swinging the rifle into firing position. "Who gives a shit about that? Why didn't you tell me Minnie was your daughter, sweet little Minnie who isn't really Minnie?" He spat the words out, each one loaded with more fury than the next. The reek of whisky soured the air.

"You're drunk," Helby said.

"She's your daughter Belle; you know she is. It's right there in the records, Dad. Cora found it. All she had to do was call Cheyenne. It was right there. A daughter born to Lil Darrow, father's name: Helby Enright. You were *fourteen*, Dad. My God, that's indecent. You let her come here to claim her share and rob our land—*my* land—Enright land—and make our name a laughing stock. How could you do that to me? A whore's kid for a sister? How could you do that,

Dad? We're Enrights!"

"Put the gun down, Jim," Max said.

"Stay out of this, Woolie." He staggered and the gun wavered to cover the three of us.

Helby moved, I think, but everything happened too quickly. Jim swung the rifle and fired. Helby cried out and sank to the pavement. I saw a flash of horror cross Jim's face. Then Max kicked out at the rifle, but not hard enough. Jim swung the butt at Max's shoulder, knocking him down, then ran for the dark end of the lot where his truck waited in the shadows. Max jumped to his feet and ran after him.

I dropped by Helby's side, but when Max moved, I took cover behind the skimpy hedge and raced unseen towards Jim's pickup. Jim stood behind the truck's open door and took aim at Max over the hood. I flung myself at the door just as the gun fired, smashing Jim's arm in the hinge. He screamed, and the gun deflected upward. I fell to the ground, terrified by what I'd done, and threw myself under the truck, dimly aware of the flashing lights and screaming sirens that rolled into the lot.

I lay there quivering, and breathed in fumes of gas and hot oil until Max drew me out and helped me to my feet.

Deputies held Jim at bay. He didn't struggle. Both doors of the truck were now open, and through them we watched him being cuffed and led away. Then something else caught my eye. On the floor of the truck, halfway under the seat, was a familiar paper bag.

"This is mine," I muttered to Max, and snatched up Minnie's manuscript.

CHAPTER 17

Helby smoothed the bent and torn frame on the portrait of Minnie and Lil, and flattened it against the kitchen table as best he could with one arm in a sling. "I had forgotten it," he said quietly, running his fine fingers over the soiled surface. We sat in the kitchen at Halfway Halt, Helby, Max and me, drinking coffee. I've never drunk so much coffee in my life.

"It was so long ago," Helby said, repeating a phrase we'd heard many times. "I was just a kid. Lil was a good woman. She took me under her wing."

And into her bed, I thought. A fourteen-year-old boy, precocious, yes, but troubled as well. However, I wasn't about to pass judgment. I did find it ironic that the young man who had impregnated a woman at the age of fourteen had remained childless until his early forties, only to become an acknowledged father again in his seventies, or whatever age he was. I hoped he would receive more pleasure from Minnie than he had from his son.

"I knew Lil was pregnant when she left Hijax,"

Helby said. "She told me the baby was mine, but I never thought much about it. We kept in touch for a while. She drifted around a bit, Deadwood, Sundance. Lil's baby sister, Minnie, the real Minnie, died there. Diphtheria, I think it was. Lil wrote me about it and I went to see her. She loved that little sister of hers. I thought she'd go crazy."

"Did you see your...The other little girl then?" I asked.

"Yes, she was just a tiny tot; Belle was her name. Lil talked a lot about starting over, thought her little sister dying was some kind of punishment. Next time I heard from her, she sent this picture and a letter from Iowa. Said she was getting business as a bookkeeper, and Minnie was doing just fine. I don't know if she was fooling herself that Belle was Minnie, or if she thought things would be easier on the girl to be a sister rather than a daughter of an unmarried woman. I never asked."

"You don't really need birth certificate verification that often in your life, and maybe even less back in the thirties and forties," I said, pondering how difficult such a scheme would be. "When you start school, even then, certainly. If she actually used the real Minnie's birth data, by that time the year-and-a-half age difference wouldn't be too noticeable. Even less so as time went on."

Max, who had been listening quietly, spoke up. "But how did Jim come up with all this? Or Cora? It was quite a jump to make, just from seeing the date on that picture."

"I don't understand Cora's part in this at all," I said. "When she came here to visit Minnie, she wanted to see pictures, old pictures of Halfway Halt. She wasn't really interested in your collection, Helby."

Helby laughed. "Cora's grandma was one of Lil's

girls. She probably wanted to make sure Minnie didn't have any pictures of her grandma to put in that book."

"But to spot the date on that picture so quickly, and to grasp what it meant. Minnie had never really looked at the picture, but I had held it in my hands, and never noticed the date."

Helby shrugged. "Cora kept a pretty tight rein on the historical society, thought she was hiding a big secret, but quite a few of us remembered. She was afraid Lamar would find out, I suspect. But none of us would have told him. He's an outsider."

"Cora was familiar enough with Lil's story," Max said. "And you said she'd just been looking at pictures that had a two-year-old in them. Besides, she'd never seen that studio portrait before. It was too familiar to both you and Minnie to attract your attention. Sooner or later you would have noticed."

Helby said, "She also couldn't figure out why I had it. That's what made her so curious. Next day she called Cheyenne. Vital statistics. That's what Jim told me when I talked to him at the jail." He paused and ran a hand over his face. "I called Cheyenne myself this morning just to check, and sure enough, there's a birth listed for Lil Darrow, child named Belle, with me as father. In those days a father's name had to be on the certificate whether you knew who he was, or not. Cora went running to Jim with the information. She was a foolish woman."

"Jim said he didn't kill Cora intentionally," I said, though I knew it offered little comfort. "I believed him."

"That's what the sheriff said. A freak hit on the temple. Killed her instantly." He shook his head. "He could have stopped there, but chose not to."

He pulled the two smaller snapshots on the table closer. They were the pictures of the hanging; the vigilantes, masked and unmasked.

"Lil took these pictures, you know. She was there that night. If I had told her then that the man was innocent she would have stopped the party. Hell, she tried to stop it anyway. Lynchin' parties weren't exactly admired by the ladies. Lil was the only one who ever stood up to my father, but it didn't do any good."

He shoved them back towards me, and got up.

"This man is named Beesom." I said, pointing to one of the figures. "I even suspected the sheriff for a while, because of it. Is he a relative of Hank's?"

"He's dead, now. Been gone a long time."

And I knew he wasn't going to tell me anything more. After all, I too was an outsider.

"Well, they're yours now, girl. You can do what you want with them, I don't care. I just came by to tell you again that I'll take care of everything Minnie needs. She'll never want for anything."

Earlier that day, the doctor had allowed the sheriff, along with Max and me, to talk to Minnie. Though she still couldn't speak, the doctor thought her condition much improved, and she would be happier knowing that Jim had been apprehended. Much as Lil had done all her life, we, too, gave Minnie a sanitized version of events, lightening the violence and pain. But with judicious questions, and corroborative nods or shakes of her head, we were able to verify that our speculations as to what had happened to her were basically correct. The fine details would have to wait until her communication abilities improved, something which the doctor assured us would increase daily.

Among us all there had been some kind of silent agreement that we would continue to call Minnie by the name her sister, or rather her mother, had used for her all those years. Belle had died with Minnie, and through Belle, Minnie lived.

When Max and I were alone again, I asked, "And how about you, Max? Are you still going to try to buy this place, Minnie's ranch?"

"You've raised quite a few ghosts while you've been here, Thea, and I guess I've gotten rid of some. No, I don't want this place, or any other. I'm not a rancher. I'm a geologist, an oil man, and that's what I want to do. Some day, some place, I might find a piece of land I want to buy, but for different reasons. This was a pipe dream, something I had to get out of my system one way or another; I just didn't expect it to happen so explosively."

His heavy-lidded eyes watched me closely, and I waited for his next words.

"Will you stay?" he finally asked. "Or should I follow you? I can for awhile, you know, but I could never live in Chicago. What about your job?"

Roger. Minnie's book. My job. It all seemed so long ago; all my frenzied career urgency had been eaten up by real life.

"I have to go back, Max. I have to edit Minnie's book. She deserves the best job I can do."

I fingered the two snapshots that were never far from our reach. "I'm not going to use these, Max." I wanted him to know the worst before things went any further. "I had planned to. In fact, I was planning a real smear campaign for Hijax. Spreads in *People* or the *Enquirer,* whatever I could get that might sell a few more books. All at the expense of the town and folks like Helby Enright, Potts, Minnie and even you, Max. I'm not real proud of myself."

He sat across the battered kitchen table from me, our home base for what, five days? Or was it six? The apple green walls still made their feeble attempt to provide cheer to the shabby old room. The dog, now a confirmed member of the household, lay at our feet beating the floor periodically with a happy tail. Max studied me as he had so frequently in the past few days.

"But you aren't going to do that; that's what counts, Thea."

"Yes, I guess so. At any rate, I've made my decisions about Minnie's book. It will be the story of Jersey Roo's Halfway Halt, as we had originally planned. If at some date Minnie wants to write about Lil's life, then that will be another book, and will wait until she can make all the decisions concerning it. But I do have to see this project through to conclusion. You understand, don't you Max? Then I can begin editing my own life. Sort out my priorities."

"Am I a priority?" Max asked softly.

"You know you are. A. Top. Number One. But if you do come with me, you'll have to wear your cowboy boots and hat, and maybe get a bandanna. Mother will be enchanted."

He stood, and drew me to my feet.

"And of course," I said, wrapping my arms around him, "I don't have to leave right now, this very instant. There's always tonight."

His face lit with that great, glorious smile. "What's the matter with right now?" He pulled me to him.

"Not a thing," I said. My lips parted under his, welcoming his embrace.

The End

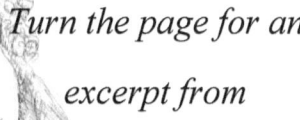

Turn the page for an

excerpt from

FROGSKIN &
MUTTONFAT

A Thea Barlow Wyoming Mystery
Book Two

Carol Caverly

Sheila Rides-Horse lay on the cot in her small room at the back of the house, her head propped up with three thin, lumpy bed pillows, the tattered quilt scrunched down around her ankles where she had pushed it to avoid the heat. She wasn't asleep. She was sure she wasn't asleep, but the walls of her narrow room were disappearing. She was outside, sitting on a rock. She could feel the hard ridges and uneven protuberances digging into her soft buttocks. Her large bare feet splayed firmly on the ground in front of her.

Her thoughts stretched out into gossamer threads that sucked up the night scents, tangled with the sharp breeze, and searched for the unusual. A meaning. A message. She wasn't frightened. She had done this before, knew how to hang on to that one piece of reality that would keep her safe.

She focused on something between her feet. A plant? A rock? Her eyes caressed the odd shape, trying to know it, but she was puzzled. The thing had a peachy glow that spoke of succulence, yet its branches...Yes, branches. A bush, a shrub of some kind. She clung to her thoughts, gripping their solidity to ward off the sweet, fuzzy haze that shredded reason.

Then the bush began to move. Pulsing with life, the branches writhed, swayed and began to reach for her. Flesh-colored but hard as stone, the tendrils brushed her legs, curled around her arms, stretched to her neck, twining, squeezing.

She grabbed frantically for cognition. "Fin...fingers..." but mind and breath began to swirl away. The cold reaching fingers tore at her mouth and reached for eye sockets. With a final burst of terror, she threw her head back and caught a pinprick of light. Clinging to the glow, she willed it closer and closer until it burst into shape. A light bulb hanging from a chain. Her room. Her bed.

"Holy shit!" Sweat poured down her face and neck and between her heavy breasts. She wiped it off with the tail of the ragged T-shirt she used as a nightgown, then stared at the shirt, surprised to find it soaked through. Impatient, she yanked the clammy shirt over her head and dropped it on the floor, then stood up on rubbery legs.

"What in hell was that all about?" she said, comforted by the sound of her voice. She had had her share of visions, but nothing with that kind of power.

The cards, she thought. I gotta get the cards. Naked, she padded to the sink on the far wall and took down a packet wrapped in a blue velvet cloth from the shelf above.

The cloth dropped to the floor unnoticed and with trembling fingers she began to shuffle the deck. The cards, worn to a limp softness by years of use, calmed her. Holding the deck in both hands, she touched the shuffled pack to her forehead and her heart, then sat on the edge of the bed. Fanning the cards face down on the sheet, she pressed them briefly into the dampness to soak up the fear. Quickly, she gathered them up again and began her spread.

She flicked the cards into patterns with the speed of familiarity, but no matter how she varied the spread the message remained the same. Danger, the Tarot symbols warned her, Anguish, Foolish Decisions, Deception and Sorrow. Always the suit of swords dominated, with its reigning king present.

So all right; she thought, wiping her hand across her face, a man is involved. The King of Swords, a dark-haired man, a man to be feared, avoided, a man who wasn't what he seemed to be.

She gathered the cards and shuffled them again, thoughtfully. Always enigmatic, the cards had their own ways of signaling urgency, demanding attention. Repetition was one of them, reinforcing the message of her vision and that awful clawing bush. Forces were swirling around her. Danger poised ready to pounce. But from where? What was the meaning of a twining grasping bush? Danger from the earth? She shook her head, bewildered. She only knew that to ignore the warning would be to her peril.

───◆───

FROGSKIN & MUTTONFAT

available in print and ebook

THE
THEA BARLOW
WYOMING MYSTERIES

All The Old Lions
Frogskin & Muttonfat
Dead in Hog Heaven
Death by Doodlebug

I was raised in a Chicago suburb and married into a Wyoming pioneer ranch family. Yes, it was a bit of a culture shock, but I quickly grew to love the stark dry landscape and, most of all, the people. I was fascinated by how close their lives were to the happenings of what I considered to be the old Wild West.

My husband's grandfather talked about how the Butch Cassidy gang trailed through a ranch where he worked as a fourteen year old kid. The gang was on their way to Hole in the Wall. They stole horses on the way, but frequently left a note on a fence saying where the horses could be found in a few weeks time. Most all ranches had a "kid" working on them and, not surprisingly, the kid usually got the stickiest jobs. So grandpa got sent on horseback to go miles away to retrieve the bosses stock. He was always afraid the gang might still be there with the horses and would tie him up, or shoot him. Enthralled, I could sit for hours listening to his stories.

So I guess it's no wonder that when I began my writing career I wanted to honor my love and fascination for Wyoming and the clash between the old and new west that never seemed to be far away. I hope you enjoy my stories as much as I enjoyed writing them.

You can visit Carol at www.carolcaverly.com